AF507379

Also by K Jwancio

A PHILLY SILLYS ROMANCE:
Nailed at Home Plate

ROMANCING THE PAGES SERIES:
Romancing the Pages
Behind the Pages

THISTLE FIELD ESTATE SERIES:
Bed...& Breakfast
Breakfast in Bed
Thistle Field Estate

SPELLBOUND IN THISTLETON SERIES:
Spellbound in the Stacks
Spells and Wedding Bells
Spells and Belly Swells

HOLIDAY NOVELLAS:
The Gift Across the Street
Long Lost Valentine

Enjoy the

Working the Mound

playlist!

ISBN: 979-8-9888132-9-3

Cover design, formatting, and interior art by Iwancio Inspired Design.
Cover character art by agingerpanda.
Interior character art by michillart.

K. Iwancio

This is for everyone who reads smutty books to heal, to learn, to enjoy, to laugh, to cry, to get turned on, and to escape the ordinary. May you never be judged, only loved, for what you enjoy.

P.S. Oh hey Dad, I'm back with another installment in my baseball romance set in Philly. Here's your yearly reminder to skip all the dirty chapters while reading this in heaven.

P.P.S. For those of you wondering, the chapters are 23, 24, 26, 27, and 29.
(Look, it takes them a while to figure out their shit, okay?)

***TRIGGER WARNING:**
This book contains two consenting adults exploring
various kinks, which include (in no particular
order): dirty talk, bad words, surprise jizz,
numerous sexual baseball innuendos, and
deliciously smutty books with spiny monster dicks.*

FUN FACTS:
"Cum" is mentioned 9 times.
"Fuck" is mentioned 80 times.
"Cock" is mentioned 34 times.
"Ass" is mentioned 85 times.
"Dick" is mentioned 23 times.
"Fucking" is mentioned 109 times.

CHAPTER PLAYLIST

1 | **Bad Kids** *Lady Gaga*
2 | **Mr. Rager** *Kid Cudi*
3 | **In Love With a Memory** *SASAMI, Clairo*
4 | **No Light, No Light** *Florence + the Machine*
5 | **My Kink is Karma** *Chappell Roan*
6 | **The Way You Loved Me** *Calum Scott*
7 | **Slow Dance** *AJ Mitchell*
8 | **She's an Actor** *Austin Giorgio*
9 | **book smart** *Amanda Frances*
10 | **Guilty Pleasure** *Chappell Roan*
11 | **Fumbled the Bag** *Jenna Raine*
12 | **Curiosity** *Bryce Savage*
13 | **Fictional** *Khloe Rose*
14 | **The Story of Us** *Taylor Swift*
15 | **Wait** *Maroon 5*
16 | **Can I Kiss You?** *Dahl*
17 | **Criminal** *Fiona Apple*
18 | **bad idea right?** *Olivia Rodrigo*
19 | **Dream Girl Evil** *Florence + the Machine*
20 | **All the Things She Said** *Harrison*
21 | **Actually Romantic** *Taylor Swift*
22 | **All Over Again** *The Shires*
23 | **This is Heaven** *Nick Jonas*
24 | **I Am Yours** *Andy Grammar*
25 | **HAPPINESS** *NEEDTOBREATHE*
26 | **PINE** *Unusual Demont*
27 | **Give You Love** *Forest Blakk*
28 | **I Must be in Love** *Aaron Taos*
29 | **Ring My Bell** *Anita Ward*
30 | **Wildfire** *Cautious Clay*
31 | **One Life** *Ed Sheeran*
EPILOGUE | Forever *Mumford & Sons*

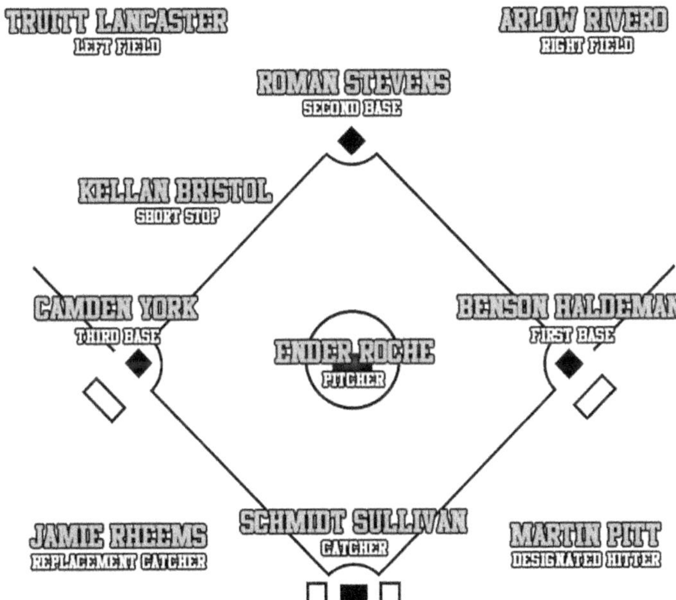

The Philly Sillys Starting Line Up

1

BAD KIDS
LADY GAGA

Ender Roche was the reason I hated men.

Hold on. Let me rephrase that.

Ender Roche was the reason I hated *real* men.

Not fictional ones. They were my only saving grace. And maybe the occasional random hookup. But that was reserved for when I was beyond desperate, and I mean desperate, to feel something outside the pages of a book.

It was rare that I felt the need for human contact. Only once in a blue moon. But most of the time? I wanted to be left the fuck alone.

If only it were that easy.

Working for Philadelphia's Entertainment League Baseball team, the Philly Sillys, did not allow me the luxury of silence and solitude during baseball season. Which, if I might add, is a really fucking long season. My only saving grace was my best friend, Cadence Andrews. Even though she was the *baseball* team's choreographer, she was the single sane person in the organization.

Work wasn't exactly terrible. I technically didn't have to *talk* to anyone while in the mascot. I could read during my downtime at the baseball games. Being the costumed team mascot had its weird perks. Despite baseball being seasonal, they paid me year-round. So, in the winter, I had all the time in the world to read and ignore everyone. It was my own form of hibernation.

My career was going great. No complaints. That was, until this season.

Because you know what's worse than having an ex from hell?

Working with an ex from hell.

Okay, fine. Ender wasn't exactly from hell, per se. Maybe "asshole ex" was more appropriate. Or "only thinks with his dick" kind of ex. Today was his first day with the Sillys. I was still doing everything in my power to avoid the man I hadn't seen since high school.

Ender was my first love. My *only* love. We were just teenagers when we started dating, but there was *something* there. The little *something* that women in romance novels always touted.

Think what you will of my teenage naivety, but we had something special. Something magical. And I've read enough romances to know that the "little spark", the "undeniable attraction", that indescribable connection was real.

Well, it felt real, once upon a time.

Our relationship started during my sophomore year of high school. Ender was only a freshman but became the hotshot pitcher on our high school's varsity baseball team. Right alongside my big brother, Cooper Campanaro.

This year's baseball season was like I was reliving my awkward high school years all over again.

Here I was, a washed-up theater studies graduate, with a fucking *master's degree*, working as an overstuffed baseball mascot. And not even a mascot for a major league team. I was a mascot for a bottom-of-the-food-chain ELB team that was nowhere near as popular as the original Savannah Bananas.

Which was only exacerbated by the fact that my big brother helped me get this job right out of school. Cooper was the pitching coach for the Sillys. He put in a good word for me when the team was contemplating bringing on a mascot as another entertainment factor. While I was grateful to the butthole for looking out for me, I never gave him the satisfaction of knowing that.

While working with my brother was bad enough, the karma gods had to throw my ex-boyfriend onto the pile as well. Ender joined the Sillys as the new lead rookie pitcher. It was like my own brand of fiery, painful torment.

At least my brother was on my side for this. Ever since Ender joined the Sillys after Spring Training, Cooper did his best to make Ender's life as close to a living hell as possible. My brother remembered Ender's and my breakup all too well.

It was only a temporary bandage over the feelings I suppressed years ago. But it did bring my sadist self some joy. A love language, if you will.

Over the years, I'd done so well repressing every single aspect that was Ender Roche. Was it healthy? Absolutely not. Was it easy? No, not that either.

Sure, I've…dated. Here and there. Nothing serious. Some of the guys were actually kind of sweet. But nothing went beyond a date or two. Most of the time I ended up ghosting them.

Because they weren't Ender.

They weren't the "I'm breaking up with you because I want to go chase some new tail" Ender. Yes, that *one*.

I know I need my head examined because, yes, years later, I was still obsessing over it, still obsessing over Ender and what he did to me.

He had given me the courtesy of at least breaking up with me first. The cheating trope in dark romance was one that I didn't mind. But in real life? Hell no.

Breaking up with me for the singular reason of trying to hook up with someone else was such a despicable excuse. At least he was honest. But that was just a drop in the bucket.

Ever since that day, I avoided him at all costs. I stopped going to my brother's baseball games. I walked on the opposite side of the hall from Ender. I went out of my way to never speak or look at him again. I'd been doing so well not thinking about him, that I was on a streak that was years long. I almost forgot the whole messy thing had ever happened.

"I know I used to tease you about it, but now I'm certain your face is just a permanent scowl after keeping it that ugly for so many years." Cooper wandered into my dressing room with a stupid ass smirk. He was easily a head taller than me, lean and athletic with dreamy sandy blonde hair. Meanwhile, I was the complete opposite, short and curvy with hair that only had a hope of vibrance from chemical torture at the salon.

"Oh look, the man that never stopped using his asshole for a mouth." I spat right back as I rolled my eyes. Cooper showing up in the Philly Sillys mascot's dressing room meant that practice was over for the team. He continually liked to hold it over my head that he got me this job in the first place. But I know it was the gripping performance of my job interview monologue that got me the part.

"Oof, the bitch's bark is worse than her bite." He teased, plopping down into my worn hand-me-down desk chair. It was better suited for a dorm room than the little office corner in my dressing room. At least I had a dressing room/office, unlike my brother. He sat crammed with other coaches in a large office off the stinky players' locker room.

"Don't you have some players' asses to snap with a towel or something?"

"Nah, their torture is done for the day. Now it's your turn, lil' sis." He shot me finger guns as he propped his grassy baseball cleats on the corner of my desk.

"Coop, you're such a disease."

"What can I say, bratty little sisters are what I feed on."

If he wasn't such an asshole about it, I would admit that he had a clever enough wit to go toe to toe with some of the guys in the romance books I read. But the last thing I ever wanted to do was compliment my brother. One of these days I'd outwit him.

"So who did you make cry today? It looks like you came here to gloat." My brother secretly loved being a hard ass to the players. He never wanted to admit it, but I knew it was because he was still bitter about his career-ending injury in college that lost him his future as a professional baseball player. Our entire family was devastated. Instead of addressing the elephant in the room, we danced around the subject.

"Just You-Know-Who." His eyes met mine with an evil little sparkle from the fluorescent lights of my office.

"Really?" I asked, a little too perky and quick on the uptake. But I couldn't help it. I took so much joy in the thought that my annoying big brother hated my ex as much as me. I hated the fact that my ex was still talented with baseball. So much so that my brother couldn't help but recruit him for the Sillys.

"Yeah, I made him do a few extra laps around the perimeter after practice. Dude looked like he was ready to have a coronary." I huffed in amusement but kept my satisfied smile under wraps. "You're welcome, by the way."

"Oh, shut it. Just admit that you're a sadist and you like making people's lives miserable. Mine included." That got an outright guffaw out of him. "Hmm…maybe I should get a t-shirt made for you for your birthday."

"You know, that's not a bad idea." Oh lord. I created a monster.

"That way, people aren't surprised since you look like a nice guy."

"Hey…" He held his hands out, attempting to look innocent. "I *am* a nice guy."

"Whatever helps you sleep at night, you fucking diva."

A knock at the door had us both snapping our heads up. Everyone was used to our bitter brother/sister feud, but it was all in love. I let out a breath of relief to see Cadence at the door. Saved by the bestie.

"Eww, girl talk time. Excuse me while I throw up." Cooper rose from my desk chair as it creaked in relief. I rolled my eyes while Cadence betrayed our friendship by laughing at my brother.

"At least she has some manners, you uncultured swine." I spat at his back as he slipped past a still-cackling Cadence. I let out an annoyed grumble as I stepped in beside my friend.

"I have no idea what your sister-in-law sees in him."

"Yeah, but I actually like her. My brother, on the other hand, I'd be more than happy to get rid of." Cadence snorted as we stood shoulder to shoulder. She was a breath of fresh air since she was someone who I could actually look straight on when talking to her. Being short only fueled my brother's teasing fire.

If only I could boot my annoying brother in favor of his wife. I was currently living in said brother's basement apartment of his Philly rowhome. My own personal brand of hell followed me wherever I went nowadays. There was a lingering moment of quiet before Cadence spoke again.

"I'm craving a beer and suffocating on some loaded fries." In our years of friendship, that only meant one thing. One of us was stressed, and we needed to drown our sorrows in some alcohol and greasy food for the night. I wasn't one for public appearances but could always be coaxed away from my hole of a basement apartment with food. I was a feral creature but with decent manners. Most of the time.

"You know, that sounds fucking amazing to me."

2

MR. RAGER

KID CUDI

There was only one thing I regretted in my life. Breaking up with Tiffiny Campanaro.

I was just a stupid teenager who wanted to follow his dick to greener pastures. The fact that we'd been a couple for a few years meant nothing. Well, at the time, it meant nothing. I just wanted to, hopefully, get laid by the popular girl in school.

Dammit.

I was such a fucking idiot.

I couldn't even remember her name. It started with an "R" or something? Regina maybe? Just goes to show how much I actually cared about her.

Had I been smarter and used less of my dick to think, I would have called out the popular chick on her bullshit. She only started to show interest in me after there were rumors around school about some big-name scouts coming out to see me play. All she could see was the potential for dollar signs and popularity.

All I could see were her pert tits.

Guys really do have a one-track mind.

My immaturity killed the one good thing in my life. Tiffiny was beautiful, smart, hilarious, and sweet. There wasn't a bad thing about her now that I had a few years to think about it and wallow in my fucking awful life choices. I let something incredible get away from me.

Over the years, I desperately tried to seek her out, but she blocked me at every turn. In the halls, she ran in the opposite direction or avoided my schedule completely. She even went as far as to switch classes so that she didn't have to get within fifty feet of me. She had cut the bridge with a rusty spork and spit in the rubble.

Over our time apart, the wound had slowly begun to heal. But there wasn't a day that went by that I didn't think about all of the "what ifs" and "could have been". Or hell, be given another shot. Not that she would let me take it.

Then again, karma was a vindictive bitch.

Ever since the moment I broke up with Tiffiny, my life has gotten increasingly shittier. It didn't start so badly. I graduated with a decent GPA and received a full sports and academic scholarship to Villanova. It wasn't my first choice of school. I wanted to go somewhere outside of Pennsylvania. But I couldn't leave Mamá on her own just yet.

Mamá had always said that school was the most important thing in my life. As much as I disagreed with her at the time, I didn't want to disappoint her or throw away the opportunity. I was the son of an immigrant. She came here to find a better life for both of us. The political climate wasn't the best in Venezuela, not to mention poverty levels were so high and jobs so scarce. As scary as it was, she made the best choice.

My father, on the other hand, didn't bother to follow us. From what Mamá had told me in bits and pieces of conversation, was that he left as soon as he found out she was pregnant. He hadn't been heard from since. Good riddance, honestly. Mamá did an outstanding job with the resources she had. We may not have always had a lot, but she made the most of it.

College went well. I maintained my grades, played baseball, and I was still able to go home on the weekends for Mamá's arepas. She always made a whole assortment of them with different things. They were just so versatile and honestly, I ate them morning, noon, and night. Hell, even as a snack. Mamá's recipe was like a drug that renewed my soul. And honestly, the comfort I needed in the best of times and the darkest of times.

My degree was in sports management, so even if I had to stop playing baseball one day, I could still be *around* baseball. Or any sport for that matter. But baseball had my heart and soul in a vice grip. Being out on the ballfield was literally paradise. Even with the endlessly screaming fans and other stadium noise, I was able to block it all out and settle into my element on the pitcher's mound. It was my happy place filled with nothing but anxiety. But I lived for that delicious contradiction.

I thought that my life was settled after college. The second I saw MLB recruiters at some of my games, I thought my career was coming to fruition. When I graduated, I was drafted by the Boston Red Sox. I thought I was on cloud nine. But even dreams can come crashing down around you when you are on the biggest high of your life.

I had been invited to my first Spring Training, which was a big fucking deal for a rookie. In the locker room, I was in utter awe of the talent I was surrounded by. If you ever want to humble yourself really fucking fast, sit in an MLB locker room for a hot minute.

Spring Training in Florida was like a dream come true. Playing alongside the current greats. Even some of the retired players came to hang out and see the rookies. I bonded with a lot of the guys, which tends to happen when we are all in dorm-like housing near the ballpark. It was almost like college all over again, but only for baseball.

Everything went well during the six or so weeks of the preseason. I trained with some of the best coaches in baseball. I learned so fucking much.

Only to be let go before the season started.

The bad thing about any professional sport is that you may be an incredible player, but if a team doesn't see a need for you, or someone edges you out skill-wise, or if their need for certain players changes, good players get let go. All those years. All that build-up. All that excitement of seeing dreams come true, only to have them come crashing down in an instant.

Nothing hurts more than getting a taste of having all of your dreams come true. To have the ultimate dream in your grasp, only for the rug to be pulled out from under you. As much as I had my heart set on staying with the Red Sox organization, I felt bitter after they let me go. There was still another chance left. To maybe, hopefully, get picked up by another team after being released.

But I didn't.

Not one other team offered to bring me aboard.

I flew home with my metaphorical tail between my legs.

I knew Mamá would be sad with me, but she was ready with a comforting smile and all my favorite foods piled high on the tiny island in the middle of our apartment's kitchen. But I didn't have the heart to call and tell her. To give her a warning that her failure of a son was on the way home, with no offers, not even a chance to play in the low-A minors.

Just when I thought karma had gotten the best of me, she was determined to make me her bitch while taking me on a hell of a roller coaster ride of emotions. One of my old high school teammates, Cooper, heard through the grapevine about my hell of a time at Spring Training. He ended up sending me a text as I headed to the Tampa airport. It was a text I'd been holding out and hoping for my entire baseball-loving life.

An *official* offer to play baseball.

Full-time.

For a team.

Great, right? Wrong.

Well, partially wrong. Because while I adored the fuck out of this Cooper and was ecstatic for the chance to play with him again, it wasn't all sunshine and daisies. He just so happened to be my ex-girlfriend Tiffiny's older brother.

And the team he coached for?

The team Tiffiny was the mascot for.

A vain part of me wished and hoped I'd get a last-ditch offer from any of the thirty MLB teams in existence. Literally any other team. Even one with a losing record. But no, destiny and karma were in cahoots because my choice ended up being either to fall back on my college degree or keep playing baseball.

But I would be pitching for the team that the woman I never got over also worked for.

I had an inkling that Tiffiny had gotten around to telling Cooper about what had happened. Because, despite extending the offer, he seemed to enjoy making my life a living hell. He claimed it was for cardio. Unlike the current MLB, it was fairly common for the ELB to bring in a pitcher to hit. Well, unless you were like the powerhouse that is Shohei Ohtani. So, it was safe to say that I was a little out of practice for running the bases.

Although I was the only one who was stuck running extra laps around the entire field along the warning track. The other pitchers got a head start in the cool showers. While I was stuck finishing my lap, ready to jump headfirst into the nearest body of water. Which just happened to be the Delaware River. If you knew anything about Philadelphia, you know that anyone with their right mind wouldn't dip a pinky toe into the river. Not unless you were okay with turning into the three-eyed fish from *The Simpsons*.

The locker room was nearly empty by the time I made it down the stairs from the dugout. That was after I may or may not have passed out on the field afterward as I tried to catch my breath. At least I could avoid the playful razzing of the rookie that the Sillys guys tended to do. They were a good group, utterly bonkers, but good, nonetheless.

I heard a titter of laughter and glanced up to see Tiffiny making her way from her office with my choreography coach, Cadence. No matter how hard I tried, I couldn't tear my gaze away from Tiffiny. Once upon a time, we couldn't keep our hands off each other. The smiles she'd slip me made me melt on impact. Despite the bitter years between us now, the woman still had this uncanny ability to stop my heart.

Thankfully, she was too distracted by whatever she and Cadence were talking about to notice me staring.

Shit.

Spoke too soon.

Her look of icy daggers froze my cleats to the concrete floor.

If I were a braver man, I would have dropped to my knees and begged the woman for forgiveness. Begged for forgiveness for all my stupid ass teenage transgressions the second I ran into her again. But she looked at me with such scorn. My heart must have had masochist tendencies with the way it still raced anytime she entered my atmosphere. Between her scary looks and the shit her brother punished me with, all I was left with was pining for the only woman I ever loved, safely from afar.

IN LOVE WITH A MEMORY

SASAMI (FEATURING CLAIRO)

I should have known a Philadelphia Phillies baseball game was the reason Cadence wanted to go out to the bar. At least one of the reasons. We both had a penchant for greasy bar food. It's not like Philadelphia was in short supply of sports bars or anything. She liked watching the games at our local sports bar because of the tiny television in her apartment. She needed a screen large enough to be able to count every strand of hair on the players' bodies. Or something.

Even though my brother had been a ball player, and the fact that I now worked as a baseball team mascot, I barely knew anything about the sport. Okay, sure, I knew some of the positions, the lingo, and what the ball and field looked like. But I still got mixed up on if I should call the guys everyone booed a referee or an umpire. Beyond that, I didn't bother to take the time to understand.

Most, if not all, of my brother's games were spent with me nose-deep in a book while in the bleachers. Until I started dating Ender. He was the golden boy of the Garden Valley Spartans varsity team. His talent surpassed most of the team, so he joined the varsity team as a freshman.

I still remember seeing him for the first time. He was tall and athletic. With tanned skin that practically glowed in the sunlight. The sight of him tore my eyes from my reread of my favorite book at the time. Fantasy was my jam, but teenage hormones were raging, okay? As much as the memory stings now, I'll always remember every single detail about that moment. So much so, I still have the book, marked to the exact page, on my shelf to this day.

It took a lot for someone to distract me from my books, let alone a real-life man. Fictional ones were far more pliable and convenient. There was just something about Ender, though. A mix of boyish charm and the seriousness of a professional athlete. But fuck, the moment our eyes met, it was that special little *zing!* Just like in every cheesy, eye-roll-inducing romance that I gobbled up on the regular.

He was running off the field at the end of the inning, his teammates congratulating him on a stellar throw of the ball. Something made him look up into the bleachers behind the dugout. Both of us were frozen on the spot for what seemed like an eternity before one of Ender's teammates coaxed him back to the present. But not before his hand lifted to the brim of his ballcap, tipping it in my direction with a smile. Like something Mr. Darcy would have done, but instead of a top hat, it was a baseball cap.

I *swooned*.

Did people swoon in the twenty-first century? Maybe I was an old soul or something. But Ender had me in a metaphorical chokehold from that very moment. As much as I wanted to maybe slide in and chat him up a bit, I couldn't. Nor could I ask my brother about him. Cooper would have asked twenty billion questions and razzed me to no end. Not to mention maybe beating the crap out of Ender for looking at his little sister *that* way.

It wasn't until my family hosted the end-of-the-baseball-season pool party at our house that I got my chance. For any normal teenage girl, having a bunch of shirtless high school guys swimming in their backyard would have been akin to hitting the hot guy lottery. What made matters worse was the fact that I couldn't work up the courage to at least attempt to be the "hot sister" and strut around in my two-piece swimsuit like every stereotypical teenage romcom movie in existence.

Except I didn't have the body of the stereotypical heroine. I had curves for days and was short as fuck. So instead, I watched from the kitchen window. I was much closer to being the subject of a Dateline special investigation than being the main character in my favorite romance.

My nose was as close to the glass as possible, trying to see where he was in the pool with the chaos of the rest of the team. Instead, he had snuck in the back door looking for what teenage guys were typically looking for: Food. Ender nearly scared me out of my flip-flops when he found me leaning over the kitchen sink.

"You're Coop's sister, aren't you?" Ender's voice startled me, which sent my arms flailing, knocking the dish scrubber and dish soap into the sink with a horrifying clatter. Yeah, not guilty of voyeurism at all.

"Uh…yeah."

"Tiffiny, right?"

Heat flushed straight up my neck and pooled into my ears with a roar. He knew my name. Wait, had he asked Cooper about me? What if he did? How the hell was I going to process that information?!

"That's me." I shrugged, fixing what I had knocked over as if it were a daily occurrence. Ender didn't say anything to make fun of me or to make me feel bad for my blunder. In fact, we ended up having an entire conversation in my family's kitchen while the pool party raged on outside. How many women can say that they had the first conversation with the love of their life when he had his shirt off?

Wait, don't answer that.

For the rest of the summer, Ender went out of his way to come over and practice baseball in the backyard with Cooper. Most of the time, I was hiding in my room, deep into a book or with my music on as loud as my mom would let me. It wasn't until Ender started lingering around to steal a glimpse of me before he left. Which soon turned into Ender just coming to see me.

Once we started dating, I was a little bit more distracted by the miracle of tight baseball pants. Don't even get me started on the knee-high socks he opted to wear. It was the least-revealing outfit for a man, but it got my motor running. Once upon a time.

"So, are you ever going to tell me what's going on with you and Jamie?" I said nonchalantly as I shoved a boneless wing into my mouth. Anything to distract myself from being bitterly nostalgic and thinking about Ender's ass. "Two weeks ago, you were annoyed any time I brought up his name, and now you can't stop blushing every time I say it."

Jamie being Jamie Rheems, the newest member of the Philly Sillys. A catcher from the Phillies organization who recently got sent down to our squad. He was here to boost ticket sales but also recoup. Cadence had the biggest crush on him and wasn't dealing with the fact that she had to be his choreography coach.

Cadence choked on her beer. "Uh…" Damn, she had a terrible poker face. Always did. But I did enjoy watching her squirm. Plus, it kept her off my back about the weird vibes with Ender that she kept probing about.

Leaning forward, I looked over at her as I stabbed a forkful of loaded fries. Being best friends meant that we didn't exactly have to be lady-like or keep up some kind of decorum. We had no one to impress here.

"Extra spicy. Got it."

Cadence almost looked possessed due to the speed at which she whipped her head around to me. She was only proving my case with every action and completely disproving hers. I couldn't help but grin, cheese and all.

"It is not!" She protested as she frowned. "Okay, so, maybe a little." Her entire body drooped with defeat as she sighed. "Oh, come on, Tiff. How the hell would you function if one of your book boyfriends came to life and you had to watch them shake their ass three feet in front of you at work every day?"

My next fork full of gooey fries stalled midair in front of my open mouth as my brain gave me a front row seat to that train wreck of a movie. Dropping my fork to my plate, my mouth snapped closed as I grabbed my napkin to wipe at a nonexistent mess. I just needed to do something with my hands before I choked her out.

"You know what, fuck you." Because, unfortunately, I knew *exactly* what that was like. But instead of fantasizing about an unattainable man, I just so happened to know what Ender's dick looked and felt like.

"Fuck you too." Cadence shot back with a laugh. Her grin was victorious. "Not so easy, is it?"

Sticking out my tongue at her, I readdressed my large bite of fries and shoved the whole damn thing into my mouth. The cheese was still warm and meshed so well with the saltiness and savoriness of the chunks of bacon. I got lost in the taste of it all, if only for a moment, before I was rudely interrupted by the fact that my distraction plan had gone to fucking hell.

"I could ask the same thing about you and Ender." Cadence glanced in my direction as she took another swing of her beer. "I know you aren't besties with the guys, but damn, Ender is like the nicest guy on the team. Yelling at him like that might get you blacklisted with ownership."

Just the other day, I told Ender to "fuck off" in front of her. In a very not-so-nice kind of tone. It was second nature at this point, lashing out at the one person who had brought me so much happiness. Only for it to turn into bitterness and sorrow. I had to get off the subject. Anything to throw her off the scent of Ender and me trying to explain the past hurt that I wasn't ready to share.

"He said audiobooks don't count as reading."

Cadence made a rather comical and theatrical gasp, complete with her hand on her breastbone to really reiterate the fact. "The audacity!" Her tone was sarcastic, but she was trying so hard not to laugh. She shared my love for books. Maybe not to the same level of obsession, but pretty close.

"Right? He's lucky I *only* told him to 'fuck off'. I could have eviscerated him with my entire vocabulary of insults and bad words from all my dirty romance books. I know at least a dozen ways to call a man a dick without actually using the word."

That got a good snort out of Cadence as she fought for her life to keep the mouthful of beer inside her mouth and not shoot out her nose. Sometimes I had a good zinger that complemented my sarcasm. This woman was the only person who kept me sane at work. Especially now that I was haunted by the ghosts of ex-boyfriends past.

"Okay, but seriously, Tiff. Just because you wear the suit doesn't mean that you can just say anything you want to the guys. Don't let the fact that you have a private dressing room go to your foam head and spinning eyes."

Rolling my actual eyes, I took a long draw from my diet soda. Never in my entire life did I think I'd get a paycheck for being an overstuffed Liberty Bell with googly eyes, making an utter ass of myself. But it did take a sort of off-kilter thespian genius to pull it off. I hadn't been nominated for Mascot of the Year last year for nothing.

"But I can say anything I want to you," My gaze darted to Cadence, downing the last quarter of her beer. "And you might want to cool it on the beers." She was on her third drink already. She wasn't much of a drinker. She was a lightweight. So, the fact that she just housed alcoholic beverages like they were water had me slightly concerned.

Cadence looked dejectedly down at her graveyard of beer bottles and sighed heavily. "You're right. I'm going to really fucking regret it tomorrow at work." Shoving the bottles aside with the back of her hand, she cleared enough space to faceplant onto the table. Well, it wasn't exactly a faceplant. It was more of a dejected, slow descent into hell.

"I can't do it, Tiff. I can't work with the hottest man I've ever seen. It's going to drive me absolutely crazy." The wooden table muffled her words, but I heard them loud and clear.

Same, girl. Same.

The words resonated with me, like a knife to the chest. How the hell was I going to survive working with Ender? Did my brother have no concern or love for his beloved little sister? Why did the universe have to punish me like this? Punish us? Why the fuck did we have this shitty luck in the first place? All I could do to survive was to keep my guard up and be my normal prickly self.

Despite absolutely hating Ender's guts, the man had aged like a fine wine. Like the ones in the fancy case at the liquor store, since Pennsylvania had to regulate alcohol to a weirdly obsessive degree. Ender was still hot. Hell, maybe even hotter than back in high school. And he still wore those tight baseball pants and knee-high socks.

I was not going to survive the rest of baseball season.

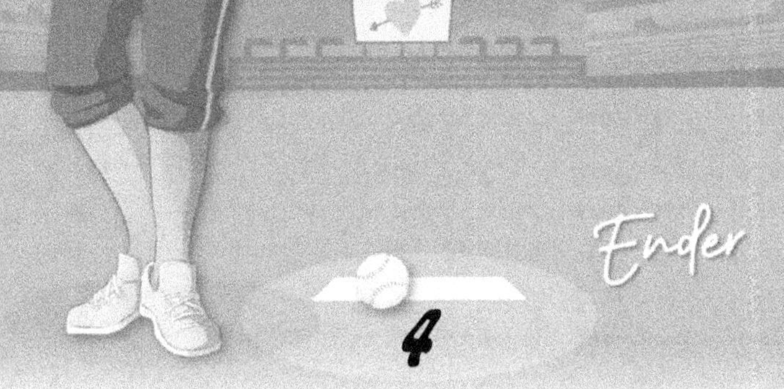

NO LIGHT, NO LIGHT

FLORENCE + THE MACHINE

Fuck.

Every day at the ballpark was just a knife-to-the-heart reminder as to why I didn't go chasing after Tiffiny after I broke up with her. After I realized my gigantic mistake. The utter icy chill she had radiating off of her had to be a superpower or something. And yet I couldn't stay away from her.

The fact that the ache in my heart was almost unbearable every time I laid eyes on her. It was as if she were a siren song, singing a tune that was so perfectly written for me that I couldn't help but be lured in. She was just…*incredible*.

Honestly, she was more incredible than she was in high school. She was confident, sure of herself. Fuck, and her curves were somehow extra delicious. The two-piece bodysuit she wore around the ballpark, when she wasn't in the Ding Dong costume, made it painfully difficult to wear a protective cup.

Despite it being Tiffiny, there was something different about her. Something changed between now and high school. She was colder, more closed off. Not the theatrical beauty that I'd fallen for. She was…

Sad.

There was a dark, gnawing feeling deep inside me that had partnered with my guilt to, very aggressively, point fingers squarely in my direction. Surely me breaking up with her hadn't turned her into this shadow of her former self? What we had in school was your standard teenage relationship. Full of big dreams, fooling around at every desperate chance, going on frugal dates with what money we had left from our meager part-time jobs.

Yet there was this part of me that never really saw anyone else in my life. Only Tiffiny. I mean, sure, my dick did when it thought it had a chance with that Regina girl. But even in that moment, in which I was about to make out with who I thought was my dream girl, all I could think about was the woman who had my heart. I couldn't escape her. Not that I wanted to.

As much as I didn't want to admit it, the woman still had a vice grip on me. Not just because of our history and this familiar swirl of feelings, but those damn curves? Something about knowing what they looked like bare and laid out beneath me was a newfound torture. I could look and reminisce but couldn't touch. I couldn't pull her back into my arms. To kiss her lips just one more time, just to see if this gut-twisting feeling I constantly had around her wasn't the overwhelming need to vomit but to kiss her.

Something that I hadn't stopped thinking about since the day she slammed that door in my face.

Not that I personally wanted to dwell there. Even though my brain sure did. It sat and pondered in my own mess, day in and day out, about the woman I let slip through my fingers.

"Ball two!"

Right now, my brain was not doing anything to help matters. It was the top of the third inning against the Erie Ghosts. I should be focused on getting my pitches across the far corners of the plate. Instead, I was too distracted by the gold lamé fabric flashing in the late afternoon sun from atop the Sillys dugout. With curves that went on for days… I ignored the fact that the only thing visible was the bell curve of the costume on the Liberty Bell mascot, Ding Dong. But when Ding Dong bent over, I did get a flash of…

"Yo Ender," All-Star catcher Jamie Rheems' voice jolted me from my daydream like a hard slap to the face. Shit. The last person I wanted to piss off was the elite Phillies catcher we acquired a few weeks ago. The man was an absolute legend, and I was honored to be able to work with him. Although he was less than thrilled to get saddled with us as a marketing tactic labeled as a rehab assignment. But he was making the most of it. "You good? Your pitches are off."

Apparently, in my sultry daydream of my ex-girlfriend, the man had called time for a mound visit. I was letting my dick think for me, and yet again, it was getting me into some deep shit. I should have learned my lesson the first time, as it was becoming a rather uncomfortable repeat occurrence.

"Yeah, s-sorry, Mr. Rheems." I stammered out, unable to meet his gaze and feeling like an utter asshat in front of the professional. The kind of professional ball player that I had always dreamed of being.

Thankfully, he let out a laugh and clapped me on the back. His hand then moved to a reassuring grip on my shoulder. "How many times do I need to tell you it's just Jamie." His laughter died down, and his face switched over to game mode. "What's got you rattled?"

I chewed on my lower lip as I kicked the grit piled on the pitcher's mound. What the fuck could I tell him? The only person who knew about Tiffiny and my prior history was her and her brother. And I was pretty sure Cooper wasn't talking. Just punishing.

"Is it a certain someone?" My head shot up as my jaw dropped. I couldn't have made it any more obvious that he hit the nail right on the head. Jamie laughed, his catcher's gear shaking with his mirth. "Ah," He hesitated a second, and I shot him a look. "I…have the, uh…same *problem* myself."

Now that took me by surprise. But it was more about the fact that Jamie had shared something personal with me. The man had been pretty stand-offish ever since he was dumped by the Phillies onto the Sillys' doorstep. Slowly but surely he was warming up to the guys. I mean, how could you not? They were just a bunch of loving goofballs who welcomed me into the team dynamic faster than any other team I'd been a part of before.

"But–"

"Look, it's totally fine to think about whoever it is all you want but," Jamie's eyes caught mine and I felt something like a student getting scolded by a teacher. "Just give me another inning of your usual fire, then you can go coo-coo for Cocoa Puffs on the bench. Right?" I nodded. This was going to be an ongoing problem if people were catching on to my thoughts about a certain bell-shaped coworker. "Focus on my glove. Listen to the PitchCom. Get these guys swinging. Hell, do one of those stupid little dances

Coach is always making us do. Anything to get your focus back. You've got this."

With a clap on my back, Jamie darted off just in time to avoid the umpire coming in to break up our conversation. The last thing I needed was another party privy to this information. Gritting my teeth, I sighed, reaching down for the rosin bag. Tossing it in my hand a bit, I used the familiar motion to try and focus myself.

Jamie was right. Although now I had a multitude of other thoughts to mull over while I was out all by myself on the mound. Not that his love life was any of my business.

The stadium DJ had put on some filler music with a good beat. Taking a deep breath, I closed my eyes and closed off the noise of the crowd in my brain. Now that Jamie was playing with us, most games of late were sold out. Everyone wanted to see the super serious catcher work with a team that dances almost as much as they play baseball.

I sat with the music for a few beats before I let the rhythm flow through my limbs. Ever since I did theater with Tiffiny back in high school, I found that I actually enjoyed dancing. While at the time I didn't see a need for it beyond the stage, it had come in handy for being a starting pitcher for an Entertainment League team.

The crowd's cheers fed my dance moves as I used my long legs to get in a few *Twilight*-like high kicks to the beat. The DJ up in the booth got the idea and quickly switched over to "Supermassive Black Hole" by Muse. All of which got me out of my funk and back on my fastball streak.

Jamie gave me an approving nod as he kicked his right foot out, crouching low behind home plate, glove ready to frame my next pitch. Breathing in, I found my stance, my heartbeat slowing to a steady rhythm. The roar of the crowd turned to dull white noise in my head. Something like the rush of blood through your veins when it's deathly quiet.

This was the one place in the world that I felt alive. Where I felt like the whole world made sense. Where all my senses blended together so perfectly that I turned into a well-oiled baseball-throwing machine. Something clicked back into place, and I pulled back, winding up before letting the hard leather slide from my fingertips.

The world moved in slow motion up until I heard that hard snap of leather as the ball hit Jamie's glove. The loud call of *"Strike!"* hit my ears. I exhaled. Okay, so far, so good. Now I just needed to do this goodness knows how many more times. I didn't like to keep current stats in my head, or else it would start to mess with my flow.

Pitch by pitch. That's how every game went. Even if this was Entertainment League baseball, it was still my lifeblood. I just had to sprinkle in some humor and maybe a dance or two, but it was still part of the track to the majors. The long way round, but still a way. And with my beloved Philly team that I grew up watching, no less.

The best part of all this new chaos in baseball is the fact that it was bringing new people to the sport. Hell, it was bringing people back to baseball in general. New generations were finding their way to the ballpark. It was almost as if the ELB was the bridge across generations to get grandfathers together with grandkids to watch the best sport.

Thank fuck for Jamie, who intervened when he did or else the game would have gone a lot worse. The fact that he had noticed something different in me wasn't a good sign for the rest of the season. I thought I could handle being close to Tiffiny again. That the years had passed without us talking and should have made this reunion less… Well, less stressful. Less trying.

Instead, I was beginning to realize that those feelings never went away. That the reason I hadn't dated was solely due to a certain short and curvy brunette currently shaking her shiny, bell-curve ass on top of the Sillys dugout.

Shit, Ender, stop. Get your head back in the game.

Blinking, I shook my head. I thought that, with exposure, being around her would have been easier being around her again. Instead, it was the complete opposite. All the memories came flooding back. All the good, all the bad.

I managed to get through the inning by the skin of my teeth and about ten more pitches than were usually necessary. Keeping my head bowed down and my eyes along the grass line, I did my best to avoid a look from Jamie that I knew was coming. The man had a sixth sense when it came to pitchers. It was both awe-inspiring and rather eerie.

"You made it out of that inning alive," Jamie smirked as he clapped me on the back with his gloved hand as we walked to the dugout. "They're still on your mind, aren't they?"

"…Yep."

5

MY KINK IS KARMA

CHAPPELL ROAN

"Hey Tiff, can you grab the last prop tote for me?" Cadence called over her shoulder as she disappeared down the stairs into the dugout. My eyes fell to the large plastic container and I groaned. Her new stupid routine kicked my ass today, and I just wanted to collapse in my private shower with the water set to frigid to offset this godforsaken Pennsylvania humidity. Although the best I could get with the questionable plumbing was room temperature.

"I got it!" A blur suddenly overtook my peripheral. I skidded to a stop to avoid the collision, but it was too late. I took a plastic tub straight to the titty.

Thanks to Ender.

I'd done everything in my power to put a good twenty yards at any given time between him and me without raising suspicion. I knew the guys wouldn't have given a shit, but Cadence was way more attuned to my quirks. But then again, she was my best friend.

Swearing under my breath, my hand immediately moved to soothe my breast, only to find Ender's gaze squarely on my cleavage. Some things never change. Men never change. I just chose to ignore the fact that his heated gaze still did some unmentionable things for me.

No, Tiff. Bad Tiff. Stop it.

"My eyes are up here, pervert." I huffed at him, still rubbing my sore breast as I shouldered past him. There was a satisfying sputter from Ender. I could only assume that he tried to find his words after I clearly caught him in the middle of some *thoughts*. I shoved the memory of some hot and heavy mutual petting after prom into the deepest, darkest recesses of the back of my brain.

"But I–"

Ender hurried after me, somehow being the last person out on the field. I could have sworn he followed the rest of the guys in. He was one of the taller guys amongst the baseball misfits so typically he was easy to spot in the crowd of Sillys.

The man stood an entire foot taller than me. Which was stupidly hot but also painful on my spine as I had to crane my neck up to look at him. It was worth it to shoot death glares in his direction. Even though I could do it at any distance. There was just something about doing it straight to his face and seeing the fear in his dreamy chocolatey stare.

"Look, I swear I wasn't staring at–"

I stopped dead in my tracks and spun around, only to have almost another collision with the man. But this time, he gave me enough of a berth, almost leaving skid marks in the field grass. The guys on the landscaping team were going to be pissy about his large shoes leaving divots. But that was Ender's problem, not mine.

"Oh, we all know you have a one-track mind, Ender Roche. Nothing has changed with you."

Whoa, girl. Take a step back. Don't trauma dump all at once on the man. Savor it.

I rolled my eyes for good measure, crossing my arms in front of my breasts to block his view. Even though my lusty ego was gulping down the attention. Ender sputtered for a moment. Then utterly surprised me with what he said in reply.

"You know, I deserved that."

Now it was my turn to be flabbergasted. Ender shrugged, his eyes hidden by the brim of his baseball cap. My heart's icy shell melted a little. Shaking my head, I steeled myself for this confrontation that I'd been both dreading and practicing for.

"Oh no, you're not getting off that easy."

"It was always easy with you, Iffy." He added softly, a husky hint to his tone. It was an absolutely dirty move dropping his beloved nickname for me. I couldn't tell if it had been deliberate or just a slip of the tongue. We hadn't been in contact in the last handful of years, and somehow we were already back into the same ol' flirtatious banter.

It both turned me on and infuriated me.

It wasn't fair that he had somehow gotten hotter when he went off to college. Or because he hit the gym on the regular ever since there were rumors of him being potentially drafted by a major league team. I wasn't stalking the man. I just may or may not have regrettably searched him on the internet in a drunken haze somewhere in the middle of my third bottle of wine a few weeks ago.

"You can't do that, Ender." I hated how strained my voice sounded. This man no longer had a hold on me. All those tears I'd shed should have flushed him clear out of my system. My voice dropped as I steeled myself, the raw emotion gone. "You can't go spouting shit like that. Like nothing happened."

Spinning on my heel, I stomped off towards the dugout. I wanted to shrink away. To disappear. To pretend that interaction hadn't happened.

And yet Ender wouldn't fucking drop it.

"But something did happen between us, Iffy." He called out after me. The box of props made a muffled staccato of sound as the contents shifted inside from his long strides to catch up with me. "Look I know it wasn't the most ideal–"

Oh hell no. We were not doing this here and now. I had to end any hope of a reconciliation that he thought he had. As much as my stomach bottomed out beneath me at the thought, this bullshit needed to stop. Just because years had gone by since our stupid breakup didn't mean that we could just suddenly be friends. The fact that we were coworkers was the only reason I wasn't screeching swear words while jumping on his back like a spider monkey.

"Not the most ideal?" I hissed, absolutely seething as my nails dug into the meat of my palms. My eyes shifted around the field, not exactly wanting an audience for what was certainly going to be an ugly conversation. "You literally broke up with me a week before graduation just so you could feel up Regina's titties. And while sure, thanks for breaking up with me before you took Miss Popular to bed. You are a stupid fucking asshole for making asinine decisions with your second, smaller head instead of the one up top."

Not wanting to continue this conversation any further, I flipped him the bird over my shoulder. I made a beeline down the concrete stairs and into the air-conditioned hallway that led to the underbelly of the stadium. I was so bound and determined to get to the safety of my dressing room that I walked right past Cadence putting stuff away in the prop storage room.

"Hey, Tiff–" Cadence started before she had a good look at me from around the edge of the doorframe. "Whoa, dare I ask?" With a brow cocked, she took a side step out of the closet. Followed by one very cautious head-to-toe inventory of me. I bristled.

"Just Ender being his usual assholey self," I grumbled, ready for aliens to take me for an immediate probing instead of dealing with this circus of bullshit. One look from her made me realize that she wasn't fully buying it. Thankfully, instead of prying, she changed the subject.

"Looks like you could use a drink."

"Ain't that the fucking truth ninety percent of the time."

"Okay, but you look extra ragey today and I think I need to coax Tiffzilla off the statue of William Penn on top of City Hall."

Thank god for my friend. She could always get me to take it down a few notches with her off-brand humor. Letting out a semi-amused huff, I crossed my arms in front of me.

"So where are we getting these anti-ragey drinks at?"

Now it was Cadence's turn to look uncomfortable. "Um…at line dancing…?"

"Oh no. Absolutely the fuck not–" It was common knowledge that Cadence had taught most of the team to dance by dragging them line dancing. They ended up having so much fun that they like to go on a semi-regular basis. But I didn't blame her for her reluctance.

"No, no! Please?" She lunged forward, grabbing my arm before I could turn and head down the hall. The desperation in her voice gave me pause so I stopped with a cock of my brow. "Don't let me face *him* alone."

"Who…?"

"Jamie."

I laughed. "Girl, you're gonna do just fine. The guys are going with you. Have them dance with Jamie."

"No!" She whined, her grip on my arm getting tighter. Pulling me in closer to her, her eyes moved to the locker room door just a few feet away. "Please? Look somehow the guys talked me into this bullshit. It's literally my last-ditch effort to teach the man some semblance of dancing before I lose my job."

My expression softened. I knew the situation with her heartthrob crush newcomer was serious, but not this kind of serious. As much as I really didn't want to go, I had to give my friend at least a little support.

"Okay, fine." I sighed, rather dramatically to boot. "But I'm bringing my book. It's either that or I'm not coming. I've had enough choreography practice for today, thank you very much."

"Oh, thank fuck, bless you, Tiff." Cadence let out a heady breath of relief. "I just need a friendly face in the crowd who actually knows my, uh, *history* with Jamie." I let out a caw of laughter. I knew my friend was smitten with the unattainable man, but I didn't realize I'd have to be her emotional support human just to get through the evening of teaching the man how to dance.

"You'll be fine. Get there early and get at least get one beer in you. You're much more fun that way." I got a hearty shove to the shoulder for that. Turning back to her, I began to walk backwards towards my dressing room, feeling slightly better at my situation when compared to Cadence's. That was until I saw Ender timidly make his way down the stairs. "First round is on you, though, babe!" I beelined it to my dressing room, barely registering the look on Ender's face.

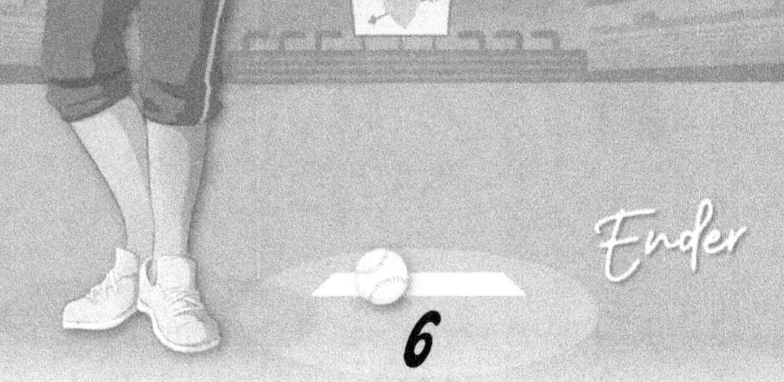

THE WAY YOU LOVED ME

CALUM SCOTT

The guys had talked about Coach's off-the-cuff approach to dancing before, but I never thought I'd have a chance to see it firsthand. The bar was lively, music pulsing in the background with a crowd moving mostly in sync in the large dance floor over on the left side. Cadence had invited us all, but it was more of an initiation of Jamie to our chaotic ranks than a formal choreography session.

Most of the bar top tables were empty save for the hordes of half-full beer bottles and baskets of nachos along a grouping by the wall near the front door. I was late, and the guys looked otherwise engaged in a rather complicated line dance. Not in the mood to jump in mid-dance, I let my eyes flit around the room, contemplating passing the time drowning myself in a very large beer of whatever was on tap.

Just when I was deciding between two of the specialty summer brews, I noticed a subtle shift of something, just off to the corner of me. Cocking my head, I glanced over only for my heart to seize in the middle of my chest. Buried with her nose in a book was Tiffiny.

She looked completely oblivious to the noise and energy of the room. Her brows were furrowed in some mix of emotion stemming from the words on the page before her. For as long as I'd known her, she was always buried in the pages of some book. Usually something with a nondescript cover, but sometimes it was ones with barely dressed men, well on their way to undressing their female counterparts. It wouldn't take much of a guess to know what those books were about.

This cover, on the other hand, looked menacing. Scary even. Had she moved onto horror instead of her usual dirty romances and faraway fantasies? The first time I had ever laid eyes on her was in a moment similar to this. Except there was a dugout and fence as the barrier between us, and not this current icy wall of animosity.

As much as I kept trying to avoid these churning thoughts of everything Iffy deep in my belly, it was utterly impossible. Not when I could look at her like this. Without her knowing. Without her spitting the well-deserved vitriol in my face.

She was never far from my mind. Not a day had gone by that my thoughts weren't of her. Reliving my stupid fucking mistake over and over again. Fuck I was an utter idiot. I had to be one to let a woman like her go.

I knew she wanted to be left alone. She had made that abundantly clear earlier when she had nearly bit my head off. Then again, it was also deserved as I kind of rammed her boob with a tote full of props.

Another hot flush made its way through my body as I remembered the way her hand massaged her breast. *Fuck.* I could remember those hot summer nights. Being as quiet as possible, touching her tits in the same way, as she grinded against me on the floor of my bedroom. It was the safest bet for not getting caught. The squeak of my bed was a rather dead giveaway as to what we were up to.

My hand reached down to subtly adjust my growing dick inside my jeans. Thank fuck the bar was mostly dim. The damn thing had gotten me into enough trouble in my life. Mostly because of the curvaceous goddess before me.

"That's not your usual genre, is it?" The words had left my mouth before I could register where my feet had led me. Traitorous bastards.

Iffy's head shot up. Her eyes were still glazed over as she tried to focus on me. Whatever she was reading, it had completely transported her brain somewhere else. I do seem to remember that she lost herself so deeply within books. I used to read as voraciously as she did, although my reading tastes were nowhere near as spicy as hers were.

Blinking through her deer-in-the-headlights look, she glanced down at her hands. Her brows furrowed in confusion for a moment. She left her finger on the page she was reading, closing the book to glance at the cover. It was as if she had already forgotten what she had been reading. Or maybe it was my presence that had gotten her off kilter. My chest swelled at that thought. If only I could be that lucky to still have that effect on her.

"Yeah." She said simply as her face evened out to passiveness. "It's not."

That was apparently all she was going to enlighten me with as she cracked the spine, whipping the book back open. There was no one else around us, so why did she bother to come if she was only going to sit here, scowling behind a book? Maybe she just came for a drink. Which, honestly, didn't sound like that bad of an idea. Especially if Cadence was going to drag my tall ass out onto the dance floor at any moment.

Giving her a nod that I wasn't sure she saw, I made a beeline for the bar. Something in my gut didn't want the conversation to end just yet. But I desperately needed some liquid courage. I wandered back from the bar with two beers just in time to see the guys come back from the dance floor for a breather.

"End Game!" Truitt Lancaster, left fielder, called out, slapping me on the back rather aggressively. With a grin, he made a move for one of my beers, but I shot him a look. He laughed and somehow found his neglected bottle on the next table over. "No fun, man."

"Dude, you make more money than me." I shot back.

"Yeah, leave the poor rook alone, Tru. Hell, you should get *him* a beer." First baseman Benson Haldeman chimed in as he looked at me with a nod. Sometimes I felt like Benson was the dad of the group. Keeping the guys in line with his cool demeanor and knowledge of the game. Like a wizened sort of Yoda. Except he was six feet tall and definitely not nine hundred years old.

"Yeah okay, *not*." Truitt stuck his tongue out at Benson but gave me a wink. The backup Sillys catcher, Schmidt Sullivan, and designated hitter Martin Pitt shuffled up to the table. Schmidt gave me a fist bump.

Before Jamie had shown up, Schmidt and I had built a whole repertoire together. Pitchers always need a good communication relationship with their catcher. Despite Schmidt's outlandish demeanor most of the time, he was a great catcher with a wealth of knowledge. Not to mention the fact that he rarely shut up, so it was always a learning experience with him.

"How's the missuses, guys?" I nodded to Schmidt and Martin, as they were the only two in the group with wives. The rest of the team were just sorry sacks of chaos. It was a wonder how Truitt managed to take home as many women as he did. Maybe it was the beard. As for me, it skived me out. But to each their own.

"Eh, mine was sick of me five minutes after I walked in the door. She said I needed to burn off some steam." Schmidt shrugged with a shit-eating grin. It took a hell of a special lady to deal with his outrageous ass day in and day out.

My eyes glanced over to Iffy, only to have her gaze meet mine from over the edge of her open book. There was an undeniable heat that rose up the back of my neck in that split second before she dismissed me, turning back to the book with a rather vibrant skull on the cover. Or was it a mask? I still couldn't tell. Either way, it looked freaky.

My shoulders sagged as I took a rather large swig of beer. My eyes reluctantly moved away from hers and scanned over the group. The whole gang was here, except for the two main reasons why our sorry asses were at the bar in the first place. I was going to be pissed if we all got stood up.

"Where's Coach and Jamie?" I asked cautiously as I scanned the room once more.

"One step away from kissing each other out on that dance floor." Right fielder Arlow Rivero said so matter-of-factly from his casual lean on the bar top just one table over from me. Everyone turned and looked at him, mouths in some stage of shock. Including my slack jaw. Apparently, we'd been oblivious to whatever was going on.

"I–" I was too stunned to speak. Arlow's words knocked the wind right out of me. From the looks of it, the team shared my sentiment.

"Holy shit." Second baseman Roman Stevens breathed out, his eyes wide as his beer bottle hovered halfway to his mouth. Sure enough, Arlow was right. He'd always been one of the more romantic at heart kind of guys in the group. Benson was a close second. I was pretty sure it was from all the romance novels he read.

All of us had our attention on the wild scene unfolding in front of us. Cadence and Jamie had lingered on the dance floor for the post-line dance songs that took place, so the caller and dancers had time to recharge in between. They were clearly so engrossed in the song that the world ceased to exist around them. The pair of them were so wildly intertwined with each other that it was almost vulgar.

Almost.

The entire lot of us had seen Cadence and Jamie be testy with each other. Ever since the moment he arrived. But now you had to be utterly blind not to see the desire and chemistry radiating off the pair of them. And we were clear across the large bar.

"Holy shit is right," I mumbled out, not bothering to move my lips much. We had to remain as inconspicuous as possible. "I mean…damn." I surmised, as we were transfixed by the obvious magic going on before us.

"It's so cute." Center fielder Tomas Lopez sighed out, his head cocked to the side as he admired the blossoming couple.

It made me ache inside. Ache for the one thing that dangled in front of me day in and day out of late, but I couldn't have. My gaze shifted over to Iffy. To most, it looked like she was still nose-deep in her book. But I could tell she was just as mesmerized by the dancing couple as we all were.

She watched the pair with a dreamy look in her eyes. Once upon a time, she looked at me like that. Grumbling to myself, I lifted my beer bottle to my lips and drained the rest of the bottle.

"Twenty bucks says they're sucking face by the end of the season." I coughed on the last gulp of my beer as shortstop Kellan Bristol grumbled around the lip of his beer bottle. The guys were a mix of surprise and amusement as we all turned to look at him. "What? Come on," He redirected our attention, gesturing with his beer bottle to Jamie dipping Cadence on the dance floor. "Even Oscar-winning actors can't fake something like that."

There were murmurs of agreement as the guys all turned back to their drinks, looking rather dejected. Aside from Schmidt and Martin, the rest of us hadn't exactly had the best luck in love. At least from what I could tell from a zillion pieces of broken locker room conversations. But that side chat with Jamie the other day made a whole hell of a lot more sense now. I smiled. Maybe it was Cadence he was talking about? It would explain all the hush-hush.

"Well, I'm fucking ready to find me a dance partner like that," Truitt stood up from his lean on the table, finishing the rest of his beer with gusto. The foam settled into the corners of his beard before he slammed the mug back down. "Who's with me?"

There was a rousing noise of agreement as the guys shuffled off, their heads on a swivel, looking for potential partners in the recesses of the bar. I waved them off, telling them I wanted to get loose with another beer first before jumping in. I wasn't too worried about Coach coming over to tell me to jump in for a few songs. She was otherwise engaged.

I had…more *pressing* matters.

Specifically, the shapely brunette in the corner. Feeling the beer in my veins, and no questioning looks from the guys, I shuffled over to Tiffiny. Her eyes shifted to me for a hot second, meeting my gaze before scrambling back, trying to look as interested as possible with whatever is happening in her book.

With each passing day it was becoming more and more painful *not* talking to her. It was as if she were my brand of drug and I desperately needed my fix. Being around her just made me twitch. Well, it made *something* twitch.

But how to crack her code? I knew she was pissed at me. Maybe I had to make it seem like I wasn't a threat? That perhaps I could be someone she could come to for anything. Just talking to her soothed the ache deep inside. Kissing her again would probably fix everything, but that was a whole can of worms I didn't want to open at the moment. And from her disgusted look, neither did she.

"So…" Shit, I should have had a better game plan in place. But yet again, my feet thought differently than my brain and dragged my sorry ass over to her the moment the coast was clear. "What's uh…um…" Her eyes narrowed at me, her gaze becoming more annoyed by the second. I needed to come up with something. "Uh, so what's your book about?"

I tried to make the question come out as evenly as possible so I didn't arouse suspicion, but Iffy was way too smart to fall for my usual bullshit. Her finely sculpted brows furrowed as she eyed me. There was conflict in her gaze. Conflict enough that my stomach flip flopped with a tinge of hope.

"It's a romance." One of my eyebrows shot up my forehead. I didn't believe her for one second. "A dark romance."

"What the hell is the difference?"

"Morally grey characters and a trigger list that makes you question how perverted you are with the kinks you're willing to tolerate."

I choked on my sip of beer. Using the back of my hand to wipe my mouth, I sputtered, trying to catch my breath as I eyed her. Iffy was never one for subtleties. It was one of the charming qualities I always admired about her. But I was a bit out of practice fending myself from her wit. She was going to eat me alive.

And fuck I wanted it.

"Maybe I should read it?" I offered as casually as possible. I was treading on dangerous ground, but getting a rise out of Iffy had always been a sport of mine. And with her being extra icy since we reconnected, it was now an extreme sport. "You know…maybe figure out some of those new kinks of yours."

I swear there were flames in her eyes. There also may have been a subtle squirming of her hips in her seat as she looked me over, silently praying that the heat in her gaze would incinerate me. Or…was it something else?

"I don't think you could handle it." Her spine straightened as she laid the book open, page side down on the table. Internally, I did a fist pump as I had successfully managed to tear her attention away from the book. Come hell or high water, whatever nasty shit she wanted to spew at me would be worth it. Just to be able to stare into her sparkling amber eyes, vibrant gemstones, even in the dim light of the bar.

"I don't know, Iffy. We did have some rather wild times–"

"I'm gonna cut you off there, desperate desperado." She held a hand up, but the other one was mysteriously out of sight. "Look, maybe I fucked your brains out too many times while we were dating, but that's not an excuse to saddle on up here and flirt with me like there isn't some hundred-foot chasm between my adorable self and your pathetic one. Not a chance in hell, buckaroo."

I snorted, unable to help myself. She was extra adorable when she was standoffish like this. Maybe I was into her ice queen demeanor after all. It didn't mean I couldn't tease her about it, too. "What's with all the cowboy references?"

She limply waved her hand around, a gesture to the Western decor hanging all over the walls. "It's the environment."

There was an awkward moment of silence between us as we both avoided each other's gazes. Why was it both hard and equally just as easy? I was about ready to burst. A great need to tell Iffy anything and everything. She had been my best friend once.

Goddamn my teenage self.

"So…uh, about the book–"

"What about it?"

"I want to know what it's about."

That skeptical look flashed back over her features. There seemed to be some internal debate going on in that pretty head of hers. And then… They softened. They softened into something like the Iffy I used to know.

"It's about a monster that lives under the bed." Okay, kind of a weird premise for a romance book, but I wasn't going to stop her now. "He stays under this one guy's bed. And well…so this guy's girlfriend comes over to stay a lot." She was slowly warming up to me. The words flowed more easily, so I nodded my head for her to continue. "And well, uh, the woman is totally dating beneath her. Her boyfriend sucks. He doesn't treat her right," I cringed a bit at that. "And her boyfriend is totally awful in bed. Anyway, the monster ends up having a crush on her and then starts fucking her and–"

The look on my face must have made Iffy stop mid-tirade. I mean, it wasn't the weirdest premise for a book that I'd ever heard, but it was pretty fucking weird. But as much as I was skeeved out, I had to admit that I was a little intrigued. Plus, if I asked engaging questions, she might keep talking to me. Warm back up to me. At least a little bit.

"Does he…" I swallowed. "Does the monster look like a monster, or…?"

Iffy shrugged, trying to look nonplussed. But even in the dim lighting of the bar I could see that her mouth had quirked up in the corner. At least she was amused by the nonsense I was spewing.

"Oh yes." She said, matter-of-factly. Looking rather smug as she did so. "He has a *tail*." I shrank a little. "It…does…*things*." *Oh…shit.* Iffy's sudden burst of giggles made my stomach do some sort of complex twist and flip in a gastro Olympics. Fuck, I missed making her laugh.

"Well…" I cleared my throat, my finger absentmindedly flicking a loose corner of the label on my beer bottle. This was hands down the weirdest conversation I've ever had. But if it kept Tiffiny talking to me, then she could cut off my arm for all I care. "I bet that's, uh…fun."

"That's one way to put it."

7

SLOW DANCE

AJ MITCHELL

I was in…
Shock.
I had to be.

If I hadn't learned my lesson with this man, I could have sworn that Ender was flirting with me. Or at least, trying to. In a really awkward sort of way. Like he was walking on eggshells. Treading over a minefield. It was kind of cute.

No, bad girl. Down, Tiff.

It was clearly evident that the man hadn't spoken to a woman in quite some time. Or maybe it was the rather questionable subject matter of our conversation. I'll admit, I was doing everything in my power to make him squirm. Testing his limits on just how long he wanted this conversation to go on for.

He was welcome to tap out any time he wanted. Then I would just hold my victory over his head for the rest of eternity. Not that he knew that.

"So…do all of your books have hot monster fucking in them or…?"

Now it was my turn to be surprised. There was no beating around the bush with that question. I was so glad that I had perfected my poker face in theater school because I had a feeling Ender was going to give it right back to me.

"Not all of them. A select few."

I surmised, pursing my lips as I slipped the straw to my glass of ginger ale between them. Cadence had only managed to grab me one round of beer before she disappeared into the throngs of people. Not that I was completely pissed that she had abandoned me. I'd gotten through three chapters of some of the hottest monster smut I've ever read before Ender disturbed my peace.

Being already hot and bothered *before* Ender walked into the bar was trouble enough. But now that my former teenage heartthrob was barely two feet away from me, asking some rather pointed questions was only adding to my fluster. I gulped down my soda.

It didn't help that he had grown into his lanky arms and legs. Each limb filled out with sinew and richly tanned skin from all the hours spent practicing in the sun. He even had the weirdly hot frosted tips that he used to sport in high school. I always teased him that he was some boy band member wannabe. There was only one option here. Deflect in an effort to ignore the humidity between my thighs so I can get out of this conversation alive.

"I still can't believe you haven't gotten over yourself." My words must have pulled him from some far-off place as his stare went from distant to a laser focus on me.

"Huh?"

"This isn't high school, Ender." I shot him a look as my nose wrinkled. My arms crossed and it must have done something to my breasts as his eyes snapped down. My amusement of his thirsty self distracted me from my snide tirade for a second.

"Uh…what?" Clearly, only some of my words were registering. Yes. I was winning this round quite handily.

"The blonde tips." Leaning back in my barstool, I gestured to his head. "Like dude, get over yourself."

That got his attention. His gaze narrowed at me and I smiled my smug little smile. Two could play at this game. If he wanted to give me shit about my books, then I was going to give him shit about his hair.

"You don't like them?" He gave me a dramatic pout as he dropped his chin. "But you loved them in high school. I thought it might churn up some interesting memories." With a smarmy smirk, he leaned forward onto the bar top, cutting the safe space between us almost in half. I'd been doing so well in this stupid showdown, and my body had to go and freeze the second he invaded my personal space even further. "Especially when you were tugging on them."

Oh fuck.

Goddamn it.

I did not need this man to say hot and sexy shit like one of my book boyfriends did. He was not going to ruin romance books for me. Business and pleasure needed to be as separate as possible.

Except his heated comment only made my insides melt into a molten puddle and settle into the deepest recesses of my belly. It wasn't fair that this infuriating man still had this hold on my body. I guess after all these years my body still didn't get the memo of 'hey, we fucking hate this dude'.

I hated how easy it was to fall back into him every time he managed to corner me and talk. I should still be pissed. I should still be prickly towards him. But some weird, obscure part of me, deep down inside, was head to toe infatuated with him. Even after all the denial. Even after the heartbreak.

Holy hell, I hated myself. That had to be it. That was the only explanation that I was sitting here at this bar talking to the man.

"Times have changed," I said simply, using every part of my theater degree to keep my face hovering between pissed off and neutral. "I only find red flag men in books hot. Not red flag guys dressed as tall as fuck baseball players with frosted tips."

I knew that would confuse him, his brows knitting together as he tried to make sense of my cryptic jab. Cadence would have known. Hell, any ladies in book world would have known what I was talking about. Fictional red flag men were perfectly fine in romance books. Red flag men in this bullshit called reality was a life sentence of misery, or worse.

"So…no to the frosted tips then?"

Holy fuck, he was incorrigible. I threw my bottle cap at him. With lightning-fast reflexes, the man's hand shot up. He didn't even move another muscle. It was just his limb, snapping to catch the cap in midair before it smacked him in the forehead. His long fingers closed over the puckered metal before maneuvering it with his digits to study the artifact.

I've never been more turned on in my entire life.

And I was reading a book where the woman was held down by the monster's tail while his ribbed-for-her-pleasure cock fucked her within an inch of her life. No spicy romance book on the planet was hotter than Ender doing baseball things with just effortless ease. The man was like baseball's version of Spider-Man.

"Yeah no, hard pass." Clearing my throat, I shifted in my seat, shoving my hand between my thighs in a vain attempt to stop the metaphorical dam from breaking. That and to stop me from reaching out and openly molesting the man in public. This wasn't fair. Not one bit.

I grabbed my glass of ginger ale and gulped down half of what was left, trying not to look like I was losing my ever-loving shit about my personal brand of aphrodisiac that was currently standing on the opposite side of the table.

No no no. I can't be thinking like this. *Be strong Tiff, be strong.* I knew he wasn't doing this on purpose. Ender didn't have a suave bone in his body. But it didn't make it any less infuriating.

Ender's lips pursed. It was almost as if he was stumped by some stupid riddle that he couldn't wrap his head around. I wasn't going to admit that I shared the sentiment, as the man and his attention on me of late felt like whiplash. As much as I wanted to give in to his awkward wiles, my integrity wouldn't let me.

The music died off, snapping us out of whatever the fuck we were in the middle of. There was a shift of dancers out on the floor as the music went decidedly more mellow.

My brain recognized it as a pop hit from our high school days. I felt the bitter pang of nostalgia. My gaze drifted over his silhouette. His tanned skin was illuminated by the colorful neon beer signs scattered over the walls. I couldn't help but think of the happier times.

"Wanna dance?" Ender's voice slammed the door on my reminiscing so suddenly that my startle couldn't be helped. I felt marginally bad about it.

Swallowing back the rush of fluster, my eyes timidly found his, looking adorably hopeful back at me. "For old time's sake?" I chewed on my bottom lip. Part of me really wanted to give in. Just for tonight. "Cadence will kick my ass if she knew I didn't dance to at least one three-minute song for practice."

Being Cadence's best friend, I knew that when it came to the chaotic players, she was a loving hard ass. I knew she'd be good for the ass kicking. Or maybe I could volunteer my foot for the kicking part.

On the other hand, maybe it was my overactive hormones trying to tear themselves from my ovaries to jump him because I was seriously considering his offer. What the fuck was wrong with me? Why was this chaos in my brain? The man was my self-imposed enemy. I shouldn't be fraternizing with the other side.

Then again…

What harm would come out of one dance? It was innocent enough. Call a truce for a few minutes. It wasn't like he was asking me to marry him or anything.

"Fine." I huffed as I stood, shoving my bookmark into my book. "Just one stupid dance. Just to shut you up. Then you can go back to leaving me the fuck alone."

Ender let out a bark of a laugh as his spine straightened, pushing himself away from the table.

Without even a second of hesitation after my agreement, his hand grabbed mine, practically dragging me towards the dance floor.

I had to bite my lip from the sudden jolt of electricity that shot straight up my arm, down my torso, and straight into the V of my thighs. I'd forgotten how big and strong his hands were. Rooted to forearms that were deliciously toned and veiny. My body immediately went into an entire court argument over whether or not it was smart to let this be more than just a dance.

Ender found us a darker corner of the dance floor, away from the rest of his teammates. Which I was silently thankful for. Sweeping me up in his arms, he pulled me in close. Too close.

I could smell him. All six-foot-four inches of him. He smelled of sunshine and fresh air, a bit of his musky cologne, and there was a hint of cooking spices. My immediate reaction was to smile.

The warmth of his body and the smell of him took me back to high school. To summer nights at the ballpark, dinners with his mom at their tiny kitchen table, stolen kisses in linoleum-filled halls. He smelled of much less complicated times.

My body was melting fast. I needed to get my head back in the game. I couldn't give in so easily.

Gritting my teeth, I pressed the palms of my hands against his chest, giving us a more visual separation that any assistant principal chaperoning a school dance would be satisfied with. This was such a stupid idea. A fucking stupid idea.

Ender thankfully got the hint and slid his hands from my lower back to settle onto the top curve of my hips. It wasn't fair that, even years later, I could easily get drunk on the way his hands on my body made me feel. My hands reluctantly landed on his shoulders, which was still a bit of an awkward stretch for me.

"Just like old times, huh?" Ender grinned down at me, his eyes sparkling with mischief.

"Don't let it go to your head. I only did this because you guilted me into it, so you don't get your ass kicked."

"So thoughtful of you." He shot back before leaning down a bit, his gaze surveying the dance floor. "Joke's on you, maybe I like getting my ass beat by women under five-foot-four."

I swallowed. I was sure that it was meant to be some silly banter, but something about the way he said it made me think it was something else. Or maybe it was just my brain being dirty again. Talking about ass-kickings shouldn't be this hot.

"Kinky." I managed to get out. I hated the fact that my voice was strained. There was a bit of heat to his gaze when his eyes shot back to mine. Excellent, I was getting under his skin again. "Maybe I can get you reading dirty dark romance books. There are some books with ass play."

Ender's foot knocked into mine, sending him into a bit of an inelegant stumble. I let out a victorious snort in amusement, still managing to stay on my feet, looking nonplused. Even in the neon lights, I could see the pink in his cheeks. Good. A literal and metaphorical stumble. Notch another one in the "win" column for me.

"I don't know why more men don't read romance novels." I was on a roll, using Ender's obvious fluster as fuel to my fire. Feeding off the fact that I was the reason he was tongue-tied. "I feel like they could learn a lot."

Ender seemed surprised by that fact, cocking his head to the side as he tried to read my face. Which, fair, I had gotten really good at sarcasm in my old age. Er, older age.

"They could learn…?" He started, his words trailing off as he got lost in thought for a moment. "Learn about what?"

"What women want."

Ender burst out laughing but immediately stopped when he saw my face. "Oh, you're serious?"

"Does it look like I'm doing a monologue on *The Tonight Show*?" I gave myself an adulting gold star for that zinger. "See, this is exactly the reason why men *should* read romance. Because men don't take it seriously and women do." A skeptical eyebrow slowly crested on his forehead. "Romance books are literally a playbook to women's desires. How they want to be loved. And honestly, it's a lot simpler than guys make it out to be."

I was passionate now. Fiery about my beliefs and putting mediocre men, who thought they were hot shit, into their place. Ender looked lost in thought as we absentmindedly swayed to the music. Maybe I had hit a nerve or something.

It's not like I wanted to give away some of my deepest secrets. But coming between a woman and her smutty books was an act of war. I wasn't going to stand idly by and let that shit fly.

"So, is that true for you?"

His soft words pulled me from my spiraling thoughts. "Is what true?"

"That romance books are just a, you know… *How To* guide to seducing you."

I was ready to kick my own ass for the unholy fluster that my body suddenly found itself in. It wasn't fair how that sentence sent my body into high alert. Why did I have to open my big, fucking mouth.

Then again…

Perhaps this could be an entertaining opportunity for me in the long run. To sit back and watch Ender squirm as he attempted to read these dirty romance books.

"I mean…" Dammit, I really dug my own grave here. The only way out was to make this man sweat. To regret that he ever went down this dark and dirty rabbit hole with me. I let my voice drop to a bit of a husk. "I learned a lot about myself reading these. Turns out I'm not as *innocent* as I once was."

Being over a foot shorter than Ender, it gave me a front row seat to the unholy bob of his Adam's apple. My dastardly plan was working. If this man was going to go out of his way to keep butting his very cute head into my life, even after I've done everything possible to avoid him.

"Yeah, well…the both of us weren't so innocent after a while." Ender shot back, recovering faster than I would have liked. Oh hell no. I was keeping the upper hand in this.

"I mean, sure." He wasn't wrong. We had taken each other's virginity so in that sense of the word, he was correct. But in my sense? "But you're too vanilla for me, Ender. I need spice. Not boring ol' missionary. And doing a sixty-nine position was spicy back then, but amateur hour for adults."

There was another visible gulp down his throat as I felt him tense under my touch. Oh, sweet summer child. Those poor women he'd been with after me. I'm surprised he didn't bore them to tears.

The music began to wind down and I took his moment of silent reflection to make a hasty exit. He barely registered as I gently slipped away, stepping away from his arms that were still hovering in mid-air, pretending to hold me. I ignored the fact that my body nearly cried out from the loss of contact.

"Crack a spine, Ender." I called from over my shoulder, quickening my pace across the bar to grab my things and get the hell out of dodge. "You might learn something."

8

SHE'S AN ACTOR

AUSTIN GIORGIO

That woman had my balls in a vice grip. Her words swam in my head as I had another beer with the guys. I was so checked out that I could barely follow the chatter amongst them. All I could focus on was Iffy's and my conversation.

After that last beer, I took a few laps around the city block to sober up. I needed to think. There was no way I could go home. As much as I adored Mamá, she could read me like a book. Which I would have found rather ironic in this situation, had it not been for my head and heart being all twisted in knots.

If our dance together had proved anything, it was that I couldn't be without Tiffiny in my life. But considering that she seemed annoyed by the very fact that I could breathe, this was going to be one uphill battle.

I'd said that I was starting from square one again, but this square one included the history of her hating my fucking guts. Instead of an adorable first glance of each other.

This was going to need a careful game plan to maybe, hopefully, let her give me a second chance. That conversation on the dance floor about books had the wheels turning in my head. I mean, why would she say such things if they weren't supposed to be a leg up on how to woo her?

I wanted to woo her. I wanted to get all tangled up with her. I wanted to tell her how much of a fucking idiot I was in high school to let anyone or anything get between us.

Because then we wouldn't have missed out on so much. Maybe we would be married. Living in some tiny townhouse on the outskirts of the city. Driving into work together. Picking up our super adorable kids from daycare…

So, what if, after practice the day after our little dance, I went straight to the bookstore and picked up the book Iffy had been reading? And so what if I stayed up to an ungodly hour on game day to get through almost half of the book? I also might have done it in spite of the fact that Iffy told me to "get bent" today when I simply said "hi" to her. I thought our moment out on the dance floor had gotten us to more neutral ground. Instead, I was met with pure venom. Yet again.

I managed to keep my cool, shooting her a look for the sudden about-face of behavior. Not to mention, Cadence was a bit rough around the edges throughout practice. She must have had one too many beers. Most of us were a bit rough yesterday morning for choreography practice. Somehow, we all managed to get through it. We even convinced Jamie to stay for extra dance lessons since, apparently, he and Cadence had a breakthrough at line dancing.

Now here I was, rounding the 48-hour mark since Tiffiny had our private moment on the dance floor, and I still couldn't stop replaying the entire conversation in my head. It was the first time I'd been that close to her in years. Maybe that was the reason my brain was so stuck in that moment and didn't want to escape.

Walking towards the ramp down to the lower-level locker room, I ran into Benson, who always looked so put together when he got to the ballpark. The two of us were usually the first ones here for report days. The man had been in this industry all his life. It was still a wonder why he was stuck playing in the ELB instead of at a minor or major league level.

"Hey Ender." Benson nodded, raising his to-go cup of coffee in my direction. "Fully recovered after yesterday?"

I let out a snort. "Chugged about half a 24-pack of Gatorade in the last twenty-four hours or so. Mamá made breakfast for dinner last night and I think that did the trick."

Benson groaned as he tipped his coffee down. "Damn, I love your mom's cooking. Any chance she could make us another tray of arepas again? Especially those chicken and avocado ones? I swear I still have dre–"

My brow furrowed as I glanced over to Benson, who had stopped in his tracks, just as we started to go down the ramp into the stadium's underbelly. Before I could open my mouth to see what had him all kerfuffled, he fisted my shirt and dragged me behind a support column.

"Dude," He whispered, taking a peek around the corner of the pillar. "Isn't that coach and...*Jamie?*"

Balking, I craned my neck to look beyond Benson and further down the hall. Sure enough, I could see Jamie taking a step back, letting a rather flustered-looking Cadence push off the cinder block wall. Their hands moved to smooth out their clothes and I blushed.

"Uh, looks like it."

"What do you think they're talking about?"

I didn't have time to answer before the two were sucking face again, this time in broad daylight in the wide walkway. It seemed to me that they must have made quite the connection at line dancing the other night. Which was wild because, up until then, they had been so testy with each other.

"Whatever it was, Jamie sure liked it."

I let out as soft of a laugh as I could muster. The two were so tangled up in each other as they kissed. Passionate and wanting, without being vulgar. I only felt a little guilty that we were spying on them. But this was an interesting turn of events. They pulled away, and their smiles could have blinded me. My heart melted before it fell to my feet. Gosh, I really fucking missed those moments with Iffy.

Shit.

The sheer fact that my brain immediately went to thoughts of her from watching kissing stimuli did not bode well for me. My brain flooded with all those stolen kisses in the hallways at school. Being around her so much was not helping matters in the least bit.

"Wait…" Benson's whisper pulled me out of my tailspin of thoughts. "Is Jamie giving Coach his number? Hold up. That's so fucking cute."

My gaze shifted to my teammate. I didn't realize that Benson had a soft spot when it came to romance. Especially sappy sort of stuff like this. I watched as Jamie typed something into Cadence's phone before handing it back to her with a smile. Benson was right, it was really fucking cute to watch a romance unfold like this in real life.

I wondered if this was the sort of bubbly, warm feeling Tiffiny got from reading those romance books she was telling me all about. Did the dark romance books with the scary covers have sweet moments like this? Or was it a different kind of intimacy given the subject matter? I definitely needed to investigate further.

The book I bought had followed me to work, tucked into an outside pocket of my bag. I was itching to pick up where I left off. Despite the storyline being utterly deranged, the chemistry between the human and monster characters was seriously off the charts. Although considering I was getting hard reading a spicy scene that was more a tease than the full-on sex, it probably wasn't a smart idea to read it at work.

Maybe a few pages wouldn't hurt.

"What the hell are you two doing?"

Tiffiny's voice yeeted my soul clear out of my body for a split second as I jumped in surprise. Benson looked unfairly cool as a cucumber as he casually turned around with a grin. The man's stoic demeanor was honestly Oscar-worthy. He must be immune to anxiety or something.

"Oh, you know, just me interrogating Ender on what the secret ingredient is that his mom puts in her arepas."

Crossing her arms, with a sharp jut of her hips to one side, led me to believe that Iffy wasn't buying his excuse one bit. But then again, she was wearing her tight spandex leggings for work. I may have been rather distracted by the masterpiece of a perfect curve that was her hip. Benson only laughed.

"Sure…"

"Well, Imma leave you two to it. See you on the field." Before I could protest, Benson gave us a two-fingered salute as he adjusted his backpack before heading the rest of the way down the ramp. Which suddenly left Tiffiny and me alone.

"Hey Iffy," I said softly, melting a little in her presence. It couldn't be helped at this point. I honestly should just surrender myself to her in every way possible lest I wilt away from pure neediness of her.

"Hey." While her tone was still on the standoffish side of things, she had at least acknowledged my presence and hadn't run away. Yet.

More than anything I wanted to blurt out that I had picked up the book she was reading. I wanted to tell her that even though I was appalled by almost half of it, it also wasn't half bad. But if I admitted that fact to her, maybe she'd just laugh in my face? Roll her pretty eyes. No, no. I needed to keep that information close to the chest. For now, anyway.

Instead, all I could blurt out was something stupid.

"Ready for the game tod–"

She completely ignored my question. "So, what exactly were you two doing?"

Shit.

I knew Tiffiny and Cadence were good friends. Most of their free time was spent in each other's presence. When Cadence wasn't supervising us on the field, she was the mascot handler for Iffy. Basically, she accompanied Ding Dong the mascot around, making sure that she took breaks when she needed to, helped her to avoid any obstacles, including not taking out small children with the bulky costume. But did Tiffiny know about Cadence and Jamie?

"Watching Jamie give his number to Cadence."

The way her eyebrows shot up her forehead led me to believe that she indeed did not know about Jamie and Cadence. Or perhaps this whole situation was new. Like, *new* new. That maybe Benson and I had stumbled onto something that had just started to blossom.

Suddenly, I found myself nose-to-nose with the most beautiful woman on the planet. Out of the blue, Iffy had grabbed a fistful of my shirt and dragged me down to her level. Fuck, this was wildly unnerving. She overpowered me in half a second. I was so close to her. I could feel her warm breath against my lips, see the golden sparkles that surrounded her irises like a halo.

Had I been a stupid man, I would have taken the opportunity to pull her in even closer. To let my instincts towards my highly denied, but indescribable need for this woman take over.

"He *what*?" From this angle, I could see just how hard her tongue pressed against her two front teeth. Her whole mouth clicked with her emphasis on the T.

"Bender and I saw it. Trust me. I'm as surprised as you are."

"That's…*wild*."

My spine had been spring-loaded with her pulling down on me, so when she did let go, I shot backwards, stumbling half a step. I almost whimpered at the loss of contact as Tiffiny suddenly snapped out of whatever had come over her.

"Uh, yeah." Clearing my throat, I adjusted my shirt, smoothing it out over my torso. Anything to distract her from the semi I was rocking in my joggers. I had a feeling I'll be reliving this moment later when I was alone in the shower. "Aren't you Cadence's friend? I thought you knew?"

"Hell no," She glanced around my body, blocking her view from where Jamie and Cadence had been standing earlier. Blinking, she stared into the now-empty space. "I'm just as surprised as you are."

"Really?" I asked, surprised. "With all the romance books you read, I would have assumed you shipped them together a long time ago or something."

Her gaze immediately snapped to mine, questions percolating in the amber depths. Oh shit. Trying to play dumb about my sudden dive into her world had apparently backfired because I used proper terminology.

After our dance conversation, I not only went and bought the book she was reading, but I also did some research into her favorite genre. There was just…so much. Tropes and ships and point-of-views and the difference between MMF and MFM. There was so much information that it was almost dizzying.

"Shipped? What are you, some closet fanfiction reader?"

Dammit. Another term I wasn't familiar with. I sort of vaguely remembered reading something somewhere. About an author named Ali Hazelhood? Hazelwood? She had written something about someone called Reylo from *Star Wars*. But I didn't remember any character by that name. The closest one was Rey from the sequel trilogy.

"Uh…a little." Maybe I could get out of this conversation unscathed with a little white lie.

Iffy narrowed her eyes at me as her hands found her hips. "Okay, which fandom?"

"Um, *Star Wars*?" I silently cursed myself for phrasing it like a question instead of being sure of myself. Thankfully, Tiffiny gave me one last lingering side glance before dropping that part of the conversation. I passed by the skin of my teeth.

"Didn't take you for a *Star Wars* fanfiction reader." She threw over her shoulder as she started to walk off, headed for her dressing room. My attention lingered on the sway of her hips, almost as if she was exaggerating the move, just a little, because she knew I was watching.

"You'll find I'm full of surprises," I called after her. It took every fiber of my being not to take a few long strides over to her, grab her hand, and pull her back to me to continue our conversation all day.

Fuck, I loved this ease with her. We talked and jabbed at each other almost as if we had never broken up all those years ago. While her iciness was still there, she was thawing out. Slowly melting when it was just the two of us together. It was almost as if she wanted to give up the charade she started. To give in to this chemistry that had never died between us.

I wanted her. No, I needed her back. Tiffiny Campanaro needed to be in my life for a hell of a lot longer than just for baseball season.

Every day at work was like an electric fence around my heart. She kept me at arm's length, a safe distance away. But more than anything I wanted to wrap her up in my arms and never let go. Our time on the dance floor the other night was the first time I'd felt complete since we broke up.

I needed to fix things. Reading her books wasn't going to do it alone. There had to be something more. Something much more. Something that would have this new Tiffiny running back to me. No corny high school nonsense.

Something about her demeanor around me was making me think that she was testing some boundaries. But she was letting me in. Little by little.

All those close encounters at games, at practices, in the locker room. The eyes I sometimes caught her making at me when she thought I wasn't looking. It all led me to believe that maybe, just maybe, there was something in the back of her head that was questioning everything.

I knew that if I didn't at least attempt to shoot my shot again, I would regret it for the rest of my life.

BOOK SMART

AMANDA FRANCES

"**D**amn, Jamie." Roman whistled as we made our way into the locker room after practice. "You get one hit in the game and suddenly it all goes to your head." The tease was playful as we all made our side glances at Jamie. Clearly, something had happened between practice two days ago and the game. He was like a completely different person. Most of today he had to fight back a grin during practice. Earlier, I heard one of the trainers giving him a hard time about his new attitude too.

While everyone was none the wiser, Benson and I shared a look. Maybe what we saw earlier wasn't something budding. Maybe it was something that was already in full bloom. Not that either of us would rat out a fellow teammate. Or Coach. Especially not in the name of love.

For the first time since joining the team, Jamie looked happy. He held his head higher. He was more involved in the conversations going on around him. Hell, he even had a great choreography practice. I guess all that one-on-one practice with Cadence really helped. Helped *something*.

I felt a bitter pang. The pang of jealousy. Jamie looked like a cat who caught the canary, but only for half a second as he tried to put his face back to his usual stoic nature. Despite feeling bitter, I was happy for the dude.

"Yeah, yeah." Jamie dipped his head, dismissing Roman but having trouble with the smile that quirked at the corner of his mouth. "Coach has been helping me with some, uh...*fundamentals*. That's all. The other day it finally...*clicked*."

Tomas gave him a reassuring slap on the back while Arlow shot some finger guns in his direction. The other guys chimed in with their approval. Meanwhile, Benson and I did our best to bite our tongues.

"Way to go, dude! I always knew you were a Silly!" Truitt came over, ruffling through Jamie's hat hair. "It was about time you removed that MLB attitude from up your ass." The guys laughed good-naturedly. I tried to stay out of the way, hunched in my corner of the locker room because I was currently at a rather climactic part of the monster romance and had to stop reading mid-page on my lunch break.

There were only three pages left in the chapter. If I could get to at least a good stopping point, I could finish up here and then get my ass home to read more. Hopefully, I got to bed at a more reasonable hour than the last few nights.

"Yo, Ender. Whatcha got there?"

Jamie's voice was like cold water down my spine. The man wanted all attention off of him as soon as possible. I slammed the book closed and shoved it haphazardly under my thigh.

"Just a book." I shrugged, glancing at him from over my shoulder. Arlow's eyes dipped to my leg as I nervously fidgeted with the pages. My finger was still jammed into the last page I read.

"Is it a creepy book?" His dark brow arched as he cocked his head. "That skull on the cover looked freaky."

Before I could even formulate an answer that didn't sound entirely stupid, Benson intervened, utterly nonchalant about the whole thing. "It's smut." I recoiled before I swallowed back my shock. How the hell did he know what kind of book I was reading? The team perked at the unusual conversation and looked clueless at the new vocabulary word. "*Porn.*" Benson clarified faster than my brain could get me out of this embarrassing situation.

Shit. Fuck.

There was a burst of chatter from the guys as they suddenly swarmed me, completely ignoring Jamie. Somehow, I managed to bookmark the page with the receipt from the bookstore I had been using to mark my place. All before it was pulled from my grasp and skeptically manhandled by the team.

"How is it porn?" Truitt grumbled, turning the book sideways and flipping through the pages. "There are no pictures!"

"Yo, wait. I just saw the word 'pussy'. Go back a few pages." Camden made a move to take the book from Truitt, but he slapped his hand away. The two put their heads together to scan the pages for the mention.

"Smut is *kind of* like porn. It just comes in a classier wrapper." Benson clarified, almost bored with the conversation. All the guys turned to him with a look. He sighed. "Come on, guys. It's all over the internet and social media." They continued to stare at him blankly. Thank fuck Benson was explaining all of this because the hell if I could.

Iffy claimed I was "too vanilla" for her taste now. Back when we dated in high school, she liked my…*flavor.* But now? She was apparently into banana splits with *multiple bananas.* At least that's how the woman was getting her kicks in the book, between extra appendages or other monsters. I only had the one banana and was in no mood to share her with anyone. But did Iffy like spiny dicks? Two dicks? Suction cup dicks? Oh, wait, maybe that was just tentacles.

Maybe I could pull a move from the monster romance I was currently reading? Or even read a few more before I figure out a proper game plan. I may have found her online reading history, complete with ratings and reviews. The majority of her five-star books were on the darker side of the romance book spectrum. Complete with darker colors with flowers or other inanimate objects. I happened to be drawn to the ones that were more colorful. With cartoon couples on the front. But those sorts of books were few and far between on her list.

Iffy was going to be one tough nut to crack. I was going to be reading some interesting books in the process. Which could be good or bad. I was more than willing to try to win her heart all over again. By any means necessary.

And I mean by *any* means.

Even if I had to read romances about couples who commit murder or about men who chase their woman through the woods at night wearing a mask. Or yes, even about hot, muscular monsters with tails and spiny dicks who live under beds.

"No, guys. The porn is *described*." Benson's insistence pulled me from my thoughts as he gently took the book away from the manhandlers. "Women like to imagine it. You know, like a self-insert." More puzzled looks. "So uncivilized. Guys, come on. They like to pretend that it's *themselves* in the story getting fucked until next Tuesday." A resounding approval echoed in the locker room.

"Wait, Benson, how do you know so much about this shit?" Shortstop Kellan Bristol interjected. Some of the other guys made noises of agreement.

Benson shrugged as he flipped through the pages. "I read it. This one was pretty good. The monster dude, while intense and didn't know boundaries, was just a big cinnamon roll." More blank looks. "He was secretly a nice monster who just wanted to take care of her."

I kept my mouth shut, but I was thankful as fuck that Benson was educating me right along with the rest of the guys. So, the guy in the book wasn't actually bad, just maybe had some bad habits. That I could work with. Not that I was really getting the "evil" vibe from the main character in the first place.

"Women are into this sort of thing?" Roman asked with a cock to his brow. All Benson did was laugh.

"You could say that. Here, I'll give you an example." His nimble fingers flipped through a few more pages before he found what he was looking for. Casting a glance throughout the locker room, he cleared his throat.

"*...like a good girl, she swallowed every drop before sliding off my softening dick. She flashed me a*

There were some rumbles throughout the room as the guys side-eyed each other and shifted uncomfortably. I couldn't tell if they hated it or loved it. I, for one, maybe finally understood what Tiffiny liked so much about these sorts of books. Even though the dude was a weird-ass monster, the sex scenes were surprisingly hot.

Romance books focused more on setting the mood. They applied the five senses of the scene so people who were reading could really feel like they were the ones in the middle of the action. Without the actual physical touching, of course. But there was emotion to it. Authors let readers see into the characters' heads to let us know what they were feeling or thinking. I was almost scared to wonder about how an author would portray my story with Tiffiny.

"Damn." Kellan whistled. "That's hot."

"Wait… Women read about chicks giving blow jobs?" Camden asked, point-blank, in utter disbelief.

"The missus likes to read those kinds of books." Martin jumped into the conversation. All of the guys now turned to look at him. "If I get into bed and see her reading one of these, it means I'm getting some kind of action." He smirked. Truitt laughed outright and gave him a high five.

More rumbles of the guys talking amongst themselves drifted through the crowd. Maybe this whole spicy book trend wasn't all that uncommon.

My spine slowly began to straighten from its cringe state. Eyeing Martin, I swallowed back my fluster and opened my mouth.

"So like…you get something from these kinds of books too?" Everyone shut up and looked between Martin and me.

"Hell yes." With a grin, Martin laughed. "She reads them and gets all worked up. I like to call it when my wife goes 'feral'."

"Holy fuck."

"Shit."

"Well goddamn."

The quiet, surprised exclamations echoed about the room. My eyes felt like ping pong balls as I tried to gauge all of the guys' responses. Suddenly, I didn't feel so weird about snooping into Tiffiny's backlist of books. All of the guys looked interested in learning more about these so-called "smut" books right along with me

"Hey, Ender, what book was it again?" Truitt asked as smoothly as possible before all the guys crowded around Benson to look at my book, still in his hands.

What in the actual hell was happening? The guys all looked rather excited about this damn thing. Some grabbed their phones to take a photo. Others stood there and ordered it on the spot.

"Maybe we should all read it? You heathens could learn a thing or two. A locker room book club." Benson suggested. The very loud and resounding agreement left me shocked on the bench. He glanced in my direction with a grin. "Thanks for the good idea, Ender."

"I–" My disagreement died on my tongue as I was surrounded by the guys giving me claps on my shoulder, offering high fives, or just general thanks and approval. "Well, uh, as long as you're the ringleader of this circus." I shot back at Benson. There was no way in hell that I wanted to be in charge of this particular kind of chaos.

"Are you kidding? I'm glad you fuckers are finally going to make the move to educate yourselves in the fine art of literature." This time, the response was only a chorus of groans. "Excuse me," Benson smirked. "*Cliterature.*"

10

GUILTY PLEASURE

CHAPPELL ROAN

The team had gone off on their week-long road trip, and I suddenly found myself without much to do. When the guys were home, we had daily practices at the ballpark with built-in off days. Cadence seemed to also be going through some sort of bizarre melancholy. Which, given the little thing I stumbled upon with Benson and Ender, might have something to do with it.

I didn't want to pry like I normally would in this sort of situation that involved besties and the men in our lives. Because I was really fucking afraid I would do this stupid thing called resonating with the situation and let something slip that I wasn't sure I was even ready to admit to myself, let alone my best friend.

I managed to occupy my days with filming social media content for Ding Dong's platform. The stupid copper bell with the goofy eyes had a larger following than the team did. Most of that had to do with me and my rather theatrical antics. It was pure cinema, if I said so myself.

Was I below my expertise level playing an inanimate object that was a symbol of my home city and our nation's independence? Of course.

Considering there were few to no job alternatives in this city, this was my best option for a regular paycheck. Despite my disappointment in me being a team mascot, I still did it with the fucking utmost integrity. And I was damn good at it.

Cadence sometimes helped me film stupid stunts or followed me around the ballpark to get content. We were supposed to be having a brainstorming session at my place, but the two of us were entirely too brain-dead. We were in desperate need of a lengthy zone-out period. So, we were flopped, rather unladylike, on my oversized couch watching *Schitt's Creek* episodes. It was either that or sitting by myself in bed for a week straight, tackling my to-be-read pile of books like a motherfucker.

A kernel of popcorn flew past my line of vision, falling dreadfully short of actually hitting the television. Cadence let out a low whine. "Ugh, they disgust me. But I love them so much." I glanced over at her, all glassy-eyed over Canada's first favorite gay couple being their adorable selves. "It's not fair."

"What, that we all can't find love with bisexual cinnamon roll hotties in small towns named after excrement?"

There was a notable scoff before a piece of popcorn ricocheted off my cheek. I grinned, nabbing the snack and popping it into my mouth.

"You know what I mean." Cadence shot back with a roll of her eyes, even though she was doing everything to hide her smile. "And then the ungodly yearning of Alexis for Ted. Like, girl, why can't you just admit you fucked up like a zillion episodes sooner?"

"Because Mutt."

Cadence let out a groan. "Right." She jabbed a finger in my direction. "Girl was crazy for thinking he wasn't attractive without a beard. Dude was fine either way."

"Preaching to the choir." I agreed, fussing with some imaginary string on my leggings. Cadence's words sat with me in a funny way for a moment. Like a lead balloon in my stomach.

What if Ender had just outright apologized to me the moment the fates decided to push us back together? Where would we be? Would I have forgiven him? If so, would he be texting me? Sending me disgustingly cute little love notes like he used to in between periods in high school? This entire baseball season could have been so different. Wishful thinking I suppose. How would a short-term long-distance thing work anyway with a baseball player who travels all over the US?

I was not a fan of the fact that I was even entertaining this alternate timeline. Ender broke up with me for a stupid reason. For all I knew, he could have a string of gorgeous, popular girl exes in his wake. Maybe I was just avoiding an utterly dramatic disaster by leaving this whole thing as-is.

But dammit. Why did it have to be so fucking difficult being in his presence? Every cell in my body vibrated like happy little gremlins whenever Ender was even in the vicinity of me. It was as if they all needed to be in his warmth in order to survive another day. My entire being was crying out for this man and I just couldn't figure out why.

"I mean, Alexis had an opportunity and she took it. That's not so bad, right?" Her words were forcefully upbeat and decidedly cautious. I had a feeling we weren't talking about the show anymore.

"Well, aside from the fact that she was trying to decide which of the two men was hotter, then no, it's not bad."

"Like, her sleeping with one guy and then the other was like a *once-in-a-lifetime opportunity*. She couldn't pass that up."

It was getting more and more difficult to keep a straight face and not let Cadence in on the fact that I suspected something. Had it been under any other circumstances, I would have pried it out of her the moment it happened. Because what woman wouldn't want to hear how an average civilian bagged a hot MLB player? Hell, that would be romcom-worthy, knowing how Cadence was. It would for sure make a wildly entertaining book or movie.

"Hell no. I wouldn't." I agreed with her and her shoulders visibly relaxed.

"And maybe that once-in-a-lifetime kinda thing is infatuated right back." I slowly raised my one brow at her. She was getting specific. I had to stay cool. "I mean, Mutt and Ted kept like, you know, fighting over Alexis."

"Yeah, but you do have to remember that she never had to fight to keep a man's attention." I leaned back on the plush back cushion of the sofa so I could look at my friend, dead on. "Then all of a sudden Ted moved on and she hadn't."

Cadence blew a raspberry in my direction. "Dude, way to bring down the mood."

"Hey! I'm just being honest." I shrugged, throwing my arm over the back of the couch. To be chased after, like that, would be hot. Instead, I was stuck with Ender teasing me to no end without having any sort of an inkling about how I still felt about him. "But yeah, it would be nice to have someone obsessed with me for once. Instead of it just being me obsessed over all my book boyfriends."

"Yeah…" Cadence sighed dreamily. "Obsession is kind of nice." I shot her a look and she immediately corrected herself. "Obsession *would* be nice. Would be."

Oh this was too fun. Maybe I could poke the bear. Just a little.

"So, how goes teaching Jamie how to dance? It doesn't look like you're out of a job anytime soon anymore."

The last thing I expected was for my best friend to go white as a sheet before turning her body to avoid direct eye contact. Shit. Right. The whole kissing-your-coworker kind of thing was still bad news.

"Oh, uh…good. Really good." She replied, each word a crisp staccato, almost as if it were rehearsed. "He uh…well, um, something got through to him at line dancing the other night, I guess. I mean, I knew that would be the trick. Going line dancing usually loosens up the new guys and helps build team morale."

Or maybe it was her and Jamie's face sucking.

"And Jamie didn't, you know, fight you on it?"

"I mean…a little. So, I told him he just needed to pretend dancing was something else. Something more…fun."

"Like what?"

"Sex."

It was the most inopportune time to have attempted to eat another piece of popcorn. I inhaled so sharply in surprise at my friend's rather frank response. After a quick coughing fit, I managed a sip of my drink before looking over at her.

"Yeah, not sure if that was the most appropriate thing to correlate dancing to."

"Look, it wasn't my finest moment, but we weren't on ballpark property. Besides, it did get him to put two and two together pretty quickly."

It sure did.

Holy hell, my inner snark was chomping at the bit to come out and join the conversation. But no, I needed to stay cool. Be my usual hilarious self as I attempted to pry the insider info on Cadence and Jamie. Even if it was on the down low.

"I mean, if you could correlate something to sex and procreation, then any organism on this planet could figure it out." That at least got a laugh out of her.

"Oh, come on, give the man some credit. He was dealt a bullshit hand by management and you know it. I had to make it slightly more entertaining for him at least."

"The two of you were pretty *entertaining* on that dance floor."

I watched with smug pride as my friend's cheeks went bright pink. Just what exactly did happen on that dance floor? Did they share some top-secret conversation? More than anything I wanted her to spill all the details. I wanted her to–

"I could say the same thing about you and Ender at the bar. What's up with you and him lately anyway?"

Shit.

In my hubris, I flew too close to the sun. Damn my need for other people's drama. What the hell could I tell her? There was entirely too much to unpack there. The only other person who knew what had gone on in high school was Cooper. And despite him being a jackass, he had at least kept his lips zipped at work. As far as I could tell.

"Uh…" I had to think of something fast. Something that would appease my friend enough for her to let it go. It had to be something boring. Stupid even. She was well acquainted with my grudges. "I don't know. His face just looks like someone you want to slap."

Cadence snorted, her shoulders bucking forward with the force of said snort. "Look, I know you and I have our differences in tastes in men but if you polled ninety-nine percent of the world on the slapability of Ender's face the majority would say zero."

Keeping up with the desperately thin charade, I rolled my eyes. "It's just too… Ugh. I don't know… Slappable." By the look on Cadence's face, I was quickly losing this argument. Or maybe she was just happy to be out of the hot seat.

"That boy has the baby face to end all baby faces in men over six feet. You are so full of shit."

"I am not." I huffed as I crossed my arms, sinking deeper into my couch, hoping the plush cushions would just swallow me whole and smother me. "I just have…very specific face-slapping measures." Cadence laughed outright at that.

"Oh, come on." She taunted, crossing her legs and leaning over the knot of her lap with rapt interest. "Just admit you have a crush on him."

"What?!" My blood ran cold as I lurched forward, my spine going ramrod straight in an instant. Fuck. *Way to make it obvious, Tiff.* "I-I absolutely *do not.*"

"Oh, come off it, Tiff. This isn't high school." I began to sweat. She knew. She had to know something to say that, right? Or at least suspect something. I thought I'd been so careful. But then again, Ender and I did dance together. In public. Fuck fuckity fucks. "We can't just go around slapping people because we don't know how to say that we like them."

"I don't like Ender," I said simply. But even I didn't believe the words. If I didn't believe them, then Cadence sure as fuck wouldn't.

"Right. And I'm the season eight winner of *So You Think You Can Dance.*" She laughed out loud, plopping against the back of the sofa. "Come on, you're allowed to have a crush. Sometimes it's also fun to have a crush on an actual guy rather than a fictional one."

"Yeah, but fictional ones don't rip your heart from your chest when they aren't interested in you. Book boyfriends always love their woman."

Cadence blew out a breath. I knew she really wanted to roll her eyes, but she also knew that I was right. "Fine." She sighed, rather dramatically. "You've got me there. But come on, Ender is a really sweet guy. Probably the most soft-spoken of the group. I mean, probably because he's still new and the guys are a bit much."

"Hah, maybe," I added dryly. Maybe this conversation was safe. Maybe Cadence didn't know about our past history. Perhaps I could just pretend this is some harmless workplace crush. This could be a smart play here. To get my friend's advice without digging up the shitty past.

"Look, I adore the sweetie pie. Maybe I could talk to him for you?"

"Isn't dating coworkers, especially players, technically frowned upon?"

Color drained from Cadence's face. "Uh, yeah...technically." She started, rather uneasily. "And technically, if you don't tell anyone, no one will know. Right? Right." The speed of her words picked up as she went. The nerves were cracking through. If I didn't have any skin in this game, I would have enjoyed this ping pong match a lot more. But something was still eating at me.

"But what if there's like some deep dark secret that, say, Jamie has. Like..." Should I even go down this route? But why not? The reasoning sounded so asinine that Cadence would probably think I made it all up. "Like maybe he broke up with you just to sleep with, like, a super-hot swimsuit model and then tried to get you back. Would you still give him a shot?"

Saying it out loud made the hurt come to the surface all over again. It sat like a bitter taste in my mouth. I glanced over at my friend, who was still mulling over the supposed situation. Couldn't I just go out on Broad Street and poll the masses like *Family Feud*?

"That is a...weirdly *specific* hypothetical." I gulped. From what I could tell, Cadence didn't look completely put off by it. "Do you know something about Jamie that I don't?"

"Nope." The P popped against my lips. Her eyes narrowed at me. Something was simmering in her brain, but not anything that bothered her enough to press the matter further.

"I mean…" Shrugging, a hearty sigh left her lips as she tossed herself back against the cushion once more. "It's kind of flattering, isn't it? That he would sleep with her, or not, and then come back? Like, maybe the sex was really shitty. Or…maybe he couldn't go through with it? Maybe he was just meant to be me all along?"

"You really have a way of looking at the glass as half full." I cocked my brow at her, frowning slightly. When she put it that way, it did sound kind of hot. Considering I never broached Ender about our past, I was, maybe slightly, curious as to how that past situation had unfolded. Clearly, the two weren't together and hadn't been for some time. Maybe he ended up getting his heart ripped out by the mean girl? One could only hope.

"Then again…" Tilting my head, my gaze focused on her face as she stared at the ceiling. "He'd have to beg to come back. Beg, plead, prove his love, and all that shit. Grovel like you wouldn't believe!"

My best friend might actually be onto something.

FUMBLED THE BAG

JENNA RAINE

I was exhausted.

And yet I couldn't sleep.

It could have had to do with the fact that we were on yet another leg of this, seemingly, unending bus trip. The first leg had been the longest. I hated those 4 AM report times with every fiber of my being. Coach Topper always said we could catch a few more hours of shut-eye on the road. But I found myself unable to sleep much at all, on the bus, or in the hotel rooms.

Because of one very curvy, brunette, bell-shaped reason.

The sun was just starting to warm the sky, the hazy orange glow setting the stillness of Lake Erie out my window aglow. We had just gotten through a three-game series with the Buffalo Wings and now were headed south to take on the Pittsburgh Stealers. Road games were fun, but they were always tough on the players. Travel, play, travel, play… It was an endless cycle on these long road trips.

Turning back to the innards of the bus, the guys were a mix of unconsciousness and awareness. My brow furrowed a bit, noting at least two of the guys reading the monster romance book. It was too goddamn early in the morning to read about a woman being split in half by two or more monsters fucking her. Apparently, Benson's words got enough of the guys to be on board with seriously starting a team book club. I sighed.

Bender had announced that the guys had the road trip to read the book, no excuses. Between the downtime of curfew at the hotel and the long bus rides, we could easily get through a good chunk of the book. That way, when we got back to the locker room for our first practice after the trip, we could all settle in for the first official locker room book club.

I thought getting away for a road trip of games would get Tiffiny off my mind. At least for a little while. Instead, I was constantly surrounded by things that reminded me of her. Namely, two guys reading her latest read right in front of my face.

I wanted the ability to be able to think straight because once we got back, I was fairly certain I was going to do something extremely stupid. That was if I didn't work out some sort of game plan. The moment she grabbed onto my shirt and brought me to her level after watching Jamie and Cadence kiss still had its flustering grip on me.

I'd already gotten off to that scene a few times this road trip. When I was stuck in the shower at the hotel with nothing but my thoughts to keep me company. Thoughts that were seemingly endless about Tiffiny.

"Dude, whatever it is, you've got it bad."

I nearly jumped out of the retro fabric bus seat. The second-to-last person I wanted to talk to about Tiffiny with was her brother Cooper. He shot me a knowing grin from across the aisle.

I didn't know if he was fucking with me or genuinely thought I had a love interest. Whatever it may be, I had to tread lightly. The last thing I wanted at 7 AM was a lecture from the woman-who-had-my-balls-in-a-vice's big brother.

"What?" I scoffed, probably a bit too dramatically as Cooper's brow shot up his forehead. "It's just…indigestion. Stupid hotel orange juice." I grumbled out, slouching down in my seat a bit more.

"Yeah, I don't think indigestion and twitterpated are even remotely in the same facial expression category. But good try." Cooper's grin only got bigger.

Ever since I joined the Sillys, he'd been on my ass for, what I can only imagine, was for whatever Iffy told him about what happened.

Because what did my dumbass self go and do?

Break her heart.

…and mine.

I couldn't exactly fault Cooper for offering up some freshly cut revenge, courtesy of Tiffiny. I deserved all of it. And more, if I were being honest. If anything, Cooper was going easy on me.

"Look, the only time you've ever had that expression on your face is when you're thinking about my sister." He held his hand up, cutting off my immediate retort, leaving my mouth hanging open. "I'm not here to razz your balls, dude." His tone softened. "I'm actually rooting for you."

I had to sit with the words for a long moment as they were nothing like what I expected to come out of his mouth at any time.

"You are?" I sat straighter in my seat, staring at Cooper. "But why?"

"Because I know how much you care about her. You always have." His gaze darted away in thought. "Well, except for the time you broke up with her."

"I–"

"But the fact that you broke up with her *before* doing something shitty behind her back, while it was still a douche move, it was at least…considerate." His voice strained on the last word.

I was a total douche canoe in high school. More than anything I wanted to make it up to Iffy. I just didn't know how. I'd give my right nut just to have that mystical knowledge of the exact steps I could go through in order to have Tiffiny give me a second chance.

Even if she wouldn't bless me with that opportunity, then at the very least I wanted the chance to actually talk to her. Uninterrupted. Above all, I wanted to say I was sorry.

Sorry for being stupid. Sorry for being a teenager who didn't think things through. Sorry for being scared of my deep feelings for her. That I thought I needed to be with someone else just to prove to myself that Tiffiny was it. All the sleepless nights on the road and being in Tiffiny's orbit again only made me revisit the feelings I wanted to bury deep down.

The feeling that maybe she was my forever.

That I'd been an utter dick to the one who might very well be my end game. In every sense of the words. Because good or bad outcome, this woman will be the utter death of me.

"Yeah, she's not exactly super happy with me. Even after all of these years. For reasons." I sighed. "I deserve it though."

"Probably. But kicking your ass is my job." I let out a huff of dry amusement. "Your job is to show my sister how much you obviously still care about her."

It felt like Cooper shoved my head up the Liberty Bell's ass and hit the damn thing with a mallet. The Taco Bell-esque *bong* was going to ring through my brain for another 250 years. Did he really just say what I thought he said?

"She won't shut up about you. It's kind of annoying really."

"Tiffiny talks about me?"

Cooper nodded, looking rather smug to be the one to divulge this sort of information. It made me want to punch him in the face. But enacting physical violence on your coach for being a smartass was kind of frowned upon. Even if he was someone I considered a friend.

"In her own little ways." Cooper shrugged and picked at something on his joggers. "You know how she is."

Cooper had told me, once upon a time, that she lived in the basement apartment of his Philadelphia row home. I knew her and her brother were close, despite the animosity over the years between them both. But it was the knowledge that she had said anything about me to Cooper was shocking. And an ego boost in a weird, roundabout way. Maybe there was hope for me after all.

"So…she still thinks about me?" I asked, cautious of these unknown waters.

"More now that you two work together. But it took her a long fucking time to recover from the douchey shit you pulled."

I winced. "Yeah… She's made me well aware of her feelings of the 'douchey shit' as you call it." With a sigh, I rubbed my hand down my face. "And I get it. I deserve it. I just wish she didn't hate me so much. I can't get within three feet of her without her going off on me."

"Join the club."

Chewing on my lower lip, I rolled my tongue about in my mouth over the words that I wanted to say, but was having a difficult time doing so. Would Cooper be open to offering up some advice? Or was I going to get reamed out again?

"Dude, the fact that you have no idea how she actually feels about you means she either hides it really well when she leaves the house or you're really the fucking dumbass she thinks you are."

I bristled a bit at the words. Not that they were wrong. It just really hurt to hear them out loud.

"She hasn't forgiven you." He said simply. But I already knew that. "But she is…open to the idea." That made me stop breathing for a second as I leaned towards him from my seat.

"Really…?" There was hope for me yet.

"I mean, you will probably have to kiss her ass for the rest of eternity, but yeah."

Oh I was willing. I was so fucking ready to get down on my knees and follow her around everywhere, kissing that oh-so-plump bottom every chance I could get. With lip balm, and gusto, and hell, even a little tongue.

"I'd do that." Cooper laughed outright at me. I was sure he was imagining it all now. Me a simpering mess while Tiffiny stood above me, slapping a riding crop into her palm. Or something like that. "But like…how? Just saying 'I'm sorry' isn't going to cut it for her."

"Oh ho ho…" Cooper huffed out, amusement evident in each breathy syllable. "I have some suggestions." I perked up with that. "And I don't think you're going to like any of them."

"Dude, come on." I pleaded, my words almost a whine. "Aside from a public shaming where people throw rotting vegetables at my head, I'm willing to do anything."

"Anything, huh?" A hand stroked the bottom of his chin as he pulled out some sort of evil villain persona. I gulped. "A good start might be reading those romance books she likes so much. I usually hear her bitching to my wife about the fact guys don't read romance novels. That they're literally a 'how to' guide."

My eyes glanced at the guys on the bus reading the monster romance out in the open. Between what Iffy had said at the bar and Benson starting a team book club after finding me with said book, the universe itself was giving me the kick in the ass I needed. I had to double down on my reading. It sounded like I had quite the research assignment ahead of me.

"Noted."

"Honestly anything regarding books is probably a good starting place." Duly noted. "And snacks. Always snacks."

"Does she still like those harvest cheddar Sun Chips, peanut M&Ms, and a Turkey Hill Iced Tea?"

A slow grin graced Cooper's face. Almost as if he knew he was right about something but wanted to be smug as fuck about it. "Throwing in some Tastykakes wouldn't hurt."

"Peanut Butter Kandy Kakes, right?"

Cooper's smile got even bigger. "You got it. You know Tiff better than I probably do. She's still the same ol' pain in my ass."

"Just…" I started out but my voice softened as my heart felt the words escape me. "More…closed off."

Cooper's face fell. "Yeah."

There was a long moment of quiet between us as the lighthearted conversation turned more serious. I knew that I had to be the reason she was like that. So guarded. Closing herself off from most of the world. Only letting a few, highly vetted individuals in. I wanted more than anything to erase all those bad thoughts and feelings inside of her. To turn her back into the bright, sunshiny, stage diva Tiffiny once was.

"I need to fix a lot of shit."

"Fuck yeah you do. And if you fuck it up again, I'll have my foot so far up your ass you can taste the rubber sole of my shoe."

12

CURIOSITY

BRYCE SAVAGE

For the rest of the road trip, I dove in headfirst into everything I could do to potentially prove to Tiffiny that I was serious about us trying something again. Even if it took decades to prove it. I was a patient man. Entirely too patient. Or perhaps it was just stubbornness.

The fact was that Iffy was not only everything to me, but she was the only woman for me. She'd been the *only* woman. My first crush, my first kiss, my first love, my first everything. My only everything. I'd never dated anyone before her, and I hadn't dated anyone since.

I always chalked the "since" part up to the fact that I was too focused on baseball, too focused on the MLB draft to want to bother. But the truth was, I *didn't* want to bother. No matter how hard a woman flirted with me, I felt absolutely nothing. Maybe a bit flattered, but all I heard in my head was the constant repeat of, "It's not her".

Sure, I could tell Iffy all that, but considering how our conversations had been going of late, she wouldn't believe me. She would think it was a stupid suave line or that I thought she was an easy lay because of our history together.

I might have deep dived a little *too* deep into Iffy's reading history since Cooper and my talk on the bus. I spent the rest of the bus ride on the way to Pittsburgh researching all about the boom in the popularity of books and reading. She'd always been a reader, but now it was socially acceptable to read. Hell, reading was *cool* now.

I may have been a little sleep-deprived reporting to the ballpark after coming back from our road trip the day before. I looked over Tiffiny's online reading tracker. It was literally a treasure trove of information and book recommendations.

To my surprise, it wasn't all dark monster romance on her list. There were romcoms along with fantasies with dragons and whatnot. Although there was also one where the female lead actually *fucked* the dragon. Nothing in literary world surprised me anymore.

In order to get ahead in my research and not go into considerable debt, I downloaded an eReader app on my phone. Someone online suggested an app where you can actually borrow eBooks from the library, *for free*, and my life was changed overnight.

Benson and Cooper were right, though. Reading some of Tiffiny's five-star reads gave me a greater insight into her current likes and dislikes. I was still coming to terms with the fact that I was, actually, very vanilla, like she said. Since Iffy was the only woman I'd ever been with, I hadn't exactly had a chance to, well, test my boundaries.

Which only led me to spiral with all the thoughts of just what made Tiffiny not so "vanilla" anymore. I couldn't exactly turn into a fire-breathing dragon with a scaly dick or be a blue man from outer space.

Okay so maybe I could but body paint was only going to make things complicated. There were other sexually suggestive things I could at least attempt to do.

I might have gotten sidetracked with a few of those trigger warning lists of certain kinks I hadn't heard of. I'll admit when I'm utterly clueless. Some of the kinks had me scratching my head and opening my internet browser. Which may have been a mistake with all of the *visual* aids that popped up in response.

Bookmarking a few for later, I decided it was probably safer to stick with just books. The safest option of them all was eBooks since no one could tell what you were reading without a cover on display. Win-win. I may have treated myself to an eReader too, as reading on my phone had gotten tedious after a while.

I knew this all might be a bit extra to some to win over the woman of my dreams, but Tiffiny was worth it. One hundred percent worth it.

Not to mention, I rediscovered my love of reading that I had back in high school. I knew I was supposed to be taking notes, but time and time again, I found myself getting lost in the book. Who knew romance books were actually pretty amazing? They literally pulled at every emotion.

Today was also the first meeting of the team book club. I had to admit that I was a little bit excited about it. The guys were more than on board with the book choice. Or maybe they really just wanted to learn the right way to romance women? Either way, hopefully it was going to be a good discussion.

I'd listened to a few podcasts about book clubs and maybe found a few videos about how to host a successful one. I really had no idea what to expect. Some book clubs just had a free-for-all discussion. While others had structured questions. I was wondering what Benson had in store for us. We'd only discussed it briefly here and there on the road trip. He assured me he had everything under control.

While still lost in thought about the book club, I made my way across the ballpark parking lot towards the players' entrance. That was when I heard something. Loud talking? It wasn't music. But the voices were talking so fast. Not quite Alvin and the Chipmunks speed, but well on its way in the right direction. Intrigued, I cautiously made my way towards the sound.

The parking lot was scattered with cars throughout as the guys showed up. But what I didn't expect was to see Tiffiny, looking utterly blissful, in her car. She only looked that way when…

Oh fuck.

I finally got close enough to make out the words coming from her car. It certainly wasn't music. Despite the windows being up, I could hear every filthy, dirty word from her audiobook.

Holy shit, how could she listen to something like that in public? Where people could just happen upon her? Damn, she had some balls on her. It was kind of hot. Especially to see her all blitzed out like that.

The words suddenly stopped and the engine cut, causing me to jump. Our eyes met through the glass of her car door. Her look of surprise immediately turned to horror before a split second later, turning into muted annoyance.

Her door popped open and she stepped out of her car, avoiding my gaze. Was she mad at me for literally just happening upon her in the parking lot? Did she think I didn't hear what she was listening to?

"Ender." She said simply in greeting, sharpness to her cordial tone. So, nothing had changed between us. No surprise.

In my pure and utter desperation to talk to this woman, my mouth started moving of its own accord as she turned and headed towards the stadium. My feet continued on, despite the invisible barrier the woman seemed to extrude anytime she was around me.

"How's the book?"

Tiffiny stopped dead in her tracks. Her shoulders hunched over as if the inertia of her suddenly stopping kept her torso in motion but her sneakers were frozen to the asphalt. Slowly, she turned around to face me. Her features were firm. But there was a flicker of worry in her gaze.

"My *what*?"

"Your book." I nodded back to her car. "The one you were listening to just now." Her throat bobbed with an uneasy swallow. From the flicker of her eyes, I could tell that she was trying to calculate just how much I had heard.

"Oh uh–"

"I thought the book was pretty cute. Deliciously spicy, but super cute."

I drank in her immediate look of surprise that she quickly tried to suppress. Gritting my teeth, I attempted to keep my glee at bay, maintaining my smile to be as neutral as possible. Save for a quick quirk at the corner.

Clearing her throat awkwardly, Iffy tried to look as nonchalant as possible. Crossing her arms and cocking that deliciously curvy hip out to the side, she gave me a slow once-over with her questioning gaze.

"You...read?"

"Yeah," I said, shoving my hands into my jogger pockets, trying not to look smug. "Mostly romance. A little bit of everything in the genre, honestly." My gaze lifted to hers, finding her trying to maintain her calm within an inch of its life. "Learned a few things."

Her eyes flashed with something heated. I suddenly found myself regretting the decision to wear athletic wear to work, despite doing it every day. I desperately wanted to pry. To ask all the questions. For her to interrogate me about my newfound love.

"I swear the TBR pile next to my bed might actually kill me one night." I laughed, throwing in a bit of the lingo to impress her further. "If only authors would stop writing awesome books–"

"...so I could actually keep up." She finished the words with disbelief as she stared at me. Okay, even I was surprised by that.

More than anything I wanted to fist-punch the air. Benson was right. Cooper was right. I studied so fucking hard. It was our first interaction, and we were already back to finishing each other's sentences.

It was so fucking cute I almost couldn't handle it.

Tiffiny blinked, shaking her head in disbelief. As if waking up from a dream. Or a hallucination. Or worse. I really hope she didn't think this was a nightmare.

I knew I was already late for practice, but more than anything I wanted to keep her suspended in this bubble with me. A bubble of just us. Talking in the middle of the parking lot, where it was getting progressively hotter in the summer sun. But there was no place I'd rather be.

"So… Do you always listen to spicy books in public?"

Tiffiny's eyes went wide. "Please don't tell me you heard that—"

"Oh…" I started, overly amused. A smile worked its way across my lips. "I did."

"All of it…?" she asked timidly, flinching as her cheeks blossomed into a rosy pink.

"All. Of. It."

"Godfuckingdammit." The words hissed through her breath, an annoyed grumble as she turned away from me.

"There's nothing to be ashamed of, Iffy," I said softly. And I meant it. After all my research into romance books and the world that loved them, I'd learned a thing or two. Reading about two or more people making love on the page was nothing to be ashamed of.

Reading romance was a safe space for people to explore. For them to find comfort. For them to heal. There was absolutely nothing shameful in any of that.

That made her stop.

"What…?"

"Listening to dirty books in your car. It makes you happy. They're fun to read and listen to. There's nothing bad about something that brings you joy. Be loud and proud about your smut-reading." Her brow cocked as she regarded me. "Like me."

That made her burst out laughing. "Ender Roche," *Oh fuck.* I was not at all prepared for her to say my first and last name in that beyond flirtatious tone of hers. There was a stirring in my joggers again. "You…surprise me."

Now it was my turn to be taken aback. Her features softened, humor glinting in her pretty eyes. But her face remained as stoic as she could maintain it, even if the Iffy I used to know was starting to crack through.

Now was the time to pull something from my book boyfriend bag of tricks. Something easy. Something that will make an impact.

Seemingly frozen to her spot in the parking lot, I slowly stalked my way to her, being sure to keep eye contact. The squareness to her shoulders faltered a little as her brow smoothed out. Tiffiny was locked on every step.

She stood, rooted to the spot, as I stepped up to her as casually in my intensity as I could manage. I could see her breasts rise with an inhale and then stop, holding the oxygen inside. My hands slipped into my pockets, showing her that I was not a threat. But the sheer imposing nature of my size and brooding stare that I'd been working on, might have been.

If only I had a wall or doorway to lean against.

My toes skewed off to the sides of her feet. Our bodies were so close that only our clothes were touching. I could feel the heat of her body warming the small space between us.

"I hope I keep surprising you, Iffy." My voice dropped low and husky. Her wide eyes flickered with something. Something heated. This was working out well. Too well. It only emboldened me further. "It's my life's passion to do so."

Swallowing back my doubts, I leaned in a little closer, her face tilting up to greet mine. Heat filled my bloodstream, making a beeline south. Her body language seemingly begging me to take advantage of the situation. But I couldn't. Not like this. Not yet.

I lingered there for only a few more beats. Her lashes had fluttered, closing to soft slits. Instead of giving in, I swallowed my fluster and pulled away, leaving her, hopefully, wanting more in the parking lot.

FICTIONAL

KHLOE ROSE

Between the spicy as fuck sex scene in my audiobook before work, that I stupidly sat and listened to the rest of the chapter in the parking lot, and Ender's little whatever it was, I was going to need a cold shower before the work day even began. He left me with an entire cruise ship full of shit to unpack. Safe to say I was a bit distracted all day.

What exactly was he trying to do? I knew the man loved to read back in high school, but this new inner romance bookworm bullshit was new to me. And the fact that he was reading almost the exact same books as I was? Highly suspect.

Part of me wilted like a love-struck female main character. Swooning over the fact that the hunky main character was reading the books I loved. That he was actively trying to get to know me again. To figure out my likes and dislikes.

He had been so close I could smell him. The crispy mint of his toothpaste and the spicy frankincense and myrrh scent he'd worn since high school. It was as if just the smell of him was like an instant time machine, taking me back to late-night theater rehearsals and stolen kisses next to the dugout after watching him at practice. He smelled of happy memories. Memories that I missed very much.

I hated the fact that I had been entirely too close to closing the smallest of gaps between us. More than anything I wanted to stand on my tiptoes and steal just one more kiss. Just to see that if those strong feelings in the past were exactly that, in the past. The fact that I felt an almost uncontrollable need to kiss him had my stomach churning in some kind of way. I didn't know whether to swoon or swear.

So what if he was trying to make things up to me? Would it be okay to let him in, even if it was just a little? Maybe if he spent more time with me he'd regret this renewed interest and leave me the fuck alone for good. But then again, did I want to scare him off?

I wished I could vomit this chaos all over my best friend so she could clean me up, reassure me, and send me back on my way with my head held high. But telling Cadence about this would open so many cans of bullshit at once.

I saw Cadence shuffling in the prop closet, getting things sorted for upcoming routines. She was, once again, bright-eyed and bushy-tailed as she worked. No longer looking stressed and uncomfortable being around Jamie. Something had changed. She'd also been suspiciously quiet via text all last night after the guys got home from their road trip.

Then it hit me.

Cadence and Jamie were fucking.

Or at the very least, hanging out together on the regular. The sudden change in attitude towards him, the heart eyes she sent him during practice today. Something was new with her. A good cock would do that to a girl. Knowing just what sort of things she had said about Jamie in the past when she watched his games, it had to be on the spicier end of the spectrum.

That's why it was so satisfying when, after confronting her in the prop closet, she admitted that I was right. My ego fluffed while my heart sank. The last thing we needed right now was both of us chasing after guys on the team. There was a bigger chance of us getting caught if two sets of players and support staff were fucking each other in secret.

It didn't mean I couldn't give her shit for it.

Which I did until the guys coming back from practice to the locker room had to break up my ego parade. Cadence looked relieved to get her secret off her chest, despite almost being caught telling it to the entire starting line-up of the Sillys. But I didn't have time to dwell on all the new information because suddenly Ender dragged me off into a dark corner behind a support column. I pouted because I really wanted to hear Cadence's conversation with her fuck buddy instead of whatever flustering bullshit that was bound to come out of Ender's mouth.

"Hey Iffy—"

"What do you want, Ender?" I cut him off with a sharp hiss, trying to glance around him. Based on Cadence's blush, she and Jamie were almost certainly talking about something naughty.

"So, uh…I was thinking…"

"Just spit it out."

"Fine." Ender huffed. The suave book boyfriend persona from earlier was now in an overly flustered state. "Would you want to go—"

"Ender, I–" I sharply interrupted, getting more annoyed by the second. Gosh, I really just wanted him to shut up and catch me in the parking lot when I wasn't distracted by my friend's unfolding sexy drama playing out right in front of me.

"...go with me to the bookstore with me?" That got my eyes to snap back to his hopeful gaze. He must have known he had me, as his lips curled into a quirk of a smile. "I needed your opinion on some new books that released this week."

My metaphorical hackles fell. What a completely innocent and utterly unexpected question to ask me in a dark corner of the ballpark's underbelly. I had to admit that it took me by surprise.

"A bookstore…?"

"Yeah…" He glanced up, uneasy, making sure the surroundings were still clear. At least that's what I thought he was doing. "How about tomorrow, after the game? Here." He shoved a folded Post-it note into my hand before he hustled away, leaving me standing there with my mouth hanging open.

Ender Roche was continuing to surprise me. Passing notes to each other threw me right back into the halls of our high school. I hated the way it made me feel all warm and fuzzy inside. Ender was not allowed to make me feel like that. Not after what he did. And yet–

A soft giggle pulled me from my stupor. Pocketing the paper, I stepped out of my hiding spot just in time to break up the two lovebirds about to kiss.

"Eww, you two are gross." The pair of them jumped apart and I smirked. "If you're gonna do that kind of gross shit in public, at least find a closed room. Preferably behind a door that locks."

Jamie was the one to blush as he dipped his head bashfully. Cadence was the one to calm him down. "Tiffiny figured out that we didn't hate each other." Go me and my sleuthing skills. At least that got Jamie to laugh.

"Right. Cady and I were just–"

"Cady, huh?" Oh, this was so far beyond the initial "just fucking" part of a new relationship. "You two are at the pet names stage? It's even more disgusting than I imagined."

Shaking my head with a cackle, I left the two lovebirds to regroup. I headed down the hallway towards the locker room. A cold shower, alone in my dressing room, had been calling my name since Ender cornered me in the parking lot this morning. Shit. I really should have reminded Cadence and Jamie they weren't allowed to use my–

As soon as I hit the locker room doors, I stopped dead in my tracks.

Holy shit.

"What the hell is this?"

I blurted out, unable to contain my shocked surprise. The sight before me was something akin to the guys conducting a seance. They were all seated in a misshapen circle on folding chairs and locker room benches. But the thing that had me the most off-kilter was the fact that they all had a book in their hands. The *same* book.

"Book club!" Truitt chirped with a grin, sitting straighter on the bench by his locker. "It was Ender's idea."

I blanched on the inside as my gaze shot over to Ender's rather sheepish face. So this was where he had to rush off to. I suddenly had the sinking feeling that my plan to mentally scar Ender with the books I read had backfired. *Spectacularly.* He slouched in his chair before quickly turning his eyes back to the book in his hand.

How the hell did Ender come up with this? Was it because of what I said about him being vanilla? He and the guys were engulfed in an open discussion about my favorite read, so far, of the year. I honestly wasn't sure if it was creepy or hot. My book girly self was leaning towards hot.

I didn't exactly want all the guys to know what kind of filth I read for entertainment. Normally, I would blurt out one of my favorite scenes in order to bond with other book lovers. But who knew what sort of nonsense that would bring here. I had to play it cool. Maybe this was the new internet sensation for guys to start book clubs with books that women were reading?

Speaking of, why the fuck weren't we funding that?

Ender took this a hell of a lot further than I ever could have bargained for. It wasn't just him who had apparently read my favorite monster romance of late. It was the *whole team.* All I could do with all of their eyes on me was pray to anyone above me who would listen, that Ender had kept the one particular dirty fact about the books I read, a secret.

"Oh…that's nice." I choked out. "It's good to see you guys expanding your horizons." That got me a few laughs. The room went quiet, and I wanted to hightail it out of there immediately.

"Hey Tiffiny," Arlow's words reluctantly glued my feet to the floor. "Do women really like reading books like this?" Before I knew it, all the guys' eyes were on me. *Fuck. Fucky fuck to the fuckiest of all fucks.* I began to sweat. The last thing I expected today was to be the female consult at an all-male smutty book club. "Benson said chicks really dig this kind of stuff."

Oh, phew. This wasn't just Ender opening his big mouth. This was Benson's fault, too. It both surprised and impressed me. I didn't take him for the kind of guy to read these sorts of things. He was like the mother hen of the group, stern and all-knowing. Although I was slightly terrified to know about just what sort of conversation they had prior to this that got them to this point of locker room book club.

I swallowed back an awkward laugh. I would have let it loose if it weren't for the fact that they were all looking at me with such earnest gazes. Shit. They were actually serious about this.

"Uh…yeah." I managed to uneasily answer. "Book boyfriends are a big thing to, uh, some people." Fuck I really hated confrontation. Why couldn't they just ask me in a text like normal people?

Anxiety, sit your ass down and shut up.

"Book boyfriends?" Tomas innocently chirped. The rest of the guys turned back to me with expectant expressions. I wanted to slap myself silly with a palm to my face. Why did I have to open my goddamn mouth? "Wait, you love these books? You call the books your boyfriend?"

"Uh…" I really despised confrontation. I was doing my best not to look in Ender's direction. But I couldn't help but catch him trying to hang on to my every word. "Yeah. Well, the guys." I stumbled over my words, trying to convey the idea while my mind was spinning in a zillion different directions. " The guys in the book. The main character guy, I mean. He's the one we call a book boyfriend. A boyfriend that lives in a book."

There was a rounding noise of revelation throughout the room as all the guys shared looks. This had to singlehandedly be the weirdest situation I'd ever found myself in. I was the off-the-cuff liaison between a room full of jocks and the romance book in their hands.

Normally, I loved yapping about books. It was getting me to shut up about them was the problem. But right now I was begging for the fault lines in the earth's crust to break apart, opening the maw of the crust to drop me straight to the molten lava core. No such luck.

"Do chicks think guys who read are hot?" Camden asked, his face dead serious. This was quickly turning into the most unhinged Q&A.

"Most of the time, yeah." I huffed out with a bit of an exasperated laugh. Because duh, women always loved a learned man.

"What do women get out of these books?" Truitt added, rather skeptically. "Is it really only the dirty parts?"

I was actually kind of surprised that the guys hadn't found some local coffee shop or library to set up shop in instead. Although this was probably the safest alternative out of everything, given their newfound popularity, thanks to Jamie.

I glanced at Ender with heat in my cheeks. The man looked stoic, locked in. But there was something in his gaze that made me wonder just how much of this conversation he was absorbing. Was he taking mental notes?

"I mean…they help." The guys quieted down. "But it's mostly the points leading up to the, uh…er…" I swallowed. "Dirty parts." Blank faces looked back at me from across the room. Okay, so maybe I had to lay it out for them.

I sighed. "Women like it when men pay attention to them. And *not* in the way you all think." I had to nip that one right in the bud before it got out of hand. "That they notice the little things like, say… How she takes her coffee, her usual order at a fast food place, her favorite thing to watch on TV, what she likes to do in her free time. That a man makes an effort to text her, hang out with her, all without her having to ask. We just want to be, well…at least one of the priorities in your life. Continuously."

There were some murmurs and nods at my words. At least part of this tirade was getting through to them. If so, there were going to be a lot more happier women in the Philadelphia area thanks to me.

"Once you have all that figured out and in a good place, then you can…uh, move to the bedroom portion." My cheeks were burning at this point as all eyes snapped back to me. "Look, first of all, I'm not giving any of you all pointers, because, well, gross. Secondly, put her um…" Holy hell, how do I make this G-rated for this room of neanderthals? "…pleasure, before all else. Make sure she gets, err…at least once before you do anything else."

I was thoroughly embarrassed now, but my mouth wouldn't stop talking. Even with an entire roster of mostly clueless men staring back at me. Maybe not so much Benson, he seemed like maybe he had things figured out. Tomas on the other hand? He was probably a lost cause. Poor dude.

"And that's all I'm even saying on the matter because I'm getting the fuck out of here before any of you assholes embarrass me further." I made a beeline past the gawkers as they slowly turned back to their book discussion. Some even waved in thanks. I was sure they now had a whole hell of a lot more to talk about now.

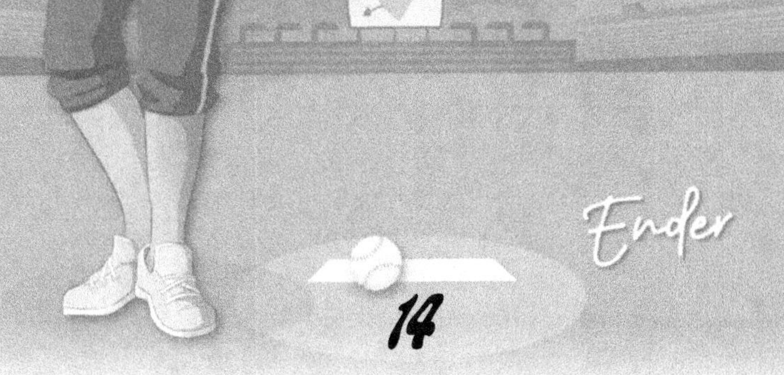

THE STORY OF US

TAYLOR SWIFT

It wasn't my day in the starting pitching rotation, so I was able to sit back and watch Tiffiny work from my bench seat in the dugout. At least the book club meeting yesterday hadn't been a total disaster. Even though Tiffiny had, unwillingly and unsuspectingly, crashed it.

I couldn't bring myself to make eye contact with her. The entire idea of the book club had been spurred on by Benson and the guys snooping on my incognito reading of Iffy's book list. If she had suspected anything wonky, she hadn't let on.

I'd been pleasantly surprised that the book club had been wildly informative, thanks to her. The guys were surprisingly into the book. More than I thought they would be. There was even a riveting discussion.

Most of the guys were in the same boat as me. Some with women they were fooling around with. Even Schmidt and Martin, who were married, took some pointers from the book to surprise their wives with. All in all, it was a success. So much so that we were doing it again next month, and we even voted on a name.

Pitching Tents Romance Book Club.

After the meeting wrapped, there had even been talks about getting t-shirts made. I don't know why I'd been so apprehensive about it all. The team was made up of a bunch of great dudes. We all encouraged each other and learned from one another. The book club ended up being no different. Maybe the guys were just a room full of budding romance readers who finally found their niche?

The flash of metallic gold pulled me out of my wandering thoughts. Tiffiny was up on the Charlotte Webs' dugout, causing the usual amount of chaos for the crowd. Ever since Jamie had joined the team, the stands were almost always jam-packed. It was like a night and day difference between now and the beginning of the season.

Like me, the crowd was absolutely enamored with her. Well, Ding Dong, the mascot. The giant foam head in the shape of the iconic Liberty Bell's yoke was outfitted with a giant foam Sillys hat and great big googly eyes that rotated from a singular top point, adding to the overall chaos of the, well…whatever it was. A cartoon version of the Bell? A monster mascot?

It wasn't easy playing a persona like that in the ungodly Pennsylvania humidity during summer days. Today was an afternoon game, so the late June sun was relentless. The shade in the dugout was somewhat tolerable. The fans in the corners helped move the still summer air. The last thing I needed right now was to be thinking spicy thoughts about a certain, deranged mascot on the opposite side of the field. Or the fact that she had accepted my bookstore visit invite for tonight after the game.

The heel of my right foot tapped on the concrete with my untapped energy. This game was going at a snail's pace. The hot weather wasn't doing it any favors.

Tiffiny had to be so hot in the plush costume. There were layers to it. But at least there were breezy layers. Most mascots were made from faux fur. I couldn't even imagine how hot those costumes were.

I may have stolen a glance or two when Iffy was walking around in nothing but the black, skin-tight top and bottom during the times she didn't have to be in costume. She worked in shorter bursts, the length of time depending greatly on the weather and how much heat she could stand on a daily basis. Cadence was usually her assistant, or someone from the back office also stepped in to help maintain the crowds that flocked to the cartoon Liberty Bell with attitude.

It always blew my mind with the fact that despite Tiffiny having a theater degree, the mascot didn't talk. I suppose it would take away the magic a bit. So instead of interacting with the guests with words, she had to do it through actions and body language alone. Which was no easy feat.

I remember overhearing a conversation between her and Cadence, in which Iffy had studied some of the current greats in the mascot world. Of course, that included local mascots. The Phanatic and, her favorite, Gritty. But she had also added the Colts' mascot, Blue, to her study. Either way, I was glad that she avoided the cake-throwing of Gritty and the pie-smashing of Blue.

She kept with most of the similar mannerisms of the Phanatic but the adult humor of Gritty. I mean the Ding Dong costume had a clapper, the ball on the inside of the bell that hit the sides to make it ring, that looked suspiciously like a cock and balls. When Tiffiny walked, it slapped along her thighs in a manner in which full-grown adults couldn't walk by the mascot without snickering. Hell, I couldn't half the time. Especially when I knew there was a five-foot-four voluptuous woman inside the thing.

The crowds loved her. She was so approachable with the kids, giving them high fives and fist bumps while doing autographs. This was only her second season as the mascot, and she already had quite the fan club. Of all ages. She only fed the fandom by posting chaotic videos on the mascot's social media channels. I'll admit, sometimes I watched old Ding Dong videos at night on road trips when I couldn't sleep.

Despite this not being her ideal acting career, she did it with such integrity. It impressed me to no end.

She was amazing.

I mean, maybe it was weird to lust after and have a crush on an inanimate object with googly guys. Especially one that was as wild as Ding Dong. But it's what's on the inside that counts, right?

As the game drew on, the long-dormant butterflies in my stomach started to flutter with a vengeance. It was getting closer and closer to the time when I could have Tiffiny all to myself. Something I'd been looking forward to ever since the idea popped into my head.

I had somehow grown enough balls to move onto the next step of my plan. To give Iffy my phone number. I'd hastily scribbled it onto a sticky note before thrusting it into her hand, like when we used to pass dirty notes in high school. I only had a moment to formally ask her out on a not-date date to the bookstore before I rushed off for book club.

I should have stayed to get her answer. But I was too chicken shit to have her turn me down directly to my face. Besides, I wanted her to have time to think about it instead of flipping me off.

I wasn't sure if her accidentally stumbling into book club had swayed her to say yes or not, but I definitely owed Truitt for the shout-out. Well, and Benson for organizing the boy zoo into some semblance of an actual, factual book club. Maybe she understood that I was serious about this. About her and her interests.

By the time the game was over, I was ready to jump out of my skin from my anxiety and excitement. I had to stay cool. Calm. Collected. At least to a point.

I waited for her outside of the agreed-upon bookstore with the excitement of a golden retriever waiting for his promised walk. I'd showered and changed in record time. I may have gotten a few suspicious looks from the guys, but I dismissed them. I was too focused on the fact that I was spending one-on-one time with Iffy. Time that she had, thankfully, willingly agreed to.

She got a head start after the game, as she didn't have after-game nonsense to deal with. The bookstore was located a few SEPTA stops north of the stadium. It was just easier to take the SEPTA than deal with Philadelphia traffic. Oddly enough, the bookstore was almost smack dab in the middle of both of our places.

My spine straightened the second I saw her round the corner of the busy Philadelphia street. I felt my heart take a rocket straight to my throat. Dressed in leggings, a sports bra, and a tee that had the neck cut out of it so it slipped over her shoulder a bit. It had my mouth watering. She could have dressed in a burlap sack for all I cared.

She seemed startled by the fact that I was so eagerly waiting outside the bright pink storefront of the romance bookstore in Old City Philadelphia, Roses are Read. She said she was *very* familiar with it already. By the looks of it, it was going to be a bookstore that I was going to be quite familiar with too, now that I knew it was here.

Shooting me a sharp look, her hand absentmindedly shook her Wawa iced coffee before she took a sip. I opened my mouth to greet her, but her words stopped me before I could even inhale to form words.

"It's not a date, Ender. We're just going to the bookstore." I went to open my mouth to expand that thought further, but she continued on. "Not even as friends either. This is purely you wanting book suggestions from the romance book master."

A delightful shiver went up my spine. Just last week, I had read a dom versus sub dynamic where she called him as such. Something in the back of my brain really liked the thought of switching roles. *Fuck.* Were romance novels becoming my personality now? Or was it just me being utterly obsessed with this hot-headed pipsqueak in front of me?

Swallowing back my little fantasy, I nodded, shoving my hands into my linen shorts as we took a few steps towards the bookstore door. While I'd been optimistic when I gave her my number, I didn't exactly get my hopes up expecting her to text me. It gave me that little spark that maybe she would let me in. Even little by little.

"Ah, uh, right. I know that. I'm just excited." Fuck, I felt like a foolish love-struck teenager all over again. "To talk books with a professional, like yourself, and all."

That got her to puff her chest out a bit as her chin raised ever so slightly. In all my new reading, I'd learned about something called a "praise kink". By the way she silently responded, it was something I was going to have to keep tucked in the back of my mind for future use. I just thought complimenting someone was being nice. I had no idea that some people got *sexual pleasure* out of it.

"What, you didn't have a satisfying enough discussion with your new book club?" I gave her a nonchalant sort of shrug as I toed a cigarette butt on the sidewalk. Her tone was teasing, even though it was meant to be a dig at me.

"Hey, no dissing the Pitching Tents Book Club."

I sure as fuck was glad that we were outside in the summer evening air because Iffy ended up spraying her iced coffee everywhere. Sputtering, she fumbled for a napkin in her crossbody purse where the heft of the thing sat comfortably between her breasts. Dabbing her mouth, she coughed. I gave her a few reassuring pats on the back for good measure, which only got me yet another glare.

"The fucking *what?*"

"Pitching Tents Book Club," I said simply, blinking at her. I, for one, thought it was hilarious as fuck.

"Jeezus fuck." She wheezed, shaking her head. Taking a few more breaths, she slowly began to regain her composure. "You boys are animals." Shaking her head, she marched up to the front door of the bookstore. I hurried after her, using the advantage of my long limbs to outstride her and grab the handle before her hand had made it even halfway there.

"They don't call it the boy zoo for nothing." The antique shop bell tinkled as I opened the door for her. "Its part of our charm. And our job, honestly." I gave her a shrug as I escorted her inside the shop. "You have to give Schmidt props for originality."

Tiffiny offered only a huff as we stepped inside. The worn wood floors were a foundation to soft pink bookshelves and whitewashed brick walls. Gold and crystal details sparkled throughout. Iffy was already perusing the new releases table. If I wanted this to work, if I wanted her to take me seriously as a reader, I couldn't get intimidated.

"Anything good?" I offered, glancing over her shoulder as I shoved my hands back into my pockets. The books were delightfully arranged on the table. A rainbow array of bright covers to dark and moody floral ones along with the charming cartoon covers that I liked to admire so much.

Her fingers caressed down along the edge of the book closest to her. More than anything I wanted to be that book. To feel the soft pads of her fingers slide down my face. It sent a delightful shiver up my spine.

"The new Talon Rivers book came out this week." I seemed to remember her mentioning something else about that author before. "I was debating–"

Before she could say another word, I plucked the book out from under her touch. She turned to look at me, her brow sliding further and further up her forehead. I only grinned.

"Consider it my treat." Her mouth opened and I tutted her smartass reply away. "A small price to pay for your time and expertise."

She hovered there for a long minute, intensely contemplating my offer. I wasn't going to take no for an answer anyway. If she wanted me to buy the entire dark romance section of the bookstore for her, I would. As long as it made her happy.

Turning her eyes away from me, a small smile quirked at the corner of her mouth as she slid along to the other side of the table. She did everything within her power to avoid eye contact with me as she carefully studied the other new releases.

"You aren't going to get a copy?" She said after a while, casting me the quickest of glances.

"Nah." I shrugged, tucking the book up under my arm after I finished reading the back. "I like to wait for your thoughts before I decide to read a book." Her cheeks slowly went pink as she tried to distract herself by wandering over to the closest bookshelf.

There had to be at least two dozen or so bookshelves, seemingly built into the older storefront walls. There was a rather plush-looking lounge area in the middle of the store with a guy chilling in one of the armchairs.

Leaning in to Iffy as she was flipping through a special edition hardcover, I whispered, "Is that the cuckold area?" The sound of her snapping the book closed cracked through the mellow music over the speakers in the shop. A few annoyed glances were cast in our direction.

"Ender, don't make me regret bringing you into book world."

"What? I was just asking a simple question." I shrugged, biting the inside of my cheek to stop myself from grinning. "Those guys are just sitting, watching their wife or girlfriend pick out a new book boyfriend. Not much different than it being a corner of their bedroom."

The soft snort led me to believe that I was getting somewhere. At least a little. Hopefully, in the right direction.

"So, what are you in the mood for?"

Kissing you senseless and doing everything to make you scream my name all night.

"Uh, maybe something lighter than the book club book." I offered, clearing my throat, making the spicy thoughts dissipate. "Maybe with one of those cartoon covers. But with spice. Nothing stingy on the spice."

Tiffiny finally looked over at me, but only for a moment. Was it judgment? Surprise?

"I have some ideas." She offered, already heading off in the opposite direction. It amazed me to no end that she knew the store so well. "Fancy a sports romance at all?" This had to be a test. Right?

"Does anyone write mascot romances?" I wiggled my eyebrows at her as I grinned. It got me a rather spicy eye roll.

"Yes…" She answered cautiously as her fingers danced along the spines of one of the shelves labeled with "Sports Romance". I should have been surprised but then again I did read a book about a monster under a bed who liked to fuck the woman who slept on said bed. A mascot romance would be pale in comparison.

Tiffiny's finger stopped on one spine before it crooked, dragging it out from its spot on the shelf. Turning to me, there was a mischievous flicker to her eyes as she did her best to avoid my questioning look. She handed the book to me.

"This one is pretty fun. As long as you don't mind that the guy gets pegged in the ass by the mascot."

I nearly dropped the book.

She was for sure testing me now. Testing my limits. Seeing where I would crack. If I were to give all of this up. That all of this was overwhelming. That I was "too vanilla".

Aside from actually enjoying my newfound genre, I was learning from the books. Learning stuff about me. About Tiffiny. New things that aroused me and things that were a hard limit.

Despite not being as big of a fan of dark romance as Iffy was, I did enjoy some of the stories. Reading romance was, well, freeing in a way. A safe place to find your limits and discover things about our sexuality that we had no idea existed.

The book wouldn't be the first book I've read with pegging, or hell, male ass play in any aspect. It was kind of hot, honestly. Considering I was contemplating additional research, pegging wasn't exactly off the table. Yet. But fuck if I was going to tell Iffy about that in the middle of a bookstore.

"Hot." I shrugged, as nonchalantly as possible, as I flipped the book over to read the blurb on the back. I stole a look at her and I was so glad I did. Her eyes went wide for a second as she mouthed something to herself. She quickly busied herself with the next bookshelf.

Another small step in the right direction. If I wanted to do this right, I knew I had it in me to be a patient man. If it took weeks, months, or hell, even years for her to give me that second chance, then so be it. Sure, it would absolutely fucking suck. But no expanse of time was too great if I meant I got to spend the rest of my life with her. Or at least some measure of time.

WAIT

MAROON 5

Was I actually having a great time with Ender?

Maybe the question should be rhetorical.

I didn't have it in me to say yes.

Ender was doing all the things he used to do when we were dating. He was engaging, asking questions, trying to do everything to get me to laugh. Laughing was so much easier then. Back when I didn't question his devotion to me.

Something in the back of my mind still replayed the memory of him dropping me like I was nothing just because the popular girl batted her eyelashes at him. Over and over again, like some sort of sick joke. It was in the past. From what I could tell, he wasn't with her. The only time he brought Regina up was when I did.

I was doing my best to embarrass the hell out of him. To make him uncomfortable. To make him question my sanity. Anything to get him to run away screaming and regretting that he ever glanced in my direction.

Yet he didn't bat an eye. Not one bit. The man rolled with the punches. Sometimes I was even convinced that he was some love-sick puppy following me around the bookstore, hanging on my every word. He was focused on me and no one else. Not even his phone. Not on any of the other women in the bookstore who were considerably hotter than me.

Don't even get me started on the fact that he was carrying around three books that I had considered buying myself. With nary a hesitation, he snatched them out of my hand and said he was treating me. I mean, I wasn't going to turn down free books. Especially not when the very notion of a man buying me smutty books turned out to be my newest kink.

This not-a-date date had my panties moister than the unholiest of humid Pennsylvania summer days. From wandering a bookstore for an unspoken amount of time, the chatter about dirty books, Ender's endless flirting, the offer to carry and buy the books I wanted… I mean, what sane book girlie wouldn't be turned on by that?

"Are those…" Ender's broken question snapped me out of my tumble of thoughts. "Um, sex toys?" His voice dropped to a near whisper as he leaned in over my shoulder, the words warm against the cove of my ear. I had to close my eyes for a second lest I climax right on the sales floor.

"Yeah. They are." I knew exactly where he was looking. Behind the checkout counter and off to the side a bit was a shelf full of discrete boxes of adult toys. I may have purchased a few in the past. Especially when something new and exciting came out. "Haven't you heard of one-handed reading?"

Ender was still so close that I could hear his breath catch. Fuck, I should not have fed into his thoughts, which were clearly somewhere filthy. Not that mine were any better. The heat of his body didn't waver as I felt his tall and looming presence mere inches from my back.

Out of the corner of my eye, I saw Ender's hand slowly reach toward me, but stopped with less than an inch to go. Instead of touching me, like my entire body was screaming for, but my brain was trying to be the voice of reason, his hand pulled back slightly, curling into a tight fist before pulling away.

"I have." The husky voice sent a delicious shiver up my spine, much to my common sense's chagrin. "Who's to say I haven't partaken of it myself?"

If he had slapped a faux English accent on that hot-as-fuck statement, I could have sworn I was living in a regency romance. Just how many different genres was this man going to fluster me with?

"*Partaken of?*" I pulled away with an overachieving scoff, chancing a darting glance. I was trying to remain cool but was positively sucking at it. "Excuse me, Mr. Darcy." Forcing out a laugh, I busied myself at the next shelf over, putting plenty of space between us.

Instead of following me, Ender adjusted the books to his left arm while his right slowly crept up to brace itself against the highest shelf as he did the fuck all sexy door frame lean, but on a bookshelf. The fluster was on full display on my cheeks. They were hot enough to fry an egg in no time flat.

"Doth the lady not desire such an educated man?"

I spoke too soon on the fake English accent thing.

The man dove in headfirst, and all I could imagine was him in a waistcoat and an ascot. I wondered if Ender would be into cosplaying–

Goddammit, Tiff. STOP IT.

If I didn't put an end to this soon, I was going to end up in a puddle in the middle of the bookstore's floor. Dammit, Ender. He shouldn't have this power over me. It's like he was my own personal brand of fluster. The man was fighting fire with fire now. It wasn't fair.

Even though I technically started it first. Now it was coming back to bite me in the ass. I had underestimated the man. A whole fucking lot.

Women would be so lucky to have a partner like Ender. Why was I holding back so fiercely? All because of a stupid teenage mistake that I turned into a lifelong grudge?

Maybe I was the one being stupid?

"Any other books you want to add to the pile?" Ender offered, casting one last look around the store to hide his smug look. That ass knew he was getting to me.

"Keep up with that attitude and I'll make you buy the whole store."

"Don't think that I wouldn't." Ender shot back, without even a hint of hesitation. "I mean, I might have to move some money around, but I'd buy you one of every romance book on the damn planet if it made you happy."

Suddenly, I had the feeling that he wasn't teasing me anymore.

Swallowing, I crossed my arms in front of myself and started to move towards the checkout counter. "I wouldn't want to put you out on your ass." I threw over my shoulder as he caught up to me in one long stride. There was a soft chuckle as he put our stacks of books on the counter.

"Damn, you're one lucky lady." The owner, Millie, said, eyeing the book piles with outright envy as she began to scan them. We had had plenty of in-depth discussions over books between me shopping and attending book clubs in the shop. "You'd better keep this guy." Ender let out a huff of amusement, but I could see the blush on his tanned cheeks.

"Oh, he's not–"

"Hell, I'd build her the library from *Beauty and the Beast* if she'd let me," Ender interjected with a laugh. Millie visibly swooned to the point that I wondered if I could get around the counter fast enough to break her fall.

"Oh my god girl, *let him*." She looked at me like I was an idiot before her eyes moved back to Ender with admiration. Oh Wayne Brady was ready to slap a bitch. Wait, why was I feeling this way? He wasn't *my* man. "I know I'd give my left kidney to have a guy like you."

There was an unholy need to claim him, itching at the back of my mind. Something ancient and animalistic. I didn't like just sitting back and watching a woman openly flirt with him. To claim him in public and knowing that Ender wouldn't mind one fucking bit.

"Actually, only this pile," Ender gestured to the taller pile of books with a playful grin. "Is for my dear Iffy here." My lips pressed into a thin line as I shot him a death glare. Blatantly ignoring me, he leaned forward onto the high counter with a smug as fuck look. "The rest are mine."

"Oh my god, and you *read* smut too?" She took a moment to fan herself. I rolled my eyes. "You certainly are quite the catch. I hope she knows how lucky she is." The conversation turned into one where they both, apparently, forgot about the fact that I was still in the room with them.

"One would hope." It was then that Ender finally looked at me. Instead of mirth in his gaze, there was only an innocent yearning there. It shot a hole right through the brick walls I had so carefully curated. Goddamn this man.

"Well, you're all set. Please come again sometime." Millie's voice turned a bit breathy as she waved us off. Although her eyes were squarely on Ender. He for sure was going to be the talk of the break room and book club for probably the next month or so.

"So…" Ender started cautiously as he held the door open for me as we made our way outside. I breathed in the fresh air, taking a few seconds to realign myself after whatever the fuck that all was that happened in the bookstore. "Hungry? I figured I could feed your brain and your stomach. If you'll let me." He paused for a moment, gauging my reaction. "I know a great place just a few stops down from here on the SEPTA."

"Ender I–"

"Please?"

As if on cue, my stomach seemingly twisted inside of itself, desperate for sustenance. The last thing I wanted right now was to go home and make myself a sad peanut butter and jelly sandwich. A hot meal sounded so much better. As much as I was in denial about it, I did kind of want to spend more time with Ender.

"Okay fine. Dinner too. Then I'm going home to read."

"You're welcome." Ender chirped back as his eyes found mine. There was a smirk of a smile on his lips as he toyed with me.

Shit. Right. Manners.

"Thank you, Ender." Despite the bite in my tone I really was thankful for the treat. My sarcasm was just a defense mechanism against him. But I was pretty sure he liked it.

"That's a good girl." He grinned, the words only for me as he dipped in close before stepping onto the SEPTA train with me close behind. This had better be a short trip.

It wasn't. It was about a twenty-minute ride. Although I had been in such a tizzy after the bookstore stop that I didn't realize exactly which stop it was. It wasn't until we went to deboard and I saw the sign. This was *his* stop. The one I rode to after date night or when I came to see him after my part time job.

I played it cool. Maybe it was just a restaurant close to where he lived. That seemed rather feasible. But when we walked around the block only to end up at a rather familiar condo stoop, I stopped.

"I thought you said we were going out to dinner."

"We are." Ender glanced at me, smiling sheepishly as he unlocked the metal entry door. It opened to the same brown shag carpet hallway with white walls that gave way to his first-floor condo.

"But…this looks like your house."

"It is."

"I said I wanted to take you to dinner. I didn't exactly elaborate on *where*."

He unlocked his front door and was immediately met with the enchanting smells of his mother's cooking. My mouth began to water instinctively.

Mamá Roche had always been my favorite cook. So while I was pissed about the destination, I wasn't completely mad about it. Although I hadn't exactly prepared myself to have a third wheel on this not-date.

Distracting myself, I took in the charmingly outdated but neat as a pin living room that was literally a time machine from our dating years. It was almost eerie. As if no time had passed. Well, aside from the fact that there were more recent photos of Ender scattered about the walls. I went to investigate.

I spotted his graduation pictures from both high school and college. A Villanova graduate? Impressive. True to his word he stuck close to home. I stumbled upon his draft photos. Damn he looked good in a uniform that wasn't as flamboyant as the Sillys jerseys. Now I kind of understood what Cadence had been prattling on about.

"Iffy! My god!" Mamá Roche's rich accent wafted from the kitchen. I noted that she still kept up with the nickname Ender had given me. Her petite form padded into the living room. Right before swatting Ender's chest with the back of her hand. "Cachetón, you didn't tell me you were bringing tu amor!"

"Mamá, it was a spur of the moment thing." Ender's cheeks had a vivid blush as he tried to smooth over the situation but Mamá Roche and I both shared a look. I knew I always liked her.

"Ah well, no matter." She dismissed him with a wave of her hand as she quickly made her way over to me. "It is good to see you, Iffy. Ender should have brought you over for weekly meals." Her petite body gave me a tight hug. It was a wonder that someone so tall could come out of a woman her size. Even though she was little, she was fierce.

"I uh…we lost touch." I managed to get out in between the crushing of my lungs from her embrace.

"Lost touch?!" She let go of me as her gaze shot over to Ender. He was trying to sneak a taste of the dinner in the kitchen and avoid the situation entirely. "Cachetón! You lost touch with tu amor?!" Something about her tone made it sound like he hadn't exactly come clean to his mother about us. "You chatter about her every day and she says you lost touch?!"

Well, that was news to me.

Mamá Roche stomped her way over to Ender and picked up her wooden spoon that was resting on a spoon rest on the counter. Before the grown ass man could react, she rapt the wood across his knuckles, causing him to drop the fried plantain back into the pan. I choked back a laugh.

"Go set the table, Cachetón. Make yourself useful." Rolling his eyes, Ender reached up into the cabinet next to Mamá Roche's head, pulling out plates and glasses. Grumbling, he wandered over to the small round dining table directly across from the tiny galley kitchen. Something told me that he was regretting "surprising" us both.

"Do you need any help, Mamá Roche?" My endearment for her slipped out of habit. I wanted to bite my tongue but the sweet look in her eyes made me pause. She lifted a hand to gently caress my cheek as she smiled at me.

"No, cariño. You go sit. You are a guest!" Shooing me away she leaned to the side to call out to Ender. "Oi! Cachetón, you'd better pull that chair for tu amor!"

"Sí, Mamá." Ender pressed his lips together as he was already reaching for the chair closest to me. I had to bite my lower lip to hinder my grin. It was a wonder as to why I stayed away from his house for so long. Mamá Roche was definitely on my side. We could have teamed up back when Ender broke up with me to teach him a lesson. Oh well.

"I am enjoying this princess treatment," I murmured to him as I sat down. He shot me a look. "Even if your mom is the only one giving it to me." There was a sharp set to his jaw as he arranged the last plate and silverware.

Finishing up, he leaned down to my ear. Much to my chagrin, he still refused to touch me. But I couldn't fault him for being respectful. It's not like he could just flip a switch after I've been so overly icy towards him.

"You know I'd give you the princess treatment day…and night. If you'd let me."

Fuckkkkkkk.

Mamá Roche broke up the sudden onslaught of heated tension between us as she brought a pan of sizzling fried plantains that Ender had already been eyeing up. Along with a pot of shredded beef. Ender had slipped back into the kitchen, bringing the rest of the meal with a bowl in each hand of rice and beans.

"So, cariño, it's nice of you to come by after so many years." Mamá Roche gave me a warm smile as she handed me the bowl of beef. "Ender has told me that you work together now?"

"Oh…" I stuttered, casting Ender a look. His mother had said something about talking about me with her. Just what has he told her? "Uh, yeah. Cooper, do you remember my brother Cooper?"

"Oh yes, good boy. He and Ender ate me out of house and home most weeks. Well, until you, cariño, came around." She chuckled warmly, taking the bowl from Ender and filling her plate.

"Well, he got Ender a position on the Philly Sillys since they played together. I've been the mascot since the beginning of last season."

"Ah, Ender did tell me that much. Although not so much about tu amor. Did you go to college?"

"I did. I got my Master's degree in Theater."

"Ah, chévere!" Her gaze moved to Ender to give him a hell of a look. "A masters, cachetón. You'd better not let her slip through your fingers." She patted the back of my hand as I felt a blush rise to my cheeks. At least she was impressed with my non-impressive degree.

"Mamá…"

"It was so nice, you two doing the theater in school. I liked your shows very much." My gaze slid to Ender, squirming in his seat. I don't exactly know what his play was bringing me home, but if it was to one-up himself, it wasn't working. Although his mom's food and conversation were.

"I enjoyed it so much I decided to make a career out of it." I gave a half chuckle, a desperate attempt to hide my awkwardness at the fact that all those years of school only got me stuffed into a polyester mascot costume during Pennsylvania summers. I could have been on Broadway. I could be running a theater program at a college or university.

"Aye, that you did, cariño. Ender has said that you are cartelúo!" Despite my Spanish being rather rusty, her warm smile led me to believe that it was a compliment. It also reiterated the fact that Ender had been saying good things about me to his mom. For years.

There was something so sweetly genuine about Mamá Roche. Like she was all the good parts of a mom and grandmother all rolled into one. If she complimented you, it really meant the world. Maybe it wasn't so bad being a bell-shaped mascot after all.

"So, Ender has been talking about me, hmm?" I glanced to my right just in time to see Ender choke on his bite of dinner. The man looked like he was regretting most of his life choices. His mom was sharp as a tack, and he had to keep his face on the right end of things lest she catch on.

"Oh non-stop! Always Iffy this and Iffy that. Even before you two worked together."

"Really now?" I leaned onto the table, hanging onto her every word. All while simultaneously watching Ender sweat some bullets. But, much to my chagrin, it didn't last long.

"All good things. I swear." He held his hands up, trying to look as innocent as possible. His mother laughed.

"Yes, all good things, cariño. That boy is madly in love with you."

"*Mamá!*"

"Oh tut, cachetón. A mamá knows such things."

Their conversation continued on, but I was taken out of it for a moment. An out-of-body experience if you will. Because nothing had taken me out like Mamá Roche's words.

Ender loved me? Still loved me? Was that what this was all about? This push to reconnect with me? To get to know me again?

What if he *never stopped* loving me?

16

CAN I KISS YOU?

DAHL

Well, that was the last time I ever brought a woman home to Mamá.

Technically Tiffiny was the only woman I'd ever brought home. I thought I could butter her up with Mamá's cooking, as I remembered her always being a fan. Hell, everyone was a fan. That maybe a dinner with us would remind her of what we used to have. And give me an excuse to spend even more time with her, away from most of the prying eyes on the team.

What I hadn't expected was for Mamá to completely nuke the entire conversation with one simple phrase. I should have known better. Mamá always had a way to say the quiet things out loud. God love her. But damn I was fucked.

I hadn't accounted for her observations of me. She had never said a damn word to me about the quantity in which I spoke about Tiffiny. Was I really that obvious? I…didn't think so. Then again, nothing got past Mamá. I should have known better. But maybe I was too far gone into Tiffiny to ever notice.

Shit.

Tiffiny was quiet as I walked her back to the SEPTA station. She had been quiet ever since Mamá dropped that bomb on all of us. Of course, Mamá was oblivious to how heavy that information had been to Tiffiny and I. Heavy for different reasons, I was assuming.

I wanted to say something to her, but what? I had no idea what she was thinking. Was it good? Was it bad? Was she absolutely outraged over all of this? I was low-key afraid that she'd bite my head off if I did ask her. Dammit, this silence was killing me.

"Thank you, Ender." Tiffiny's soft words suddenly broke the silence as we walked. The June evening was thankfully cooler than the humid mess it had been during our afternoon game earlier. Which was a godsend because I felt like I was sweating bullets. "For dinner." She added quickly, still avoiding my eyes. "And my books."

"Uh, yeah. Anytime, Iffy. Mamá always likes having you over. Surprise or not." I offered with an awkward chuckle as I shoved my hands into my pockets, a desperate attempt to avoid touching her. Not without her consent, first and foremost. But fuck I wanted to. I would be content with just a warm hug from her. "It was really nice spending time with you."

The quiet resumed as we walked the last few yards to the station to await the next train. A few others mingled on the platform, but we had plenty of space for our own little bubble. One that I was afraid would burst. But here we were, hovering in this unsure balance. I didn't want to make any sudden movements.

I wanted to linger here. To linger in this warm connection that was ever so slowly sparking back to life, little by little. My stunt today might have backfired. Not only with Tiffiny, but with me as well.

If this woman couldn't be in my life permanently, I would surely wilt away into nothing.

Who knew that a simple visit to a bookstore and dinner with my family would make me fall that much harder for her? Oh, who am I kidding? I only breathed easier when I admitted that my feelings towards this woman were so much more than a high school infatuation. Years had gone by, and my yearning for her had never diminished. Working with her again only made that yearning ever more powerful. So powerful to the point that it hurt.

Every second she wasn't paying me any mind, I took those moments to study her. To drink her in, just in case moments like these would have to last me the rest of my life.

I wanted to memorize how every muscle moved when she smiled. How her graceful fingers liked to trace down the spine of a book she was considering. Or the fact that her lips pursed when she was deep in thought.

Right now, she looked so beautiful with her skin kissed by the warm orange and reds of the sunset. The breeze filtered through her dark tresses, making them look silken. She was always beautiful. Inside and out. Even when she was grumpy.

As much as I hated to agree with Mamá, she was right. I was in love with Tiffiny. So desperately, head-over-heels in love with her. And the truth was, I'd always been in love with her. Nothing had changed from the moment our eyes locked above the dugout way back in high school. Okay, so a whole hell of a lot had changed. But it was more evident to me now that my feelings hadn't changed. Only how much I was in denial about them.

Tiffiny stopped so suddenly in her tracks that I went two strides past her before skidding to a stop. I'd barely turned around before I found her practically toe-to-toe with me, staring at me so intently that I was frozen to the spot. Oh shit. I was in for it.

"Is it true, Ender?" Iffy said sharply to me, meeting my gaze. It was almost as if she had come to some conclusion all of a sudden. "What your mom said?"

All these weeks and months since Tiifiny was thrown back into my life had led me to this moment. My heart immediately began to race as beads of sweat formed along my temples. I never thought this moment would actually come to fruition, despite all my fantasizing over it.

I wanted to confess everything. All at once. Just to get this unbearable weight off my chest. To tell her about that night with Regina. To tell her that I never stopped loving her. I'd practiced this hugely elaborate speech that was poetic and romantic.

And what did I finally manage to say?

"Yes."

I barely had a second to breathe before she moved. Her paper bag of books hit the concrete with a thud as her hands shot up toward my face. I was ready to brace myself for her onslaught, whatever it might be. A noogie. A nose pinch.

But the last thing I expected her to do was the one thing I wanted most.

She *kissed* me.

Her hands grabbed hold of my jaw as she pulled me to her. I almost lost my footing in the process from the sheer power of her at that given moment. It was desperate, a spur-of-the-moment move that brought us back together. Something akin to a big bang.

My mind exploded with a zillion thoughts at once but was suddenly silenced as I gave in to her mouth. It was all hard and soft at the same time. A delicious contraction that had my knees bowing under the weight of it all.

I felt the stars align, the planets fall into sync, the earth moved beneath my feet. Everything shifted as if it went back to the right timeline. The timeline where I didn't make a stupid mistake. A timeline that Tiffiny and I were both still head-over-heels in love with each other.

I finally managed to rub my two currently working brain cells together so my body could respond appropriately. My arms wrapped around her, crushing her body to mine. The way her body fit against me made my eyes roll back into my head. My broad hands smoothed over the tasty lower curve of her back while the other staked its claim across her shoulder blades.

There was an uncomfortable hunch to my back with her hanging onto my face, but I didn't care. I didn't care if the crook in my spine was now permanent. The fact that I was finally kissing this woman after so many years was all that mattered.

I may or may not have made a rather obscene noise of utter relief as I gave into her the rest of the way, completely disregarding the fact that we were in public. I felt her voluptuous body melt against mine as I gave into her. My god this was fucking fantastic. I didn't care if I never came back up for air, I'd be content to wither away while in the middle of this moment.

"That was a hell of a thank you." I breathed out when I felt her melt away from me. Her feet gave out from standing on her toes for god knows how long. I hated that fact, but maybe it was safer that way. Who knew what we would get into if we had some room?

"Don't let it all go to your head." Tiffiny rolled her eyes as she tipped her chin down to hide the smile that she was so sure I didn't catch.

"Oh, feel free to say, 'thank you' anytime you want." I grinned down at her. It was taking every ounce of my strength not to pull her in for another one. "Although if that's the kind of thank you I get, I'll take you to the bookstore and buy you a book every damn day."

"Ender…"

"What?"

Tiffiny sighed with a weight that I didn't want to dissect. "Just because that kiss was *fucking amazing*, doesn't…doesn't mean anything."

I cocked my brow at her. "So…you just go around kissing any ol' guy that buys you books because it 'doesn't mean anything'?"

"Yes." Immediately she squinted her eyes shut before shaking her head. "I mean, no! *Fuck.* Stop…being so, so confusing."

I couldn't help but chuckle. Reaching down, I timidly extended my fingers, half afraid she'd pull away or run off. But she didn't. In fact, her body relaxed as the pads of my digits traced the plumpness of her cheek before circling down to draw a line along her jaw.

"I think a kiss like that is pretty straightforward, don't you think?" My voice dropped to a low murmur. I cocked my finger under her chin and tipped her reluctant gaze back up to mine. "Because if that kiss is the last kiss I'll ever have, I'll die a happy man. But I really hope it's not the last."

Even in the dusk, I could see the color rise to her cheeks, which had nothing to do with the cotton candy sky. I couldn't help myself with her being this close, this pliable and wanting, despite her sharp tongue speaking otherwise. The subtle way her body leaned in towards me was the last bit of consent I needed again.

This kiss this time was soft and gentle. She melted beneath me as her hands reached out, slowly fisting into my shirt. My soul was singing, my body in this weird limbo of feeling complete and yet utterly overheated.

I wanted to dive in deep and drown in her. She had a power over me, and I had no problem relinquishing control over to her. This woman was my everything. Today only reiterated that fact.

The squeak of the train's brakes as it came into the station pulled us reluctantly apart. Her tongue darted out, dragging along her plump bottom lip for only half a breath. She took a step back, turning away from me to grab her bag of books off the sidewalk.

"Iffy!" I called after her, my heart sinking at the thought of calling it a night. She looked over her shoulder as she quickly made her way to the awaiting SEPTA. "Think I can take you on a proper date now?"

A sliver of sunshine made its way across her face with her smile, but it was gone just as quickly as she pressed her lips into a line. I lost her as she slipped between the doors, turning away from me to find her seat. I let out a breath as I watched the train pull away. It was then that my phone pinged with a text message.

Yes

17

CRIMINAL
FIONA APPLE

"Alright guys, from the top!"

I watched Cadence twirl in place, spinning around so her back was to the guys so they could follow along with her guidance. The team was in the last rehearsal before the big performance tomorrow. I was stretched out between three rows of bleachers, lounging in the shade of one of the corners of the stadium, taking a break from social media posts for Ding Dong's pages.

Mainly, it was the fact that I was still processing exactly what went down the other day with Ender. He's kept his respectable distance since our kiss. We hadn't exactly talked about what his mom said, just kissed.

It was easier than taking a deep dive into the feelings I'd kept bottled up ever since that day he threw me aside. But we needed to talk. I needed to rip the bandage off. Put down some clear boundaries for myself. Especially if I was going to embrace the insanity of maybe, perhaps, probably getting back with Ender.

Part of me was put back together on that SEPTA platform. While the rest was utterly confused and torn over the whole situation. I didn't want my heart broken again. But how could I say no to something that felt so scarily right?

My eyes drifted over the infield, finding Ender's tall form as he danced with Jamie. The man had some moves, no doubt there. He was for sure teaching Jamie a thing or two. I couldn't wait to see the man in a pink rhinestone-studded jersey that Cadence had somehow talked him into wearing.

Letting out a sigh, I took a long sip from my emotional support water bottle. I was trying really hard not to dwell on the fact that Ender's and my first *date* date in years was tonight after practice. There had been a lot of back and forth between us as to what to do. As much as I wouldn't have exactly minded going to another bookstore again, I was sure the poor guy was still licking the wounds in his wallet after our last trip.

Considering I wanted to avoid hanging out with his mom for the time being, and the fact that I wasn't really up for a night out, I had the stupid idea of a movie night at my place. My brother and his wife had plans elsewhere. So honestly, it was the safest bet to keep this nonsense a secret. But it was a really stupid idea on my part to be alone with the man behind closed doors.

That kiss…

Oh, holy fuck that kiss.

I shoved my hands between my thighs, pressing them together as I tried to think of anything else except the absolutely sinful talents of that man's mouth. Just how much practice had that man had? I didn't even want to consider his bedroom talents.

The man had been so vanilla when we first dated. Clearly, his kissing game had improved. Or was it just me? It wasn't like I dated around much. Just here and there, when I let my hormones be my brain instead of my common sense.

The ways I could corrupt Ender now…

The music abruptly stopped and Cadence did a happy little cheer on the field. The guys had their shit together enough for her to be satisfied about tomorrow. It was getting late in the day. Typically, they did choreography practice in the morning when it was slightly cooler. But when they had a big performance, they snagged a little bit of extra time after field practice the day before just to work out the kinks.

I wish Ender would work out my kinks.

Oh, absolutely the fuck not.

The man was coming to my basement apartment after practice was over. I couldn't be thinking about smutty shit like that. I had to have my wits about me.

Besides, I was an adult, dammit. If I wanted to ride my high school ex-boyfriend like a bucking bronco into the sunset, I should be able to. Without guilt. Without the pretenses of a relationship. It was just sex. We weren't getting back together. Like ever. We could go on dates platonically.

Right?

There was a soft little catcall from the field as Ender had pulled away from the milling mass of Sillys players. Suddenly, I was back in high school, sitting on the bleachers, waiting for Ender's practice to be over, passing the time with a book. I subtly tipped my chin up to look his way as I was the only one in the stands.

Noting that the coast was clear, the man had the outright audacity to *wink* at me. A wink! What the hell. What in the actual hell?

I sat up, my mouth hanging open to yell at him, but he was already running off to join the rest of the guys. It's not like I could say anything, not without someone catching on to what we were trying to hide. What I was trying to hide.

The knock at my front door, which was technically the back door based on the layout of my brother's townhouse above me, jolted me off the couch. It wasn't fair that I was a nervous mess for this *date* date. I had already dated Ender once before. The second time around should technically be easier, right?

My hair was in a messy ponytail at the nape of my neck. It was paired with an oversized T-shirt and leggings with my bare feet. There wasn't a need to impress the man. He knew what he signed up for. Why would I give up my comfort for him?

That was one thing I never understood about the dating world. Why wear layers of makeup and fake lashes and shapewear to try to snag a man, when all you are is lying to him from the get-go? I mean, I understand women wanting to feel pretty themselves, but don't do it for the sole reason of attracting a man. If they don't like you at your worst, they don't deserve you at your best.

Ender had seen me all hot and sticky after wearing an overstuffed bell costume in weather that was so hot and humid that you could almost drink the air. Me wearing something that I wore to bed on a semi-regular basis wouldn't be a surprise. I wanted this evening to be as low-key and low-stress as possible. Maybe have a little fun. Maybe make out a little. But just a little. At least one kiss.

Swiping a hand over my hair to push aside any strays, I steadied my breath before opening the door. Ender stood there with a boyish smile that made my heart warm to a bubbling simmer. In his hands was a bouquet of mixed flowers in various shades of purples and pinks, along with a white bakery box. I had to bite my lip to keep my face neutral.

"I know you said pizza tonight was your treat, but I figured I could at least bring dessert." Ender offered the box as his smile only grew. "And flowers. Show those book boyfriends of yours how it's done." I swallowed back my smile.

"These aren't those donuts from that one stand at the Reading Terminal Market, are they…?" I asked cautiously, noting the subtle logo on the box as Ender stepped inside, closing the door behind him.

"They might be. Hopefully, you still like them. I know they were always your favorite back, uh well…in high school." He laughed nervously as he smoothed his hand down his thigh. Gosh, he was as uneasy as I was. "I got a dozen." So much for not letting his man spend another dime on me for this evening. He paid a pretty penny for the heaven-on-earth handmade pastries.

"You're crazy." I huffed at him as we shuffled deeper into my tiny L-shaped kitchen. "But thank you. I haven't had these in forever." Which was true,

I rarely got over to the Reading Terminal Market. Maybe that was a potential future date for us.

Already planning for the future, hmm?

Shut up, brain.

This was all just…

Well, what was this exactly? Ender and I hadn't exactly discussed what the game plan was for, well, *this*. Placing the donut box on the counter, I glanced up to see Ender casually leaning on my tiny little butcher block island. Staring at me. Staring at me as if he was doing something to me in that positively sinful brain of his. A delightful shiver went down my spine.

It wasn't fair that he came looking all hot and sexy. A fitted, button-up short-sleeve shirt with a collar that looked cool and effortless. His dark hair was all mussed, as if he had been running his fingers through it on his way over here. Linen shorts were loose on his hips and he had already kicked off his flip flops on my rug at the door.

I found myself drifting closer to him, the quiet between us not at all uncomfortable. Kissing him on the SEPTA platform the other day had opened a door that I had kept locked for the longest time.

No, I couldn't give in that easily. I had to make him work for it. To prove himself. To prove that he wanted this. Wanted me. That he wasn't going to repeat the bullshit from before when someone prettier and skinnier came into the picture once again.

A sharp knock at my door made us both jump away from our dangerously close proximity to each other. I let out a nervous laugh as I stumbled over to the door, tripping over his one shoe. "I guess that's the pizza." I gestured vaguely towards my living room, trying to swallow back my fluster. "Go pick a movie to watch."

Thankfully, Ender just shot me a playful grin and did as he was told. I quickly addressed the delivery driver with a tip and a smile as I brought the pizza box inside. With the latching of my door, we were finally alone.

Something about that both excited and unnerved me. There was a comfort to being around Ender. But it was also kind of weird, too. Now we were adults with free will. That was just asking for trouble.

Delicious trouble.

"Need any help?" Ender called from the living room as he peeked over the back of the sofa, remote in hand.

"I-I'm good!" I reassured him as I grabbed two beers from the fridge. Tossing some paper plates and napkins on top of the box, I picked up the pile and headed into the living room.

Ender seemed right at home, a half-smile on his lips as he flipped through my movie options. A few titles seemed to get a chuckle from him. Most of my watch list was comedies, the complete opposite of my dark romance books. Reading trauma was so much easier than watching it. I needed something to laugh at after reading so much darkness.

Setting the box down on my coffee table, I spread out all the accouterments as Ender finally made his choice. All I could do was let out a laugh as I plopped down on the couch.

"*Happy Gilmore*? Really?"

"Man, I haven't seen this movie in forever." He grinned as he eased himself onto the sofa next to me, dropping the remote on an empty spot on the coffee table. "Do you remember we used to quote this movie like, all the time?"

I couldn't help but smile at that. Happy memories over the lunch table danced through my head. Our friend group, spouting lines from Adam Sandler's more memorable movies of the late 90s and early 2000s.

"I watch it a few times a year. I don't care if I know all the lines. It's still so outrageously stupid. It never fails to make me smile. A good comfort movie of chaos."

Leaning forward, Ender opened up the pizza box, diving in for a cheesy slice. Grabbing a plate, he sat back with a laugh. "I think *Billy Madison* is much more chaotic."

"Ah," I had to join him in his amusement for that. "For real. *'Stop looking at me, swan!'*" I spouted one of our favorite lines from Billy Madison, doing my best to put Sandler's goofy twist on it. It took Ender by surprise, mid-bite. He let out a snort before coughing, choking a bit on his pizza. I patted his upper back.

"Iffy, warn a man before you start doing impressions. Holy fuck." He wheezed, managing to clear his throat. Watery eyes were bright as they looked to me before he grabbed the beer bottle off the table. Taking a swig, he let out a breath. "I still have no idea how you can do that."

"Do what?"

"Just say random movie lines. Out of the blue."

I shrugged, smiling to myself as I nibbled on my pizza slice. "I don't know, it must be my theater brain, I guess."

"You were always good at that. Learning lines and music lyrics. I remember you being unbeatable at Music Bingo." Ender took another bite of pizza, chewing thoughtfully for a moment. "Oh hey, maybe that could be our next date? Kicking my ass at Music Bingo."

My good mood went to serious as he ended up bringing up the talking point I wanted to touch upon. Although I wanted to at least digest my food first before talking about schematics. Resting my plate in my lap, I sighed.

"Ender, that's what I wanted to talk to you about."

The slide of pizza stopped halfway to his mouth. His dark gaze shifted over to me, his brows softening to something of worry. His mouth hung open for a second before he closed it and uncomfortably swallowed.

"Yeah…?"

I cast a cautious glance at him as I shifted in my seat. Why was this so hard? I should be able to voice my needs and wants. Especially after he shit all over them way back when. Life was too short to sit in pretenses. I'd rather this all get out in the open instead of having expectations that he knows nothing about. It wasn't fair to him, or me.

"This whole…dating thing…"

"Yeah?" His boyish face brightened a bit and I had to bite down on my lower lip.

"If we were going to try it," His expression fell just a bit. "I think we need to set some ground rules and such. I don't want a repeat of last time."

Ender looked hurt at that. And he should. I would have rubbed his nose in his past mess if I could. If only to save other women from the same fate. Yet here I was, seriously debating putting myself through it again.

"Okay." He nodded, a set to his jaw. "That's fair."

"I mean…you can't just expect us to, well…" I wasn't exactly sure how to put this delicately without straight up calling him out on his past bullshit. "…pick up where we left off."

There was a soft bob od his head. "That makes sense."

"Look, I know we have history together. I-I'm not saying we should forget it but…"

"Maybe we just start fresh?" His chin dipped a little so his gaze could catch mine. "Go slow? Whatever makes you happy, Iffy. I told you. I'll wait for as long as you need. Just as long as I can be in your life regularly again."

My molars jammed together, setting my jaw tight to stave off the emotion that was threatening. Setting his plate down, Ender reached for my hand, clasping it between his two large ones with the utmost care. It wasn't fair. The instant his touch graced my skin, I felt calmer. At peace. Like I was home.

Ender's hand tenderly cupped my cheek, drawing my attention back to him and out of my swirling thoughts. His gaze was full of tenderness as he drank me in. He pulled me closer, just a little bit.

"Look, I know I did some really stupid things as a teenager. The stupidest thing was letting you go."

My breath caught. My lips parted, a preemptive move to inhale oxygen once again but I couldn't bring myself to find the ability to do so. More than anything I wanted him to kiss me. To press me into my sofa and never have a chance to breathe because he was too busy kissing me senseless.

But…he didn't.

"For now, let's just hang out and eat. I just like being here with you, Iffy."

He kissed my forehead before pulling away with a soft smile. Picking up his plate, he brought his piece of pizza back up to his mouth. Leaning back against the couch, he gave me one more lingering look before turning his eyes back to the movie.

Well, the line was drawn in the sand. And drawn by him, of all people. All I had to say was one thing and he was heartily all for it. Respectful of it. Which I was thankful for.

So why was I feeling a little disappointed?

Did I really want to jump back into things? Or was it just my long-neglected lady parts crying out for help? No, no. I needed to stand my ground. I needed to take this easy. Dip my toes back into it.

Finishing my second slice, I slid my empty plate across the top of the pizza box. Ender had long since finished off his fourth slice and was completely transfixed on the movie. I could feel my body calling out, voicing its incessant need to be close to him. Innocently though.

Swallowing back my hesitation, I scooted myself closer to his body, draped over the corner of the couch. His arm was thrown across the back of the cushion, so it was all too easy to curl my body up next to him. The moment our bodies made contact, he startled a bit, glancing down at me with my sheepish look.

The biggest grin illuminated his face as his arms moved to embrace me. That's where he left it, his one arm around my shoulders. I both loved and lamented the way this made me feel.

I couldn't remember the last time I'd been held like this. The few guys I'd actually had some sort of sexual fling with was just that, sexual. No softness. No cuddling. The truth was I didn't want this sort of thing with a stranger. It was just so…fake.

Yet again I couldn't shake this feeling of contentment when I was this close to Ender. That all the chaos in my mind settled into a calm quiet. Like he grounded me.

Keeping my chin tucked towards my chest, I finally let myself relax and smile. Would it be so bad if we…

"This is nice." Ender sighed, giving me a little side hug as his arms tightened around me before releasing.

"It is." I agreed, before I even had a moment to think.

"Coming around to the thought of us giving this another go, huh?"

I glanced up at him, shoving my lips aside to hide the smile that quirked there. "I invited you over, didn't I? Don't let your ego blow it." My cheek bounced against his chest with his chuckle.

"Hey, if I could stay in this moment forever, I would. No question." His response was much softer. "Maybe one day you'll believe that you're it for me, Tiffiny."

Slowly, I lifted my chin from his warm torso, chancing a look up into his eyes. They were warm and adoring with a gentle smile to match. Nothing in his words, his tone, or his look led me to believe that he was bullshitting me. This was pure honesty.

Then, I felt it. That slow, powerful draw back to him. It was like a scene from any romantic movie in existence. The distance between us grew less and less as our eyes slowly closed. I could feel the warmth of his breath just a moment before his lips met mine. Everything about it felt as perfect as before.

BAD IDEA RIGHT?

OLIVIA RODRIGO

Fuck.
We slept together.
Okay, no wait.
We couldn't have.

I was still clothed. That was the first thing that came to my mind. Next was Ender's vice-like grip of his powerful pitching arms around me. I did a head-to-toe check-in with myself. The only thing that my body was screaming about was the ache in my lower back from waking up on my couch after apparently sleeping there all night. So we hadn't *sexually* slept together.

We just slept side by side. All tangled up in one another's arms. As if we were dedicated lovers who couldn't bear to be a breath apart from one another.

This was not going to bode well for me.

The last thing I could remember was sitting on my couch watching a movie. Completely innocent. He had been the epitome of respect. Maybe we had snuck in a kiss or two. Ender had been adamant about setting boundaries with rushing things. It had just been some G-rated kissing and cuddling.

Yet here we were. Desperately hanging onto each other as if we were back on my twin bed in high school. While my couch was L-shaped, it wasn't exactly the size to accommodate Ender's over six-foot form.

His arms had completely enveloped me to the point that I felt like some kind of stuffed animal. Ender was on his side, his back to the backrest of the sofa. His long legs were bent beneath my ass, with my legs thrown over his, and me on my back. We fit together like Tetris pieces on a very small game board.

Thank goodness I woke up, staring at the ceiling. If I had been face-to-face with him, I might have found it a lot more difficult to wriggle free. I knew I would be too engrossed in staring at his handsome, sleeping face. Either way, I wasn't in any hurry. This felt…nice.

The warmth of his body made my thoughts fuzzy. *Needy.* Maybe it was because it was the morning and I hadn't had my coffee yet. Or maybe it was me suddenly becoming aware of the hard cock jammed up against my right butt cheek.

I cast a glance from my peripheral vision, and I was relieved to see that his eyes were still closed. The fluttering warmth of his exhale caressed against my collarbone, sending a bloom of goosebumps across my skin. His breathing was still in a soft rhythm. We really needed to get up for work, but his arms were like my own personal brand of weighted blanket.

He needed to be there a whole hell of a lot earlier than I did for practice. Especially today. Today was Jamie's big dance number. The last thing we needed was to be rolling up to work at the same time. One that Ender had a pretty sizable part in.

I was actually looking forward to the performance. Being a theater geek, I was foaming at the mouth from the second Cadence said "Dancing Through Life" from *Wicked* was what the next big routine was. Of course, the bigger shocker had been the fact that Jamie was the one who suggested it.

I, for one, was both shocked and excited by the fact that my friend was living her best life by sleeping with her years-long crush of a man. She was so lucky to have that delightful specimen in her life. I needed some eye candy to look at.

I hated that my brain immediately went to thoughts of Ender. It wasn't fair that she had gotten hotter as he'd gotten older. Nor was it fair that the man had me pinned to his rather hard body on my sofa. I mean, I probably should wake him. I didn't know what time it was. For all I knew, he could be late to the ballpark already.

One quick study of his face wouldn't hurt, right? At least before I disturbed this little bit of peace. I just wanted to study him without him judging me. To drink him in and burn the vision of his handsome face to the depths of my brain.

Ever so slowly, I turned my head towards him. In high school, he was such a lanky guy with a baby face. But between college and getting some training behind the scenes in the majors, his body bulked up. I could feel the subtle muscles of his torso, and I definitely felt the sizable muscles of his biceps on more than one occasion. Not to mention his sculpted forearms. Delish.

His face had the biggest transformation. There were fewer soft lines as the bone structure of his face came into play. A subtle sprinkle of stubby facial hair was scattered across the jut of his chin. His long lashes made me jealous. They matched the mussed waves on his head. The bleached tips still made me chuckle.

But why were they so fucking hot?

I wanted to give in to him. To kiss him senseless, to have him hold me for hours on end after just as many hours of sweaty, passionate sex. To devour this man as a full-bodied woman. Maybe teach his vanilla ass a thing or two.

He was eager to learn about smutty romances. Maybe he would be just as open-minded in the bedroom? His world was opening up to new sexual possibilities with all of his new reading material. Corrupting this sweet man even further would be too much fun.

Did I want to sleep with Ender?

Yes.

Was it going to complicate literally everything?

Also, yes.

There was just something about this man that brought out the me that I'd kept inside since that fateful day. Why did I feel like there was something he wasn't telling me about that whole thing with Regina? I should have pressed him before, but the words always caught in my throat.

Why did being an adult have to suck so bad?

We as humans shouldn't have to resort to having an early morning inner dialogue debate between sleeping with the hot guy, cuddling us, or being pissed because his teenage-self broke up with our teenage-self half a decade ago. We were an advanced species with free will for fucks sake.

"Morning."

I nearly jumped clear out of my skin seeing Ender's chocolatey gaze staring back at me. Alarm bells started going off in my body as my anxiety kicked in, full steam ahead. Like I'd been caught with my hand in the cookie jar. I panicked.

"Do you know your dick gets really hard in the morning?" I bit my cheek immediately after the words slipped past my lips. No coffee and being caught mid-spicy thought removed my brain-to-mouth filter entirely.

"I, uh…" His now wide-awake gaze blinked at me in utter shock. I suppose he didn't exactly expect that visceral of a response first thing in the morning. Especially with the offer to sleep with me. I was literally ruining everything. "I mean, yeah. But look who's in my lap."

"Ender…"

"I can't help it. Especially when what I want, more than anything, is to wake up in my arms." He whispered against my cheek, his nose brushing against my temple.

"Ender–" Why did my voice have to sound so needy?

I suddenly found myself pinned to my sofa, wide-eyed and breathless as Ender had somehow untangled our bodies in the span of a breath to top me. Apparently, it was my turn to have my mouth gaping like a fish out of water in surprise. There was a determined furrow to his brow as his hands tightened around my wrists.

"Tiffiny Elizabeth Campanaro."
Yes sir.
Fuck.

Him saying my entire name did things to me. Like regulating my entire nervous system that, up until that moment, was short-circuiting.

"As much as I want to make your body permanently fused to a mattress, I really want to take my time with you, Iffy. When you're ready. Contrary to whatever belief you've conjured up, I haven't been doing all of these things to sleep with you just because we are back in each other's lives again."

I–uh, what?

I squinted at him. Did he have a direct line into the chaos of my brain conversations? How was this even fair?

"Because if I ever end up in your bed, I have every intention of making it a *permanent* thing, not a one-night stand." My jaw dropped open, but no words came out. "I don't expect you to believe me, but it's the truth. It's always been the truth. And I have to remind you every day for the rest of my life, so be it, I will."

Goddammit, that was it.

The straw that broke the camel's back. The cat was out of the bag. He hit the nail on the head after spilling the beans. Along with any other idiom that suited this auspicious occasion. Although why I was so hyper-fixated on idioms and not Ender's disgustingly sweet confession was beyond me.

Fuck it.

Fuck this.

Fuck everything.

Fuck me.

Fuck Ender.

Which is exactly what I planned on doing. The day be damned.

Somehow, I tugged my hands free of his grip, inhaling sharply as I grabbed his face. I didn't plan on coming up for air for a very, very, very long time. I felt Ender's smile against my mouth as his body relaxed against mine.

I groaned against his full body weight, finally settling on top of me. I felt ready to combust from the sensation alone. His hands found their way back to my body, heat-seeking missiles straight to my hips. There was a hesitation at first, so I deepened the kiss, slanting my mouth across his.

His fingertips dug deep into the jut, finding my hipbones beneath the depth of skin. The grip went from timid to desperate, which only made me want to arch my pelvis straight into his. The kissing only grew more feverish. I realized how things can go off the rails so quickly in romance novels when the heat was turned up like this.

When caution was thrown to the wind. When inhibitions were uninhibited. When stupid things were said.

"Just so you know, I'm going to hold the fact that you broke up with me over your head for the rest of eternity," I mumbled against his mouth. The kisses helped distract me from the icy sting of my words that slipped like bitter vomit from my mouth. Why did it still have to hurt after all these years? And why the fuck did my past pain decide to choose now to rear its ugly head?

I wanted to pretend that it still didn't hurt. I wanted more than anything to forget that it had ever happened. But it was a bump that my brain just couldn't get past, despite my body wanting to. More than anything. There was just something about it all that–

"I couldn't do it."

Ender mumbled against my lips so much that it took my brain a few extra moments to register what he said. Or was it the fact that his fingertips had slipped under the hem of my shirt? If he said what I thought he said, this wasn't a conversation we should be having while we were both actively trying to fuck each other.

"What…?" I breathed against his insistent lips. It seemed that he was more determined than ever to skip over the talking part of our private moment. But every synapse in my body was screaming at him to clarify what the actual fuck he meant by what he said.

"I couldn't go through with it." Ender finally pulled away from me, all the way, sitting up at the end of the couch. All I could do was lie there, absolutely aghast.

He… He couldn't go through with it? What? Sleeping with Regina? Kissing her? I did everything in my power to stay away from all the school gossip, and well, to stay clear of Ender just in general.

"What…?" I was beginning to sound like a broken record. "Couldn't go through with what…?" I hissed at him in my impatience as I sat up to confront him. Why couldn't he just spit it out?

"You know what."

"No, Ender. I really fucking don't."

He raised a brow at me. I was being honest. I didn't want to know a single thing about him after he uttered those fateful breakup words. My imagination was bad enough. I didn't need confirmation of what he and his overly eager dick got up to after we broke up. The man had wasted no time.

Ender pulled away from me, his head bowed to the floor as he avoided my questioning gaze. My eyes slowly widened as I realized the man looked utterly distraught. What in the actual fuck actually happened with what's-her-face?

"I couldn't go through with it." He repeated, more firmly this time, a sharp bite to his tone. Hunching over his bent legs, he dropped his face into his hands.

"I gathered that much. Care to elaborate?" I eyed him as if he was some kind of feral animal who was more terrified of me than I was of it. But if his words were true, why did he look ready to bolt?

"I didn't sleep with Regina, Tiffiny." The words halted me in my advance towards him. My eyes felt wide enough that my actual eyeballs felt like they would fall from the sockets. "Hell, I didn't even kiss her. I ran out on her before we even got close."

I'm sorry, but I beg your finest pardon?

"You… You…didn't…?" My hand was still mid-air as I was precariously leaning towards him, propped up on the other. "But–"

Ender's head lifted from his hands, casting a hooded look over at me. It froze me there on the spot, rooting me deep into the plush sofa. He looked positively wrecked. I felt utterly perplexed and well, rather awestruck.

It felt as if neither of us took even the slightest breath as the air grew thick between us. My gaze softened. Something was happening here. All as I was stunned into disbelief.

Maybe it was because I was in utter denial that maybe, just maybe, all the years of animosity towards the only man I truly ever loved was all for naught. That we had thrown away so many years for no reason whatsoever. The fact that both of us were stubborn assholes who thought the other never wanted to speak to the other for the rest of eternity. Although Ender broke first.

"I couldn't." Ender finally turned to face me, one fluid motion that literally had my heart frozen mid-beat. He looked like a man close to the tipping point of no return. As much as I relished in seeing him struggle, I needed to hear the words that I felt, well that I *hoped*, were on the tip of his tongue. "I couldn't do it, Iffy. I couldn't do it because all I could think about… All I could think about was *you*."

And my heart ceased all function at that moment in time.

He…he couldn't go through with it?

Ender wasn't with Regina?

I mean he was with her, but not for any measurable amount of time. That even though he went and broke up with me in order to mack it with another chick, he couldn't go through with it? All his brain could focus on was me, instead of the hot, popular chick?

Tears pricked at the corner of my eyes. I furiously tried to blink them away. My mind was going at light speed trying to connect all of the dots at once.

Was he really speaking the truth? Did his mom know? Why didn't he come crawling back to me? Why didn't he tell me?

The surge of emotions inside me was too much to bear. I wanted to yell, scream, throw a shoe at him for his stupidity. Although whatever I did to him, I'd have to do it to myself. Because I was just as stupid in this entire situation. We were grown ass adults, and somehow still acting like teenagers.

"Ender, please be serious right now." I breathed out, still in disbelief that this was all happening. Right now. In my fucking living room for fucks sake.

He sat up straighter, his palms pressing into the tops of his hard thighs. "What makes you think I'm not serious about this?" There was a desperation to his eyes as his brow softened.

How the hell could I explain to him that it was my utter disbelief that made me unable to comprehend his confession? For years I'd been so sure that he had moved on from me at the drop of a hat. Instead, he's been *pining* for me. Which was only exacerbated by the fact that we were now coworkers, thrust together on a daily basis through some god-awful meddling of my brother.

"I know I should have told you directly earlier, but I wasn't exactly sure that you wouldn't bite my head off if I approached you." *Fair enough.* "Its not exactly something you can bring up in casual conversation. 'Oh, hey Tiff, by the way I wanted to let you know that you're all I've ever thought about, so much so that I've never been with another person.'"

Say what now?

"Wait, you haven't been with anyone…?" My voice went hushed and breathless as I tried to blink back tears. "Like…*nobody* else?"

"How could I when all I think about is you, Tiffiny. I think I'm beginning to sound like a broken record here."

I sat in silence and mulled the words over. My tongue moved inside of my mouth, as if I was dissecting the flavor of said words in order to give them an accurate assessment.

"You've always been *it* for me. Believe it or not. I don't know how many different ways I can tell you that." Ender adjusted his tall body against my petite couch. "Look, I can understand if you never forgive me for what I did to you, but more than anything, I'm sorry for ending things as I did. I'm sorry for not coming after you. I fucked up big time, and I was too chicken shit to admit it, to you and to myself."

I was frozen in my spot on the couch, staring at Ender, wide-eyed. I couldn't believe it. He did it. He really did it.

Ender *apologized*.

"I was too afraid to admit this out loud. I didn't think I'd ever get to see you again. I knew that you didn't want to see me. I spent the last few years coming to terms with the fact of my being alone for the rest of my life. And then Cooper contacted me out of the blue, and I saw my chance. I saw my chance to try to make it up to you. In every way possible. In hopes that maybe, one day, I could finally admit the truth to you. Not that this was how I imagined it. Waking up on your couch, tangled up together..."

"Oh my god, Ender..."

"It's fine," He shook his head as he waved me off. "I'll go. I'm sure you need space–" He moved to stand, but instead I pounced on him. It was a gut decision, but I didn't want him to leave. Hell, I didn't want him to ever leave.

There was a drenching downpour of surprise, shock, and relief all at once. I was going to be reeling over this in therapy for sure. How did we both word vomit the things that the other one wanted to hear? Needed to hear?

"Ender…" I whispered, half on him, while he looked like some mix of surprise and delight. "Stay. Please?"

I felt him slowly relax beneath the cage of my body. "You're…not mad?" His brows perked up.

"Oh no, I'm fucking furious with you."

His face immediately fell. "Oh."

"But I also want to kiss you senseless."

"*Oh*…" I thought his eyes were going to fall from their sockets with how much they widened.

"Can we stay in the 'kiss me senseless' part of your fury?"

I snorted. "Maybe." My stomach churned with the emotions of his confessions this morning. "But why didn't you just get this conversation over with, oh I don't know, weeks ago?"

"I was scared, Iffy. I really thought you'd run away again. I didn't want to take the chance." A timid hand reached out, tracing his fingertips along the apple of my cheek as his eyes followed the movement. "And last night? Last night was amazing. Having you in my arms again. I didn't want to mess that up. Although…I didn't exactly mean to fall asleep last night either." It was then that his gaze found mine, a sparkle of mischief there. "I'm not exactly complaining."

I shifted even closer to him, a wry smile ticking at the corner of my mouth. "I'm not either."

It was then that our mouths finally met again. Deep and all encompassing, drinking each other in, gulp by delicious gulp. The uncertainty was dissipating between us, the mutual attraction becoming more heated by the second as our brains and bodies worked through the implications.

With each kiss, the intensity grew. It was almost as if we were both slowly letting our walls down to let the other in. The air in the room changed to something more lighthearted, yet there was a charged undertone.

Ender must have sensed it too, as his hands reached back out to my body, grabbing hold of me. And that's when all hell broke loose.

Letting out a soft whimper against his mouth, my hands fisted into his shirt as I pulled myself somewhat into his lap. Ender's hands eagerly slid around my body, grabbing heaping handfuls of my ass cheeks. *Oh, fuck yes. Yes, yes, yes.*

That was when things got hazy, almost as if the heat between us steamed up my brain cells. I was suddenly so desperate to have this man. To reciprocate my own set of feelings into this madness since Ender had gone above and beyond to put his heart on his sleeve. To maybe start mending my heart back together since the only man with the magic to do so was currently kissing me senseless.

I wanted to mount this man like he was a prize steed going into the Kentucky Derby.

Was it stupid?

Yes.

Was it a horrifically awful idea to rush into bed with this man?

Yes

Was I going to do it anyway?

Also, yes.

Pulling Ender towards me, he lifted his back off the couch, eagerly wrapping me up in his embrace.

His kisses got harder, more fervid which only sent me chasing after the point of no return. With zero fucks left to give.

Despite not having a drop of caffeine in me, I felt supercharged. Everything about this man intoxicated me. While we probably should talk about what the future held for Ender and me, that was definitely a to-do list item for future Tiffiny. But present-day Tiffiny wanted the man flat on his back for riding purposes, of course.

Using what strength I thought I had, I attempted to manhandle a man who was so much taller than me. I managed to back up slightly on the couch, Ender chasing me every inch of the way. Bracing my knees on the plush cushion, I tried to heave his body around mine to lie flat on the long part of the sofa behind me.

Instead, I lost my grip along with Ender leaning far too much into me, which had us, a tangle of arms and torsos, tumbling forward. I cried out as I felt Ender's weight suddenly counter mine, pulling me with him as he tumbled towards the floor. My cry turned into a laugh at the absurdity of it all until I heard a sharp CRACK as the back of Ender's head hit the edge of my coffee table.

"Ender? Ender?!"

Oh fuck.

19

DREAM GIRL EVIL

FLORENCE + THE MACHINE

This was karma.

It had to be.

The karma of my past was finally catching up with me. At the most inappropriate time in the history of ever. Because I'd been *this close* to getting another taste of Tiffiny. After yearning for the woman for so many damn years. At this rate, perhaps my *only* taste for god knows how long.

Instead, I had somehow found myself on my back in the local emergency room, nursing the most wicked sort of headache. The bright room was slightly blurry, framed by boring curtains and a rather irritating, slow beep. I wasn't moving, but I was dizzy. My stomach was not a fan of the feeling either.

The back of my head was utterly throbbing, so much more so than just a garden-variety headache. With an uneasy hand that was somehow attached to various tubes, I made a move to inspect the damage, but a worried voice stopped me.

"No! Don't bother it! They just got the bleeding to stop."

I blinked.

Bleeding? What in the actual hell happened? A car accident on the way to the game? Did Tiffiny deck me in the head after I finally apologized to her? Why couldn't I remember anything past kissing her?

Wait, Tiffiny was here? With me?

I smashed my eyelids together in a vain effort to try to get my eyeballs to refocus. Reopening them slowly, I found two very worried Tiffinys staring back at me. A crooked grin washed over my face as my arm moved to reach out to her instead.

"Iffy? Baby!" My words felt like molasses in my mouth. Somehow, I managed to get my hand behind her head and pulled her closer, puckering my lips because I wanted to pick up where we left off earlier.

"Oh my god, Ender, no." She hissed at me as she cast a glance towards the open slit in the curtains. "Just relax." Her hands reached up to at least convince me to go back to my bedside. But I was too hyper-focused on the fact that Tiffiny finally agreed to kiss me after all this time.

"Come on, I wanna ring that bell!"

Her eyes widened as her cheeks went bright red. "Ender, please be quiet. You-you have to rest—"

"Noooo, how can I rest when I can finally have you again?" My words felt uneven coming out of my mouth, but I was still insistent. Why did I feel so funny?

Shifting on the extremely uncomfortable hospital bed, I made an awkward attempt to reach for her again. All of my senses were fuzzy, almost as if I'd been drinking. Or was it that all my blood was surging south again? I'd been so sure that we had been headed to sexy fun times before the blackness had settled in.

A sudden metallic scraping grated against my ears as the hospital curtain suddenly parted, revealing a middle-aged man in a white doctor's coat. He was followed by a nurse in navy scrubs pushing a mobile computer desk into the cramped space of this corner of the hospital.

"Oof, that looks rough, kid. But don't worry, we will get that taken care of. Can you take those shorts and any undergarments off?" The doctor patted my shoulder reassuringly. I blinked, lost in the pain of my head and the stupor it left me in. Surely, I didn't need to take off my clothes for a headache? "Nurse, let's get a syringe of phenylephrine ready, if you please."

"Uh, he's not–"

I watched as the female nurse tried to intercept the doctor. A syringe?!? How bad was this?

My eyes caught the worried gaze of Tiffiny. She was chewing her lower lip, her eyes darting across the linoleum tiles on the floor. I know she felt bad, but it was just a headache, right? Although she had mentioned blood–

"Tell me, sir, you are a little young to be taking such a drug. But how long ago did you take the Viagra?"

My eyes went wide and I felt the heat in my face. Despite the chaos of this hospital visit, my aching brain was still focused on the fact that Iffy and I had been *this close* to getting back into bed together. Then I suddenly found myself in a bed. Although my common sense hadn't come to terms with just where said *bed* was located.

"Uh, it's not–"

"He's just big." Tiffiny dismissed the medical professional. Insistent and so nonchalant as if she had been talking about the weather outside instead of my dick. Because there were more pressing matters to attend to.

My ego almost inflated as quickly as my cock, the blood rushing south so fast again that it made me woozy. I was already desperately trying to get my semi to abandon ship, but it was bound and still determined to blast off just from the fact that Iffy was still adamantly by my side. And that she had complimented my cock.

My aching head was swirling with so many thoughts. Because clearly, she had been thinking about my one appendage. Or at least remembered it quite *fondly*. I secretly hoped it was both.

"Look, doctor dude," Tiffiny cut in sharply. "Ender here hit his head and kind of blacked out for a hot minute and has been acting weird ever since. I just want to make sure he's not concussed." The doctor stood there, blinking at her. "So how about you check the bigger of his two heads before the other one swells to match."

"I, uh… Yes ma'am. I apologize."

Tiffiny sticking up for me like that was not on my bingo card for today. Hell, even this year. Despite the dig at me, it was so badass of her. Fuck why was that hot?

I couldn't get turned on any more right now. The stupid ass doctor already thought I OD'd on fucking Viagra. But no, the swelling in my dick was only Tiffiny's fault.

Think unsexy thoughts. Think unsexy thoughts.

Tiffiny had mentioned the possibility of a concussion. The last thing I needed today was to be down and out with a fucking *concussion*. Not on today of all days. At least I was pretty sure today was still the day.

Because if I wasn't as far gone as I thought I was, today was supposed to be the big dance routine day for Jamie and the team. We'd been practicing for weeks, and I, begrudgingly, was supposed to play Glinda to Jamie's Fiyero in the big "Dancing Through Life" number as Jamie made his way out onto the field.

Hopefully it was all nothing. Hopefully, I had just bumped my head and triggered some weird vertigo incident. Maybe I needed just a stitch or two. The doctor here just had to toss me a few extra-strength painkillers so I could get on my merry way.

"Look here." Before I could even obey the doctor's command, a pen light was shining in my eyes. I had to squint from the harsh glow. It only exacerbated my splitting headache. "Keep your eyes open. Follow my finger."

I did my best to follow his lead, but the concentrated light was making my temples throb even more. He moved the digit back and forth and then worked on me being able to focus on distance. The look on his face was not what I wanted to see.

"Nurse, schedule a CT scan." He stated over his shoulder before turning back to me. He placed a reassuring hand on my shoulder. "Sorry son, looks like you're out of commission for the next 24 to 72 hours. The scan will give me a better idea of the severity of the damage, but it doesn't seem like anything too concerning. Limit physical activity and screen time. What do you do for a living?"

"I uh…play professional baseball."

The doctor let out an amused huff. "You'll need to follow up with your team doctor then. I'll be sure to give you a copy of your records for them to take over your care. But no field time or any related physical activity for at least the next few days, until the headache and dizziness goes away and stays away. Your nurse here will see about getting you stitched up."

He nodded briefly before he left the room, turning me back over to the nurse for the list of follow-up care. I melted into my pillow, feeling defeated for something that was, mostly, out of my control. But was it worth it for a hot as fuck make out session with Tiffiny?

Yes.

Even with the doctor calling out my concussion-aided erection in public?

Technically, also yes.

Great. Just fucking great. How the hell was I supposed to explain this to my coaches? To the guys? I couldn't exactly say "Hey guys, sorry I missed the big routine, but I busted my head on a coffee table while trying to mack it with the mascot". It sounded like something out of some made for television high school drama.

The nurse explained that she had to grab some things for the stitches as she typed in the request for the scan. Once she was finished, she parted the curtain again with a smile. Suddenly, it was just Tiffiny and me in the tiny exam room together.

"Never a dull moment with you, Ender." Her arms wrapped around herself, trying to escape the chill of the air conditioning that I had barely noticed. She shook her head, fighting back a smile. I managed to relax a little. But only a bit.

"Just put 'death by blue balls' on my tombstone." I laughed, but only ended up wincing from the pain. I had to use humor to distract myself from the fact that it was probably going to be another week before Tiffiny and I could even attempt something like that again. That is, if she didn't change her mind before them.

"Oh, what's a week or so more?" She smirked. But there was something in her eyes that made me wonder if it was something else. "Maybe we can actually manage something…not so spur of the moment. Instead of some random quickie because we couldn't get our hormones under control."

Flames heated my cheeks. "Uh…yeah. Right."

I hadn't meant to spend the night at Tiffiny's. It had just been an innocent movie night. A movie night in which she fell asleep in my arms. No funny business. Just two past lovers hanging out. I didn't have the heart to wake her. Which only led to me falling asleep, waiting for an opening to sneak out undetected.

What I hadn't counted on was sleeping late and waking up to her staring at me with such a wondrous, dreamy look in her eyes. Or was it that our bodies were all tangled up together. It just felt so…normal. So perfect.

Every morning for the past few years should have been like that.

I needed to stop reminiscing. I could feel myself getting hard all over again. And from the smirk on Iffy's face, she could tell too. Guys who wore loose shorts had a literal death wish when it came to wearing those and getting flustered.

"It…doesn't mean we can't still hang out." She added softly. Hesitantly. Almost as if she was sure I wouldn't want to see her face again after such a disaster of a day.

"I don't know…" I started, trying to remain stern, but it was so hard not to tease Iffy. "You might get bored with me much faster that way. Or make another attempt on my life."

Tiffiny gave my shoulder a fist bump in reply, causing me to squawk a bit. Immediate worry flickered in her eyes as her hand turned back to soothe the area. "Shit, sorry. It's just weird for me to think that all six feet of you are actually fragile."

"I mean, you can make it up to me…" I shot her a slow, wicked grin, albeit slightly crooked from the ache in my head.

"Oh yeah? How so?"

"You can dress up as a nurse and take care of me." I took a chance against the pain and gave my eyebrows a suggestive wiggle. Tiffiny just rolled hers. But I could tell she was trying to keep her smirk at bay.

"Ender…"

"What?"

A heavy sigh filtered through her lips. "Look, I know things got heated. But maybe we should pump the brakes a bit."

"…and?"

"I…" Chewing on her bottom lip, she avoided my gaze. "I'm going to need some time. I-I rushed things…"

My heart and soul fell to the linoleum floor. "Time…? For what?"

"What you did back then…" Her words were soft, painful. A gut punch right to my heart that was suddenly bleeding out on the floor. "It hurt me. Like, a lot. To throw me away like that. Like…none of our time together mattered." I watched as her palms slid up and down her arms, almost as if she was reassuring herself. I should be the one holding her, instead, I was stuck in this hospital bed. "And then for you to go and say that nothing happened with Regina, that everything I've told myself over the years was a lie, it's… It's a lot to process.

The make-out session was hot as fuck, but uh," Licking her lips, she chanced a glance at me. "Maybe this uh…*whole debacle* came at a good time." Her hand lifted as if to pause the thought. "I mean, not that your concussion is a good thing. But maybe it was like a, well, proverbial squirt bottle on our over-heated hormones."

That was a lot of big words for my throbbing brain right now, but I had to agree with her. What made me think that we could just jump right into where we left off years ago? We were different people now. With different experiences. We had to learn about each other all over again.

I knew I had taken the right step by asking to date her again. Why I thought getting into a heated make-out session with her was the next logical step was beyond me. I hadn't expected to unexpectedly wake up in her arms either. Had I been able to keep my impressive dick, her words not mine, on the down low, I wouldn't be stuck in the ER, about to get stitches and miss a week's worth of games and practices.

It was safe to say that my dick was the reason for all my troubles in my life. I needed to stop listening to it. If I knew what was good for me. For us.

"I think that's a good idea."

The nurse and a nurse practitioner came in with a small cart of what seemed like torture chamber tools. I just wanted to get home and shower and—

"Oh shit! The game!" I shot forward as my brain slowly came back online. Tiffiny's arm landed on my shoulder, stopping me from lurching forward any further. The movement in which I was already regretting.

"I…" Easing myself back down on the bed, I glanced at Tiffiny, who was chewing on her lower lip. "I texted Cooper." She winced at that. Oh fuck. I didn't know just how much Iffy had bothered to tell anyone about our, well, whatever we were. I knew Cooper knew how I felt about his sister, but I wasn't sure if she had any idea that her brother knew. "I didn't know how to unlock your phone to call the head coach or whoever else."

"No," I sighed as the nurse urged me to roll over on my side so she could address the apparent head wound that I had yet to know how bad it was. "Cooper would be the one. Cadence, too, technically." Tiffiny frowned at suddenly having a front row seat to the mess that was hiding in the knot at the back of my head. She hightailed it over to the side I was facing. It was nice to see a comforting face. "Was he…pissed?"

"I think he was more worried than pissed. I'm just waiting to get an angry text from Cadence, which should be–" An incessant buzzing sounded in her pocket. Now it was Tiffiny's turn to sigh. "There's no way I can explain why I was with you at the time of your…*need for an ER visit*. Or that I was the cause of said visit."

I laughed, which turned into a hiss as the nurse gently pulled off the gauze against the back of my skull. She was prepping the area for the numbing part. Which included needles and I was already apprehensive about that part of the process.

"What are you gonna tell her?" Not that I wanted to pry, I just really needed a good distraction at the moment.

"Well, considering the fact that she's sleeping with Jamie, something tells me she might not be overly shocked."

I coughed on my inhale. "W-What…?!"

"Mr. Roche, you're going to have to lie very still."

Managing to get some of my bearings once more, I looked up at Tiffiny, wide-eyed. I dropped my voice to a near whisper as my injured head tried to process the rather scandalous information. "Are you serious?"

"Well, she didn't exactly tell me in so many words, but best friends kind of pick up on shit like that." She shrugged. "So I called her out on her bullshit."

"Okay, Mr. Roche. Big pinch." Tiffiny's hand shot out to hold onto mine as I felt the burning sensation from the numbing agent. Fuck that hurt. "Just a few more spots."

Tiffiny almost looked as pained as I felt. Her brow was furrowed as she watched the nurses work. My fingers were tight around her hand as the painful sensations started to melt away.

"Don't mind the buzzing, but we have to shave some of your hair so we can properly address the wound before we stitch you up. The numbing medicine should kick in quickly."

I offered my agreement, shrugging off the fact that I was going to have a bald spot somewhere along the back of my head. But it was Tiffiny's reaction that had me more gutted. A deep frown had settled onto her face as she looked over my shoulder at the nurses working on me.

"What?" I asked, slightly disturbed by her reaction.

"Not your frosted tips…" She whimpered, her brow melting with concern.

"I don't think they're touching my tips, Iffy." I laughed but remembered that I needed to stay still, so it morphed into a snort instead.

"So now we will get you sewn and bandaged up. Then you just have to wait for your scan. If it's all good, then you'll be discharged."

A long moment of silence passed between us as Tiffiny held my hand while the nurse administered the local along the edges of my wound. It hurt like fucking hell, and I couldn't find the ability to speak anyway. Despite the wince on her face from my firm grip on her hand, she stood steadfast by my side. Now, and hopefully forever.

ALL THE THINGS SHE SAID

HARRISON

I still wasn't sure if it was a good or a bad thing that I agreed to hang out with Cadence. She'd been avoiding me ever since Ender's ER visit. Well and the fact that I technically never called her back afterward. But I couldn't exactly explain the entire awkward situation with Ender to her. At least, not yet.

Because I didn't really even know for sure where we were. For the most part, I was elated that he finally confessed everything to me. But was it because it was just something to keep me placated in the heat of the moment, or was it really true that he hadn't done anything with Regina?

One would think that it would be easy to recover after hearing the supposed truth about something you'd spent such a large chunk of your life believing. But it wasn't like you could just flip a switch and sweep it all under the rug like it never even happened. I wanted to talk to Ender more about it, but I didn't want to do it while his brain was still recovering.

He'd been holed up at home, almost driven crazy by Mamá Roche nearly smothering him with love and attention. She was literally cooking up every morsel of food she had in that little kitchen, just to keep herself distracted with Ender's recovery.

Thankfully, his CT scan was negative for any long-term effects, but he was going to have some residual issues as his brain slowly healed. I felt so fucking awful. This was all my fault. I did my best to stop in and see him after games or practice, if it wasn't too late. Our texting game stepped up a lot as it was easier to spare a few seconds to shoot a text off than attempt a visit through Northeast Philadelphia.

The talking part with Ender was easy. Back in high school, he had been not only my lover, but my best friend. I told that man everything. My stresses, my worries, my thoughts of our future together. We just had this easy communication between us. Always had. I'd missed that.

I glanced at Cadence walking next to me. Going to a Phillies game wasn't exactly my idea of fun when we had a lot of fucking shit to talk about. Close proximity was a nightmare when there were secrets between you and your best friend.

Or, well, the old Philly Sillys catcher. The night after the performance, Jamie apparently got the call to go back up to the Phillies. Just like that, Cadence's little stressful fairy tale was over. Er, well, it moved a few miles further up Broad Street. But that had been the only info I'd gotten out of her. It was all the guys could talk about, aside from Ender's post-concussion recovery.

Which led to a very awkward start to a baseball game between Cadence and me. Even though I wasn't exactly a huge baseball fan, I knew the seats we were sitting in were no laughing matter. They were just a few rows back from the fence in the

Diamond Club. I knew neither Cadence nor myself, could afford such luxury at the drop of a hat for a random weeknight game with no planning.

"Where the hell did you get seats like these?" I cautiously asked as the crowd roared. For a moment, I thought she hadn't heard me. That was until I realized that her eyes were glued on whatever the hell was going on, on the field in front of us. "Yo, Cadence. You, okay?" I'd only been half paying attention to the Phillies game as I mentally processed my trauma of the past few days. Right now, she was breathing heavily with her hand tucked between her thighs.

"What?" She replied, her words more air than voice. "Huh? Oh…uh yeah."

I'd only been slightly aware of the roar of the crowd around us just a few moments ago. Something must have happened in the game. From the way she was acting, she was either on her way to an orgasm or working her way down from one.

"Are you *sure* about that?" I cocked my brow at her.

"Look, you're just going to have to give me a moment." She breathed the words with a charged exhale. "My *boyfriend* threw a literal bullet to second base to get the runner out. His mask flipped off… And with the backwards hat…" The flush in her cheeks deepened once again as she relived the moment.

"Well, sorry. I guess it's my fault for speaking when your Man Meat Express is squatting. But uh...boyfriend huh?" My look went utterly smug. Apparently, I had missed a lot. They weren't just having sex. They were *serious*. Cadence shot me a side eye that should have vaporized me on the spot. Instead, her annoyed resolve cracked like the thin chocolate coating on a Drumstick ice cream cone. "Care to share with the class?"

Cadence leaned back in her seat, looking like she was ready for a cigarette or another round of well, whatever *that* was. Running a hand down her face, her shoulders rose then dropped abruptly. A dopey grin lit up her face. Uh oh.

"Long version or the short version?"

I snorted. "The long version, duh." Anything to keep her distracted from whatever questions were burning inside her brain to ask me about the whole Ender situation.

"I'm dating Jamie!" She could barely contain the squeal in her voice.

"I gathered that. But come on, I did ask for the long version. I need the juicy details." I let my voice drop, hoping to get my point across. Despite the chaos currently going on in my life, if my friend had something good or drama-induced going on, I wanted to hear all about it. "The *juicy*, juicy ones."

The look she shot me gave me a pretty good idea of where this was going. And it was going to be good.

"Girl, if you can…" Leaning in, she bit her lower lip as she glanced around. Lowering her voice, she added, "Definitely date a baseball player. Because goddamn the *stamina*?" Settling back into her seat, she fanned her hand in front of her face. "I don't think my toys could ever keep up with him."

Well…shit.

"Obviously, the sex is good, but what the hell made it go from 'just sex' to 'serious shit'?" Not me fully prepared to take mental notes.

Cadence fully turned back to the game, lounging in her seat as she ruminated over the words. "I mean…it's obvious, isn't it?"

"Not…really? Look, I only put two and two together a few days ago."

"Oh, come on, Tiff. Don't tell me you've never had it bad for a guy."

Shit, red alert. Red alert! Distract her. Get her off the subject.

"Maybe once or twice." I shrugged, perhaps a bit over the top in that nonchalant way. If Cadence noticed, she didn't say anything. "Nothing that ever really lasted. Okay, let me rephrase. When did you know it was more than just…*you know.*"

"It's all the, you know… Little things. *In between.*" A dreamy sigh left her lips as she prattled on. "Like brushing your teeth next to each other, making dinner together, just talking on the phone during a long road trip. You look forward to *all* the moments. Not just the sex. The sex is a bonus."

Suddenly, she launched herself out of her seat, and that's when I realized that she had been claimed. She was wearing Jamie's Phillies jersey.

Fuck, I wanted that.

Wait, what?

A familiar song played over the ballpark's sound system, and it pulled me from my thoughts. It was just in time to see Cadence cheering Jamie on as he walked up to bat. Sure enough, the man made time to point his bat at her and shoot her a wink. Hell, even *I* swooned. And he wasn't even my type.

"For fucks sake, get over the pretenses and just ask him to wear his gear to bed already." I rolled my eyes.

Cadence glanced at me quickly before she looked away and slouched back down in her seat, desperately trying to fade into obscurity. I let out a solid note of laughter as my eyes widened. My best friend had already beaten me to the punch. "You whore! You dirty, dirty whore." I hissed. She smacked my bicep.

"It was just...once..." She could barely breathe the words. "After he got called up–YEAH JAMIE!" A sharp crack from his bat resonated throughout the stadium as I watched Jamie make a pretty nice in-field hit. Enough to get him to first base and for Cadence to turn her attention back on me. Her cheeks had reddened to a shade that was pretty damn close to the Phillies' signature shade.

Crossing my arms, I gave her my most judgmental look. "Yeah. Uh-huh. And I can pickle cucumbers in my vagina."

She shot me a double take before her face slipped back into thinking mode, desperately trying to keep her unexpected laughter at bay. "Wait, no, I think you actually can—"

"The legalities of me pickling a girthy vegetable in my vajayjay is completely beside the point I'm trying to make here."

"So, what if I asked him to wear his gear to bed *once*? It's not like you to kink shame."

I couldn't help but laugh. "What is it with you and catchers anyway?"

"Fuck, well..." Cadence fussed with her ponytail and a few flyways that had sprung free. "I mean...who doesn't love a man on his knees?"

Oh, fair point.

Ender wasn't a catcher, but damn, the thought of the tall man on his knees sounded delightfully unhinged. I remembered our earlier conversation. That I should have him on his knees, begging for forgiveness. Perhaps a bit of worship was in order. Knowing the sort of books he was now reading probably wasn't out of the question…

"Come on, Tiff. Have you seen the way that man straddles a plate?" Cadence hummed through her smile as her eyes were glued to Jamie's ass. Another start to an inning meant another practically front row seat to the catcher's round bottom as he knelt down into the dirt behind home plate.

I rolled my eyes. "Good god, woman, take your dirty ass drool somewhere else."

"Oh no. You can't say shit like that. I always have to hear about what the dude's, or whatever he was, dick looked like in those monster romances of yours." Cadence stuck her tongue out at me.

"Oh, don't you dare tell me you didn't enjoy the not-safe-for-work character art for those books and their said *appendages.*"

She decided not to designate that with a direct response. "Besides, my boyfriend *encourages* my behavior. He nabs me a ticket right behind home plate just so he can hear me gush later about how good his ass looked turning the game. If I ask nicely, he gets me two."

I made a mocking gag. "Gross."

"Those corded thighs of his are so strong after straddling the plate for almost two decades. He's been playing since he was little. The man can piston like a superhero--"

"Okay! That's enough." I pressed my palms against my ears and shifted as far away from my friend as my seat allowed. Before she got into more explicit details about her boyfriend's stature and sexual prowess. The dude was a hunk, but he didn't exactly do it for me. A certain 6-foot-4-inch man with frosted tips did. "You're going to make anyone within a ten-mile radius vomit."

Cadence cracked up in laughter as she relaxed back into her seat. Carefully, I lowered my hands from my ears, hoping the coast was clear. At least for the time being.

All kidding aside, it was really nice to see my best friend positively glowing. She had found her happiness. Hell, she hit the fucking lottery. Any of us would be so lucky to find a man who was not only hot, but successful in his career, worshipped the ground we walked on, all while fucking us ten different ways to Sunday.

Ender had done that for me, once upon a time. Although with a lot less intense fucking. Now the fates had us thrown together again.

The poor guy was still on the mend after his rather unfortunate accident. I still felt rather guilty about it. Even though he insisted that he didn't mind one bit. His apartment was small, and I knew Ender was going stir crazy with his mom hovering. But the more he rested, the quicker he could get back on the field. And the sooner we could get back to trying things again.

"So, what's up with you, girl? You've been…distant lately." Cadence's words pulled me from my thoughts as she gave me a curious look. "Everything okay?"

"What? Me?" I huffed out a dry laugh. "Yeah. Totally."

Way to oversell it, Tiff.

"You…sure?" Cadence was on to the bullshit I was trying to sell.

"Yep."

"This wouldn't have anything to do about Ender, would it?" The teasing tone in her voice made my nails dig into the heft of my thighs. "Cooper said you were the one who took him to the hospital."

Goddammit Cooper. So much for swearing my brother to secrecy. He was such a gossip in his old age. I hated it.

"I…did."

Cadence popped her brow up at me. "Care to elaborate?"

"Not really."

Pressing her lips together in a thin line, she tipped her chin down to look me square in the eye. Suddenly, her eyes lit up. "Oh, I get it. You like him!"

"I," My back went ramrod straight as my gaze shot to her. "I do not."

"Oh, come on, Tiff. You're allowed to have a crush on him. He's a sweet guy."

I suppose having a crush on Ender was one way to explain it. I cast my eyes away, suddenly distracted by a discarded peanut shell on the concrete floor next to my shoe. "It's…complicated," I mumbled.

"Oh my god," Cadence leaned forward all of a sudden, concern etched across her features. "Please tell me you haven't already slept with him and he was an asshole or something."

"What?!" I sat up, blinking at her, aghast. "I…uh… Fuck, no."

"Oh." Her shoulders dropped. "Well, good. I'd hate to have to kick his ass."

I couldn't help but laugh at the thought of that. "What, all five feet of you?"

"Shut up."

"Munchkins from Munchkinland would have an easier time." That got me a piece of soft pretzel thrown at my head. At least that got her off my back. Even if just for the time being. Until I could figure out how to explain this to her. To actually see what the immediate future has in store for Ender and me.

Maybe this is all just a quick infatuation. Something to get out of my system. A nice blast from the past. To close the door for good on that part of my life.

Ender and I could be two totally different people once we dove a bit deeper into this resurgence of feelings and attractions. Both of us so desperately lonely, or something. To finally tie up the loose strings with how we ended things. Well, how he ended things.

Perhaps I'll tell her the whole story.

One day.

21

ACTUALLY ROMANTIC

TAYLOR SWIFT

I was so happy to be going back to the ballpark in full uniform tomorrow. I'd been cleared by the doctor for game play. Finally. I spent yesterday and today on the sidelines, watching practice and taking notes on the choreography. I was a little scared about the resurgence of dizzy spells, but thankfully, they all seemed to have dissipated.

As much as Mamá enjoyed having me home for such a long stretch during the regular season, I could only survive two complete rewatches of *The Golden Girls* series before I started talking with Blanche's accent. The guys kept me occupied with video calls and crazy texts. Not to mention the social media team had me doing some "sick day" content. Which ended up being pretty hilarious, thanks to Mamá's cameos.

Then there was Tiffiny.

She stopped by every day with some sort of treat. The first few days, my head hurt too much to read, so she gifted me some of her favorite spicy audiobooks. That helped pass the time in my recovery. It even managed to reduce the swelling in my head as my blood tended to rush south because of them. While the gesture was super thoughtful, it just added to the edging insanity. Except this time, I couldn't exactly *take care* of things like I usually did.

Tiffiny never stayed long. Mamá was always hovering. Maybe she thought that Iffy would finish the job by biting off my head like some praying mantis. Mamá didn't exactly believe me that nothing happened on the night I accidentally fell asleep at Tiffiny's. Hell, I ended up in the hospital because of it. But Mamá wasn't exactly mad about the fact that Tiffiny and I were hanging out together on the regular now.

We chatted mostly over text, once I could stand the glow from the screen. Now that everything was out in the open, conversations were so easy. No tiptoeing around things. It was like I had my best friend back. And I couldn't stop smiling.

"Yo, Ender! You with us?" Benson's voice pulled me out of my reminiscing. I was glad that I was able to finish the Pitching Tents Book Club book selection this month. I'd been able to listen to the rest of it while I lay in bed.

"Oh, uh, yeah. Sorry. I was trying to…uh, narrow down my favorite character."

"Dude, it was like, impossible." Truitt chimed in, leaning towards me. There were murmurs of agreement.

"I love me a good billionaire, especially when he's secretly the biggest sweetheart and down-to-earth man beneath it all. Money was just a construct to him." All of our eyes slowly turned to Roman, who had chimed in with his rather insightful comment. He swallowed. "I mean, it's true."

"He's right." I agreed, breaking the awestruck silence. "But I couldn't help but like the love interest, too. She was an anxious hot mess, and then randomly met a man who was absolutely infatuated with her from the start. The bonus was the billionaire part. If only we could all be that lucky."

"I could totally go for a sugar daddy," Camden added, serious as all get out. The room erupted in laughter.

Tiffiny would be so proud of me for actively engaging in book club. I would have loved for her to join, but I liked the aspect of the guys-only attitude. It was only the second month of our meetings and we all had already learned a lot. This month's selection had been one of the romcoms with a cartoony cover. A few guys groaned with the choice. They rather enjoyed the monster romance from last month.

With the lighthearted cover, none of us expected the absolute filth inside. Hell, there was squirting. And toy play. Even a scene with anal. One would have had absolutely no idea from the unassuming cover and title of the cute-looking book. But the smut made up for the "dark" or questionable parts.

That was the best part about books. They surprised you in new and fun ways. While yes, some were disappointments, I have to say that, for the most part, I'd been pleasantly surprised. Like a special gift from a special someone.

"This book was nice. Refreshing. I liked it better than the last one." Tomas added with a bashful smile. He seemed a lot tamer in the romance department than even me.

"I didn't have high hopes for it, but hell, it was dirty as fuck." Truitt's brilliant grin highlighted his words.

"Who knew that an innocent cover would have such awesome filth inside," Camden added, and the rest of the team heartily agreed.

"So, gentlemen," Benson's voice turned serious as he commanded the attention of the book club. "What did we learn from the book?"

"Communication is key!" Arlow immediately chimed in.

"I don't think I'm a fan of that." Grumbled Schmidt.

"Of what, the miscommunication trope?" I added with a cock of my head. Because the man never stopped communicating.

"Whatever it is. Like dude, just be two adults and talk out your feelings. Even if you can't believe them yourself." Schmidt's response was like a slap to my face. I mean, duh, yes. But real life wasn't as easy as it was in books.

I didn't want to think about how shit would have gone down if I had immediately walked up to Iffy and was like, 'Hey Tiffiny, so I've been hopelessly in love with you ever since the moment I laid eyes on you'. I would have gotten a smack clear across my face. And honestly, I would have deserved it.

Sometimes, a miscommunication trope was needed. Or maybe miscommunication wasn't exactly the correct explanation. It was more a withholding of feelings until you tested the waters. Or something like that. I might have to search romance tropes later because now I was curious as to what trope Tiffiny and I were living. I knew it was a second chance, obviously. And a workplace romance. Ugh, right.

We had to tread carefully. The last thing I needed right now was to lose yet another job with a baseball organization. A baseball organization that I absolutely loved. I loved this team. I loved the coaching staff. And I loved the fact that Tiffiny was here.

"I like that they tried new things. He encouraged her to push past her self-imposed boundaries. Even though she was scared, he stood by her side. Every step of the way. Even before he realized he loved her." Roman's soft words next to me startled me from my deep thoughts.

We all looked at him in wonderment. There was a quiet pause before the room burst out in chatter. Truitt even offered his hand as a high five to Roman.

Damn, who were these guys? They were some of the biggest goofballs I ever had the pleasure of meeting. Yet, because of this book club, I realized that they were instead beautifully insightful goofballs.

I glanced over at Benson, who was almost beaming like a proud papa. When he brought the book club idea in front of the group of us, I really expected all of them to turn it down. But they'd been open-minded. Excited even. Which, when you had active participants, it made any sort of discussion that much more exciting.

To me, it looked like all of the guys were learning a thing or two about how resourceful romance books were. They were making us reflect on our inner selves. To make us better men. Better and more attentive lovers.

I had already learned so much just by reading Tiffiny's books outside of the book club picks. Iffy had let me know how much of an asshole I was. The books I'd read only reiterated that fact. If I had to spend the rest of my life making it up to her, then so be it. I was ready for it.

I wanted to spend the rest of my life reminding her just how much I cared about her. That I loved her so much that it physically hurt to be apart from her. Most would say it was corny. Well, all I had to say on that was they'd probably never felt anything like this. Because when you fall for someone, genuinely fall for them, it hits you like a freight train. Running you over, again and again, all while you lay there, beaten and bloodied, with the biggest, stupidest grin on your face.

Fuck, I had it bad. There was no denying that. Tiffiny was my everything. I even shed actual blood because of it.

22

ALL OVER AGAIN

THE SHIRES

Our first official date.

Round two.

Ender was respecting every boundary I had set. As right as all of this felt, I had already learned my lesson with the whole giving Ender a concussion thing. I still felt so incredibly bad about it. He kept insisting that it was all okay. I was trying to take it as a reminder to take our time with this second chance. To go about it with adult thinking skills instead of teenage hormones.

Ender insisted we go somewhere public. Which made sense, considering the last time we were alone together, it ended up with him in the hospital. We settled into one of my favorite coffee shops in Old City, right around the corner from my favorite romance bookstore that we had our "not date" at. It was halfway between where Ender lived with his mom and my place. A perfect meeting spot. And another excuse to visit the bookstore.

Brunch was iced coffee, an egg and cheese bagel, along with some delectable pastry that had enticed me from the moment I walked in. By late morning, the coffee shop was much quieter than the before work rush. For the most part, it was just me and

Ender, seated at a wooden and metal cafe table by the large storefront window.

With his hand on mine.

I tried so hard to keep my smile at bay, but it was just easier to let it light up my face. Not that I was in any rush to remove it, I could eat one-handed.

"My soul is happy now," Ender said softly with a smile to match. I felt a flush bloom across my cheeks.

"What, going all sappy on me now?"

"Oh no. I've always been sappy around you. You just choose to ignore it."

I stuck my tongue out at him, and he laughed. That warm, sensual husk of amusement that made that hot flush in my cheeks rush south. I had to keep reminding myself to pump the brakes. I really didn't want to. He made me feel good. He made me feel wanted. Desired. As if I were the only singular thing in his entire universe. And he was in no way mad about it.

"So, what's new in book world that I should be looking for at the bookstore?"

"Wait," I nearly spat out my drink mid-sip. "You want to go back to the bookstore?"

"Why not? I thought you'd want to, since we're only a block down from it." He shrugged, the side of his thumb making lazy caresses back and forth across the back of my hand. "Figured it was worth taking another peek."

"Oh well…I'll never say no to a trip to the bookstore. Even if I was just at one yesterday. Hell, even the same day."

Ender laughed. "You never know what you might miss. I swear I find something new every time I go. How can you not?"

I couldn't help the dreamy sigh that slipped past my lips. "Can I just say how much I love the fact that you're into books? And not just books, *romance* books."

He leaned forward with an amused smile, resting his elbow on the honey oak table top. "Oh yeah? What else do you love about me?"

I shot him a look before turning my attention back to my half-eaten pastry. "Don't get ahead of yourself, Romeo."

"Hey, the praise kink goes both ways, Iffy."

My eyes shot right back up to his. His gaze had darkened. The normally milk chocolate irises had gone to something decidedly richer in the cacao percentage.

I swallowed.

His opting for a public place for this date was so fucking smart. Because I was about a half-second away from vaulting over the table and tackling him to the floor. I didn't want to get arrested for lewd acts. Nor did I want a lifetime ban from the coffee shop that made the best fucking gingerbread lattes for me year-round.

"Learning some things about yourself while reading those romance books, hmm?" I say, my voice rough. I take a long drawl from my iced latte, but damn, my mouth is still entirely too parched.

"Maybe…" His attention turned to my hand, still pinned beneath his. Shifting in his seat, his other hand joined the first, clasping my hand into his. He took a moment to admire the shape of it in his hands with a stray brush of his thumb. All before bringing my knuckles to his lips for a whisper-soft kiss.

New kinks weren't the only things he was learning. Phew.

"Sometimes we learn something new about ourselves. Or…find a new turn on." Ender's Adam's apple bobbed as he slowly swallowed, his eyes positively glued to mine. Things were getting too heated for a public space. Maybe I should steer the topic in a different direction.

"This is true."

"Or maybe a new trope."

Ender let out a huff of amusement at my about-face in conversation topics. "Also, true. I found myself rather obsessed with second-chance romances lately." Now it was my turn to swallow whatever had settled into the back of my throat. "Sports romances too. Not to mention mascot romances." *Dammit.* Ender literally just grabbed the steering wheel of this conversation and put us right back into the smutty lane of traffic.

"I, for one, happen to enjoy slow burns the best. Where the woman is the badass. Makes a man get down on his knees and grovel." Ender's hands still held mine. His gaze was fiery, drinking me in with big gulps. If I didn't know any better, I was pretty sure he was plotting his next move. "As much as I am absolutely ravenous for these yearning books, sometimes I just want to take the guy and–"

Ender kissed me.

Mid-sentence.

I couldn't even finish my thought before his one hand shot out towards me as he leaned across the table, making our coffee cups clatter. He had been hanging onto every word up until he grabbed the corner of my jaw and brought his mouth to mine. It was sweet with an underlying lick of heat just simmering beneath the surface. We were out in public, so it's not like he could throw me on the table and have his way with me like I wanted him to.

"What was that for?" I breathed out, blinking at Ender as I was still coming out of my haze.

"You're cute when you're excited." He sat back, licking his lips as if to savor the quick, sensual moment between us. I had to press my thighs together. "Couldn't help myself." He shrugged with a swagger that made Indiana Jones' flirtations look like amateur hour. Like, how was that so randomly fucking adorable? And so damn hot?

I felt the blush creep up from the top of my breasts, up my neck, to blossom across my face. I felt like one of those Peanuts characters with a squiggly line for a mouth. Ready to burst at the seams from pure sweetness overload.

Ugh.

Why was I, this dark romance girly, living in her own personal, fucked up romcom? Was I secretly a softie at heart? Was I a sucker for all the handholding, forehead kissing, and random words of endearment?

Oh, for fuck's sake.

I was.

I had been. So long ago. Back when Ender and I first dated. Back when things were far less complicated. Back before he broke my heart.

But today, and well, every day since we were thrown back together, he's been little by little putting me back together. He was the only person who could reassemble my heart back to what it once was.

"You're lost in thought again." Ender mused, pressing his lips together to keep his grin at bay. His hands went back to cradling mine again, his calloused fingertips caressing along the back of my knuckles.

"Oh, uh…yeah. Sorry." I let out a humorless laugh, avoiding his stare. I'd spent so many years turning myself off from my feelings. Using sarcasm as a bandage over the sadness inside.

"Hey," Ender's playful gaze turned somber as his hands cupped mine, bringing the knuckles back to his lips for a reassuring kiss. "You don't have to apologize. I just hate that I'm the reason that light from your eyes goes dim. I'm the one who has to say 'I'm sorry' for eternity."

I felt like I swallowed knives. The saltiness of held back tears stinging in protest of not being able to be set free. There was a long moment of quiet between us before Ender sat up, downing the rest of his coffee.

"Come on." He insisted, standing up, his hand outstretched to me in invitation. "Let's go to the bookstore so I can spoil my girl some more and find some of those tropes we like."

Millie was all too happy to see us again. At this rate, our trip to the bookstore might end up being a semi-weekly thing. Not that I was complaining. Especially not when Ender let a "my girl" slip while talking about taking me back to the bookstore.

This time we walked in, hand-in-hand. I caught Millie giving us a knowing smile from her spot behind the counter. The last time we were in here I was so adamant about the fact that Ender and I weren't together. Now here we were, fingers interlocked, and Ender not letting me get further than an arm's length away from him before he was reeling me back in.

Since I still had a book or two left to read from the last bookstore haul, I insisted that Ender only treat me to one book. He had also paid for breakfast. Even though our purchases were less insane this time, we still lingered in the shop for over an hour.

Ender was keeping a mental checklist of my suggestions as we went. The man hung on my every word, asking pointed questions about aspects of each book. Not once did he wander away or go sit in the bookstore cuckold chair. His attention was solely on me and our time together.

The trope conversation snuck back into the depths of my brain as I stood in front of a shelf full of a book series, trying to remember where I left off. Ender and I were locked in the slowest of slow burns in the history of ever. And yet somehow, we gave enough "spice" just to keep the other on their toes until the real fireworks began.

This date only reiterated the fact. Ender's touch never strayed far from some part of my body. The unending tease of awareness and affection was beginning to consume me from the inside out.

The moment we stepped back outside the shop, I breathed in deeply. Despite the weather being hot, the breeze was light and fresh. A salty tang to it from the Chesapeake Bay. We headed down Arch Street toward Independence Hall and the SEPTA station.

"So, what's next, shortcake?"

I whipped my head around, craning my neck to give him the stink eye from down below. "Shortcake?"

"Don't like it?" Ender cocked a brow at me as his face turned thoughtful. "I thought I might try out something new. You are short," My eyes narrowed at him, a warning to ward off any short jokes. "And have *quite* the cake." A hearty tweak of my ass made me squawk and jump in surprise, completely forgetting to be mad at him about the "short" comment.

"Okay, fine. It's not *that* bad." I rolled my eyes at him, trying to suppress my grin. "It's not my fault you're freakishly tall."

Ender stopped by an alcove that led to an apartment building. "Oh yeah, but if I weren't freakishly tall, as you say, then I couldn't do this." It was then that he raised his arm above his head a bit, leaning it against the open doorway of the alcove. "Sexy book boyfriend door lean anyone?" He threw in a Flynn Rider smolder for good measure.

I pursed my lips together in a vain effort to ward off the eye roll and the playful grin that were both trying to break through at the same time.

"First of all, that's not even a door." I snidely remarked as I stepped up to him. My body leaned towards him, feeling his magnetic pull. Finding myself without a reason to move away from him. "And your smolder could use some work."

Ender tipped back his head and laughed, his arm reaching out so his hand could grab ahold of my hip, pulling me against him. As if in reflex, my arms wrapped around his torso, holding him close. Despite the summer weather, I couldn't deny my need to be smashed up against him.

The hand on my hip slowly rose, catching the jut of my chin with the pad of his thumb. His pointer finger crooked, giving my chin a soft perch to rest on as he tipped my face up to his. A warm smile highlighted his face. I could feel my insides turn to goo. This man must have taken very detailed notes from the romance books I recommended and studied them to fluency.

We stood there in the breezy sunshine. The sounds of Old City drifted away as we sat in our own little world. His thumb lifted, arching to caress my bottom lip. My lashes fluttered, closing my eyes to small slits. More than anything I wanted him to kiss me.

As if he heard my chaotic inner monologue, his head dipped down, capturing my more than willing lips, and I happily submitted to him. This was the kiss that those cheesy romcoms were made of. The way our lips danced together, soft and coaxing caresses as we drank each other in deep.

"Is it bad that I want to pick up where we left off? Just no ER visit this time?" I whispered in between gentle kisses. Nothing vulgar, but goddamn, I could feel them shoot straight to my thighs.

"I thought we were going to take it slow?"

"We've had a week. A very fucking long week." I reminded him, my words slightly more desperate. His chuckle was warm. I could feel the vibration of his chest against my breasts.

"At least you could do something about it. I was under doctor's orders *not* to do anything that would be…uh, *straining*." I sniggered. "But damn do I want you." His breathy tone, laced with want, had my chuckle dead on arrival in my throat. "Hell, I've wanted you for all these years. I–I didn't tell you what happened after."

"After?" I pulled away from him a bit so I could look into his eyes. He stepped away from the doorway, putting us back on the sidewalk, hand in hand. There was a long stretch of quiet between us. Something about his stature led me to believe there was something there he wasn't telling me.

"I drove straight to your house. I stood out there on your sidewalk looking in. But I couldn't bring myself to go and ring the doorbell." He offered softly, staring straight ahead as we walked. "I…I felt like such an ass. I deserved every second of punishment from you. I didn't deserve to have you back. Even though I really wanted you in my life. Forever."

Of all the places to drop such an epic truth bomb. The city of Philadelphia sidewalk was not the ideal place to have such an intimate conversation like this. Once again, I was blown away by the sheer devotion that this man had for me for so many years.

He left me to process that tidbit as we made our way into the park in front of the Independence Visitors Center. Given it was around lunchtime on a weekday, there weren't as many tourists wandering about. Mostly local employees out enjoying the summer breeze and sunshine on their lunch break. Being out in a wide-open quad with a line of trees off to the side felt a lot more private than walking down Arch Street.

"Goddammit, Ender. Can you just stop making me…feel things?" I suddenly grated at him, pulling him towards the shaded path along the trees. The white steeple of Independence Hall in the distance. "Especially on a public fucking sidewalk."

"I don't want any more secrets between us, Iffy. Like zero. We've had too many, and I want us to have a fresh slate. Especially," He tugged me back in close, whispering into my ear. "If I'm going to drag you back to bed."

My cheeks flushed.

"Maybe we do something a little bit gentler than throwing down or dragging. No more ER visits, remember?" I offered breathlessly as he pulled away.

"You're right. We should do this the right way."

His words made me stop breathing for the moment. A slow, meandering heat began to lick its way through the pit of my stomach down between my thighs. My breath quickened as I licked my lips. There were numerous implications in his tone, and I wanted them spelled out. No more dancing around this issue. Not when both of us so clearly wanted to explore the more intimate side of all of this.

"D-Do what right…?" I managed to get out in a shaky whisper as he pressed himself back in closer to me. We found a little secluded nook, tucked away in the shade and from prying eyes. The way his gaze was staring at my mouth was heated and full of unspoken promises.

"Make love to you." His words were a delicious balm over the length of my entire body. "This… Us…" I felt the gentle caress of his fingers and palm against my cheek and jaw as he took a moment to admire me. "It's so much more."

His fingertips danced around my temple before sliding a lock of my hair behind my ear. It was so soft, so gentle. The Ender that I always knew.

"There's never been anyone else." The darkened look in his gaze softened, right along with the tone of his voice. "There…will *never* be anyone else."

The words hit me like a fully loaded tractor-trailer. I didn't know what to do with that admission. Was it a slip of his subconscious? Or was he truly serious?

Unable to process his words, my hands fisted into his shirt as I brought his body to me, our lips meeting in a heated clash. It burned brightly for a singular moment before his mouth eased everything back down to a simmer. How the hell did this man have this kind of restraint? Especially at a time like this? I had so many questions, and yet, I couldn't find the words.

"After all of these years apart, I can wait a few more days to savor you. I want to make it special." He snuck in another kiss. "Dinner out, flowers, hotel, the works. No sneaking around at one of our apartments like teenagers." I had to laugh at that, but it was short-lived. "Because the things I want to do to you," His voice dropped to a honeyed husk. "I want to be able to hear you scream out my name and beg for more. So much more…"

Oh…fuck.

My brain exploded into a zillion different thoughts at once. But mostly, the only thing I could think about was just how his words made me feel. So wanted, sexy. Desired.

Did I really have my very own living, breathing book boyfriend? One that spoke dirty as fuck but also did romantic nonsense? Romantic nonsense that I swore I'd never be a part of again?

The harder I fought these feelings, the more they bubbled up. This wasn't just potentially friends with benefits. Ender wanted me. All of me. All the time.

"I…I'd like that." I managed to choke out. "You're worth the wait."

Ender turned with a smile, tugging gently on my hand to follow him back towards the street back to the nearby SEPTA station. The entire conversation left my head in a delicious tizzy with all of the implications. He wanted to be respectful of my body. Of my time.

Planned sex was way hotter than spontaneous sex. Look, I loved me some spontaneous sex, but there was something in that delicious edging that really got my gears going. Because today? This entire past week? So much edging. The anticipation. The implications. The mind was a powerful tool when it came to intimacy.

"But…what if I don't want to wait?" I whispered, casting a timid glance in his direction. Ender's cheeks went pink. His throat bobbed with his heavy swallow. "I've had all week to think about what I want. I'm an adult. Clearly, we care about each other." Ender's brows slowly rose as he got a whiff of what I was reasoning.

"So, when do you want to…*you know*…?"

"Now?"

Ender blinked at me, taken aback. "N–Now?"

"I have it on good authority that my sister-in-law is at work until late and my brother is off at the in-laws helping with some project. So, my place? It's…quiet."

CANNED HEAT

JAMIROQUAI

Oh holy fuck.
Holy shit.
It's happening.
It's really happening.

I was on a one-way trip to heaven with the most beautiful woman on the planet. I tried so hard to keep my cool as I sat next to Tiffiny on the SEPTA train. She looked just as nervous as I felt. Which was silly.

As she said, we were both grown-ass adults. We could have sex any time we pleased. Well, within reason. So what was the apprehension?

Was it the fact that we had already done this before? Why was that making it so much weirder? Okay, so maybe weird wasn't the right word. I wanted this woman laid bare and writhing in my arms for all of eternity. There was nothing weird about that. But still, there was a churning in my gut that had nothing to do with digestion and everything to do with the beautiful, curvy woman next to me.

Her hand shot out, grabbing hold of mine. I saw that her feet were fidgeting on the metal floor of the train, even though she seemed mostly calm and collected from the waist up. But once my eyes looked at her face, I saw a reflection of myself.

"Please tell me you're as nervous as I am."

She took the words right out of my mouth. "I am."

Her shoulders relaxed, almost sending her torso into a heap in her lap. "Oh, phew."

I couldn't help but laugh. "We're crazy, right?"

"Maybe a little," Iffy admitted, leaning back in her seat with a sigh. "It's just like a weird, excited kind of nervous."

I thought about my inner turmoil for a moment, only to realize that was exactly it. "I guess that's a good thing?"

"As long as it's not the kind where you puke all over my shoes because of it."

"I'll be sure to give you a warning." I chuckled.

A moment of quiet passed between us before I draped my other hand atop our joined ones. I smiled at her and got one in return. There was nothing here that we needed to worry about. We were both beyond comfortable with each other. That part hadn't changed.

Maybe it was because I felt the need to make everything up to her. To physically show how deep my feelings were with the woman that I've always cared about. If that wasn't a gut-wrenching sort of thought process or overwhelming expectation, I didn't know what it was.

Tiffiny's hand squeezed mine, and it brought me back to earth. I brought hers to my lips, taking the time to kiss each knuckle. It was slow and sensual, and despite her relaxing just a bit more, the air was suddenly a bit more heated between us. I smiled down at her, sure to keep eye contact while hers slid to soft slits. The less we thought about the schematics of this, the better.

Few words were said between us as we got off the train and hightailed it to her place. My skin was prickling with awareness as we slipped inside her basement apartment. The true implications didn't hit me until I heard the front door lock engage.

"Nothing happens until we are on a soft surface. Got it? Because if I have to take you to the ER again, so help me god, Ender Roche–" She reminded me, a bit breathless. Biting her lower lip, she tried to hide her bashful grin. Kicking off her shoes, she slid past me, but I caught her hand.

Without a word, I toed off my shoes too before I enticed her back to me with an almost rough tug, snapping her body back towards mine. Instead of enveloping her into my arms as she got close, I stooped down, wrapping my arms right under her peach of an ass and lifting her into the air. Iffy squealed in surprise, her hands quickly moving to my shoulders, holding on for dear life.

"Last chance to change your mind." I breathed against her lips as I encouraged her legs to wrap around my waist. My hands slid, worshipping the shape of her hips and bottom before grabbing a hold of each ass cheek.

"Absolutely the fuck not." She huffed against my mouth before she kissed me. Hard and deep, finally giving in to the thing that had been simmering between us all morning and afternoon. "I'm yours, Ender. Better make it worth my while."

I'm yours, Ender.

Those fucking words had me rock hard in an instant.

There was a bit of a bite to her tone, but the idea of a challenge made me suddenly ravenous about the entire situation, shoving aside all previous nervousness and hesitations. I now had a chance to show her what I learned. To branch out from my vanilla ways from the last time our bodies connected so intimately. More than anything I wanted her screaming my name so loud that the neighbors complained.

"I'm going to make you mine, Tiffiny Campanaro," I murmured back to her, nipping at her lips. She still tasted sweet from her late morning latte. "Just need to get to the soft surface first."

Iffy was caught somewhere between a groan of delight and a giggle as she vaguely gestured in the direction of her bedroom. It probably was self-explanatory, as her apartment was fairly straightforward. My elbows and forearms got a few jabs between furniture and walls before we made our way down the hall to her bedroom.

It was bright and airy with an entire wall filled with floor-to-ceiling bookshelves. Not that I was surprised by such an impressive sight. But as much as my curious mind wanted to look through her collection, there was a much more pressing matter that had my hands full.

We tumbled down onto her bed with a soft bounce. I was sure to avoid the end tables she had along the one end of her bed. Her body wordlessly made way for me, notching my hips right into the V of her thighs. Fuck this felt right. Hell, it felt amazing. She felt amazing.

There was a starry-eyed look about her gaze as she looked up at me. I smiled at her, caressing a finger down along the curve of her face. There was a rosy bloom there and I was pretty sure I had one to match.

"Still good?" I asked, giving her an out if she wanted me to pull away from this.

She gave me a curt nod, her voice breathy. "Absolutely."

Grinning, I leaned down, recapturing her lips in a slow and meandering sort of kiss. I relished the way she melted beneath me. All the chaos and nonsense between us, fading away. Fading away into pure and utter bliss.

I wanted to take my time with her, but I wasn't sure if I had another hour of patience when she was pinned beneath me like this, writhing and practically begging for more. I'd been dreaming of this moment for years. I'd been fully prepared to never have another intimate moment with her for as long as I lived. So there was no way I was going to fuck this up by blowing my load early.

Fuck.

I really hoped I wouldn't blow my load early.

During our prior heated make-out session, I'd only gotten a fleeting feel of Tiffiny's body, so my hands eagerly sought out her curves. I was rewarded with a delicious moan that landed on my tongue. It only encouraged me further. With a firmer hand against her hips, sliding along the curve of her waist, up along her ribcage, before cupping her breast that filled my hand and then some.

Tiffiny wriggled beneath me, her fingers fumbling with the fabric of her shirt as she tried to shimmy it up and over her head. I was ready to assist, shifting my body out of the way a bit to make quick work of it. Tossing it aside, I glanced down at her, drinking her in.

Her bra was nude in color, no fancy bells or whistles to it. I wanted to give it all the five-star reviews because, *goddamn*, the cleavage it gave her? That was the kind of vision Renaissance artists could only hope to convey in their statues and paintings.

"You're even more beautiful than I remembered." I breathed out, completely aware of the fact that I said them out loud. Tiffiny's cheeks flooded with color as she chewed on her bottom lip.

Reaching up, I cupped her cheek, using the pad of my thumb to pull her lip from the hold of her teeth. Her eyes timidly moved back to mine. I couldn't help but smile down at her. There was a moment of quiet as I saw something pass through her gaze. Her head tilted a bit just so she could give me a kiss against my lingering digit.

I had to clench my teeth just to keep my groan at bay. It was just a teasing little kiss, against my finger for fucks sake. But dammit, it drove me fucking wild.

Pulling my hand away, I leaned down, kissing her so hard that the breath slipped right out of her and into my mouth. Her body arched into mine as her arms tangled around my neck, keeping me close. I wanted her bare. I wanted her stretched out on the bedding, writhing, whimpering, begging for everything that I was giving her.

My hands moved quickly, slipping between us to flick the handy front clasp of her bra open. A sigh of relief from her tickled my lips. I could feel the shake in my hands as I timidly nudged the loosened garment off her body.

Warm, silky skin greeted the palm of my hand. The hard pebble of her nipple sent pleasurable jolts down my limb and straight to my already straining cock. A breathy whimper was fed into my mouth, and it made my hand close around the mound of her breast reflexively.

This was torture.

Sweet, delicious torture.

I reluctantly pulled my mouth from hers so I could trail heated kisses down along her jaw. To the quickened pulse at her throat, to the bare skin of her shoulder. Iffy's soft sounds of delight danced through my ears as I added my other hand to join in on the fun. My mouth slowly made its way back, only to end up with my lips against her ear as I used every shred of what sanity I had left to whisper against her ear.

"Tell me how you like it now, Iffy. I want to learn all the ways that I can make you fall apart."

The way her body arched towards me in that moment had my eyes rolling back in my head. Her hands grabbed hold of my cheeks as she briskly moved my mouth to hers. She slanted her lips against mine, slipping her tongue inside my mouth as she tried to devour me right then and there.

"Taking all of my clothes off is a good start." She mumbled against my mouth, sucking my bottom lip into hers for good measure. I felt the teasing sting of her teeth into my flesh and that was when I let out a husky groan, grinding my hips into hers in response.

I didn't move until her teeth let go of me. Briskly, I sat up, my vision still a bit hazy from the desire for the woman beneath me. But there she was. The woman of my dreams stretched out between my thighs. Her skin flushed pink, lips swollen from my attentions.

I took a few steadying breaths as I studied her, before my hands guided the straps of her bra down her arms and off into some corner of her bedroom. As much as I didn't want to move off of her, getting rid of her pants was detrimental to the whole having sex with her part. Shifting my body up and off of her, I gritted my teeth, feeling my cock straining against the fabric of my shorts that were less than forgiving.

Adjusting my dick, I moved off the bed as my hands reached for her hips. My fingers dipped into the waistband of her pants and panties. Holding my breath, I eased the fabric over the jut of her hips, down over her ass as she lifted it off the bed to help me make quick work of it all. In one smooth move, I stripped the fabric down and off her body, letting it collapse into a heap on the floor.

Immediately, I was greeted by the scent of her desire. Thick and heavy in the heated air between us. Ripping off my shirt, I sank to my knees at her feet. My hands hooked under the crook of her leg, jerking her body to the edge of the bed. They immediately slid to the inside of her thighs, parting her legs like the gates to heaven.

My cock bobbed in my shorts, and I regretted that I hadn't fully undressed when I had the chance. But I didn't want the temptation of touching myself to impede getting at least one orgasm out of her before the main event happened. Just seeing her glistening pink center had me ready to release an entire week's worth of cum right into my boxer briefs without a single touch.

"Well?" Tiffiny sat up with a cocked brow. It was then that I realized that maybe I had hesitated a bit too long, completely distracted by my admiration of her beautiful cunt. And well, not blowing my load because of it.

"Can't a man admire a piece of art?" I got a snort of amusement in reply. "And I'm trying really fucking hard not to uh…"

"Oh…" The pink color in her cheeks went straight to rose red.

"I…just need a breather, is all. Because the second I taste you, it's only going to make *that* matter worse." I swallowed, trying to control my breathing and convince my cock to wait at least another half hour. Bare minimum. "Show me. Show me how you like to be touched here." I grazed the pad of my thumb upward along her slit, brushing past her swollen clit, which got me a sharp inhale.

Her throat bobbed as she gave me a timid nod, reaching her hand down. I gave her a few kisses along the inside of her thigh as I watched her pointer and ring finger part the sides of her folds, spreading herself open for me. Her middle finger traced along the same path my thumb had. But instead of just a glancing caress of her clit, I watched with rapt interest as it applied pressure as it rolled the spot in a counterclockwise motion.

My eyes shifted up to her face. Her head was tilted back, her eyes closed, her lip caught in the trap of her upper teeth. I watched her fingers work for a few more rotations before my hand took over. The skin of her thighs prickled with goosebumps as my thumb and middle finger kept her spread open while my pointer found her clit.

That got me a full-on moan as she collapsed back to the bed. "Yes," she breathed. "Just like that. A-Add a bit more pressure like–*oh fuck yes…*"

If I survived giving her oral without orgasming myself, it was going to be a goddamned miracle. I kept at it for only a little longer as I was eager to see just what else would make her curl her toes. My mouth kissed its way up to her core, brushing a soft kiss against her mound. I was rewarded with a shuddering breath.

"Ender…more…please."

Fuck me. I'd only kissed her between her thighs, and she was already begging for me. My tongue took a meandering glide around her clit, flicking it with the tip before her hips jerked in response. I grinned.

Slipping my tongue into her slit, I did a long, slow lick from bottom to top, gathering her slick into the curve of my appendage. I pulled the harvest into my mouth, humming in the utter and glorious satisfaction of the sensual taste of her. Diving back in for another round, I took my time caressing her silken inner walls before drawing back up, pressing the breadth of my tongue against her clit.

I made sure to listen to every sound, every whimper, every cry, every sharp hitch of breath she made in response to my motions. She was so responsive, and it made my job of rediscovering her that much easier. My tongue moved to thrusting as deep as I could manage, in and out, in and out. My top lip hit her right in the clit, and I pressed harder, applying pressure there as she liked before pulling away, giving it a good round of flicks with the tip of my tongue.

Her cries were music to my ears, egging me on. I pressed back in, sucking the swollen nub between my lips. That earned me a sharp, grated moan as her fingers tangled into the bedding, sending soft ripples across what had been a smooth surface.

"Gentle, Ender." She reminded me through clenched teeth. "I do happen to like my clit." I let out a breathy exhale of amusement. Oops, I got overly excited for a moment.

I decreased the suction, adding the tip of my tongue to flick against her clit. That earned me a whole host of new noises. I made a mental note of that for future reference.

Pulling away, I caught my breath, but not without continuing the pleasure. This time with my thumb. Licking my lips, I inhaled, diving back in to try out a trick I'd read in one of the cartoony cover romances.

There was a running gag in the book about the guy using his tongue to trace the alphabet while deep inside her cunt. He wanted to see how far he could get before she orgasmed. Or which letter was her favorite.

Letting my thumb keep up with her favorite sensation, I set to work with my elementary skills, and the reaction was immediate. Tiffiny's fingers tangled into my hair, pulling hard by the time I hit G. M was when I got the loud moans. Q was when she yelled at me.

"Suck my clit and for the love of all that is holy put your fingers inside me." She choked out. I was all too happy to oblige.

Chuckling to myself, it was a thankful distraction to my painfully hard erection. My lips moved back to her clit, finding the depth of suction that had her crying out once again. Gingerly, my middle finger traced along her slit, earning me another groan. That only fueled the fire as I pressed the digit inside.

I'd never heard a more beautiful sound than the one Tiffiny made as my finger slowly penetrated her.

Immediately, I felt her vaginal walls clutch me, greeting me with a warm hug like an old friend. Groaning around her clit I felt her hand jerk in my hair again, pulling the strands sharply.

Slowly, I began to slide my finger in and out of her. It glided in and out of her with wondrous ease. I couldn't help but moan all over again from the implications.

"More, Ender…more…" Iffy whimpered as her walls fluttered around my digit as her hips rocked to meet the motions of my hand. Fuck, I could never deny this woman anything.

I slid my pointer finger inside of her and her entire body shuddered with the sensation. I picked back up on the worship of her clit. That was the moment I felt her resolve begin to crack. So desperately I wanted her to cum all over my face. To fill my mouth with her essence as she screamed my name.

I remembered another trick from yet another one of Tiffiny's favorite romance books of late. Rotating my fingers inside of her so I was now palm-up, I crooked both digits in a come-hither motion. I did a few quicker thrusts with this positioning as I was looking for something.

The pads of my fingers brushed against a textured patch of skin just slightly deeper inside her. There. That was it. On the next few thrusts I did my best to push the tips of my fingers right into that area, making her back arch off the bed. I quickened my pace and I suddenly had the feeling that I was on the precipice of something great.

"Harder! More! And whatever you fucking do, *don't stop*. I-I'm so close…" There was a desperate grit to her voice and I immediately obliged. I was delirious from the auditory and sensory stimulations as her walls tightened around my fingers.

In a few more strokes, it was a glorious endgame. Her hips bucked off the bed as she cried and screamed out my name. Her head tossed back and forth as her body writhed with her pleasure. I could scarcely move my fingers inside her as her vagina had clamped down on them so hard, pulsing with the waves of her earth-shattering climax. It sent me reeling.

I kept up her demand, only easing off my sucking and thrusting when she begged me to. Her words were breathless and broken. The fingers knotted in my hair relaxed and fell away onto the bed with a soft bounce.

"Pants. Off."

The woman couldn't even speak in full sentences. That only made my bare chest puff out with pride. I felt lightheaded as I stood, taking the moment to suck off my fingers with ravenous enthusiasm. It also allowed me a chance to try to pull my shit together because the woman wanted me and my cock in the worst way.

Gingerly I eased my shorts and boxers off my body, only to catch her staring with a darkened stare. It sparkled in the late afternoon sun that filtered in through her blinds and sheer curtains. She sat up, still looking a bit woozy, patting the bed next to her. I hesitated.

"Look if you put that mouth anywhere near this thing," I gestured to my cock as I slowly eased myself back onto the bed, stretching out beside her. "I can't be responsible for its actions."

"Is that a threat or a challenge?" She grinned wickedly at me before turning her gaze to my dick that jutted straight out from my body, loud and proud. Just the fact that I knew she was staring at it made it bob. Which only enticed her further. With one hand she pressed me flat to the bed while the other headed south. I opened my mouth to protest, but she was entirely too quick for my blood-deprived brain as it had all rushed to my dick.

"But what if I…" Her soft hand wrapped around the shaft. My fingers immediately dug into the comforter, strangling the home good on impact as I gritted my teeth. Fuck her mouth. If she moved a single finger, I was a goner.

"Iffy d–" An approving hum sounded deep in her throat as her hand only slid up towards my tip. But my warning came too late as I felt that point of no return sink in. Pure electricity settled into my balls before exploding out of my tip as I fell back against the bed, shuddering and groaning as my overly full balls emptied in mass.

I barely registered her jumping in surprise as the thick white ropes pulsed out of my tip, going as high as her eye-level. All before falling back on me, painting my body and her cocked thigh with hot splats. My vision went hazy the second her fist pumped my cock through the rest of my orgasm, urging every last drop I had stored out of me.

Watching her through hooded lashes, the look on her face was pure desire, awe, and euphoria. She managed a few more pumps before she was sure I was milked dry. Fuck. Of course, I had to go and ruin this chance too.

"Fuck, that was the hottest cum shot I've ever seen."

My still hard and extremely sensitive cock twitched in her hand, making me inhale sharply between clenched teeth. I may have completely lost all of my brain cells in my ejaculation, but did she really say that was...*hot*?

"Iffy, I–I'm sorry. I couldn't help it–"

She tutted me as her eyes drifted to the puddles of cum on both of our bodies. As good as her hand felt around me, she thankfully let me go. Although I wasn't exactly sure I'd get soft ever again.

"Damn, I guess you really did have a bad case of blue balls."

I couldn't help but laugh, my body relaxing as I melted back into the bed. "You're telling me." I felt the heat of embarrassment hit my cheeks. "I swear I can last longer than that."

"Well, I would hope so. Especially after that impressive display." My cheeks heated for a different reason. "Let me go grab a washcloth. Then maybe you can get me to cum on your face a few more times before the grand finale."

Holy fuck.

I AM YOURS

ANDY GRAMMER

Ender got me to cum not once, not twice, but three fucking times between his mouth and fingers. I had died and gone to heaven. That was the only explanation. With every movement, he asked for consent and direction. By the third O of mine he worked on, he was like an old pro at it.

Typically, orgasms for me were harder to achieve the longer the session went on. But damn, Ender was having me go from zero to off the charts in less than a minute at one point. It was as if he knew exactly what to do and how to do it. Or maybe I was just a really good teacher. Or he was a straight-A honors student.

I was a literal puddle on my bedding. Fully relaxed, straight down to every single molecule in my bones. Ender had me tangled up in his arms as his fingers, that had just been inside me, traced wet, heated circles on the curve of my hip as I came down from my high.

While he had been a little rusty at the start, he was a quick learner. I couldn't help but ruminate on what he said the other day. The fact that he claimed he hadn't been with anyone else since me. From the dinner conversation with his mom, it didn't sound like he had been lying about that fact. Or he was really good at hiding his exploits from his mother. Given the fact that they were on the road so much, it wouldn't be that difficult.

Despite the breakup, the man had never lied to me once in our entire existence together. Why start now? Why lie about something like that?

My head was spinning, and Ender must have noticed as fingers caressed down my cheek, drawing my attention back to the present. Back to him.

"You doing okay?"

My heart squeezed and twisted with the fact that he kept checking in with me. Every step of the way.

"Yeah… Just a bit blitzed out of my mind. Thanks to you." I shot a soft smirk at him. He chuckled.

"Not…completely out of your mind, right?" The husk suddenly in Ender's voice had my synapses sparking back to life, one by one. He leaned in slowly, grazing a gentle caress of a kiss against my lips as he gently nudged me onto my back. "Because I'd very much like to claim those last few brain cells. If you'll let me."

There was nothing directly dirty about his words. But the connotations behind them had me feeling like lava was ready to suddenly boil over between my thighs. I had to swallow back my fluster and pray that my voice didn't give me away.

"O-Oh yeah…?" My cadence was a little shaky, but my smirk gave me that little nudge of confidence. "Finally recovered?"

"I recovered two orgasms of yours ago. But I enjoyed hearing you get off too much to stop."

Holy ever-loving fuck.

I was beginning to regret calling Ender "vanilla". While the man hadn't tried anything kinky yet, he sure was batting a thousand in the dirty talk aspect of things. Goddammit. Now he even had me thinking dirty, sexy baseball puns. What was wrong with me?

"Should we stop?"

"Hell no."

Ender threw his head back and laughed. A full-on, deep, belly laugh. "That's my girl."

He came back to me, molding his body right up against mine. Another caress graced my cheek. This time his fingertips continued their journey. Down the column of my neck, out along my shoulder, further south around the outside curve of my breast. I had to bite my lower lip.

His touch continued around my navel, over the curve of my hip, before dipping back down between my thighs. My breath hitched sharply as his fingers grazed my swollen and sensitive clit. Normally, I'd be more than happy with four orgasms in one afternoon. But this man was making me *feral*. In the nicest of ways. Respectfully.

"Mmm…" The musing was warm and honeyed as his eyes strayed from watching his fingers work and moved back up to mine. "I can see that your body agrees with that sentiment." Leaning in, his mouth found mine. It was gentle and sweet, something less heated than earlier.

"Can I make you mine again, Tiffiny?" His words were hot but sweet, a hint of desperation there. I could feel just how badly he wanted to. His cock thick and heavy against my thigh. A sound of desire rumbled in his throat as he felt my cunt flex with his request.

"Yes…" I whispered to him, desperate myself. He slipped two fingers inside me as his mouth completely claimed mine. His body pressed me into the bed as he shifted his body so he was caging mine in.

"Condoms?" He managed to get out in between deep and breathless kisses. Shit. Did I have condoms? How long ago did I buy condoms if I had them? A year? If so, phew. I was fine.

"Top drawer." I thought better a second later. "Let me get one. No more head injuries allowed." Ender rolled off of me with a laugh, his cock loud and proud, pointing straight at the ceiling. Goddamn it should be a registered weapon at this point. A registered weapon that was going to be deep inside me very shortly.

Biting my lower lip, I spun on the bed a bit, shifting myself up towards my pillow, and plopping on my side to address the drawer. Opening it, I shoved my hand in there blindly, hunting around for a single silver packet. I also realized that I really needed to clean out this drawer.

Just as I fingered the square packet, Ender's hands were on me, gripping my thighs as he quickly rolled me back onto my back. My breath caught as I suddenly found myself staring at the ceiling, successfully holding the packet of projection aloft. But I was entirely too distracted by the giant of a man, face-first into my crotch.

"Not fair!" I gasped out before the last syllable turned into a moan as Ender pressed open-mouthed kisses right against my core. Hadn't this man had his fill of my cooch today? Not that I was complaining.

"Couldn't help myself." He mumbled against my throbbing center. I held onto the condom for dear life as he left me writhing on the mattress. But I didn't want another orgasm from oral. I needed him. All eight inches of him. Or at least that was my best guess. The man's cock was nothing to sneeze at.

"Help yourself to me." I rasped out as my hips arched into his greedy mouth. A breathy chuckle vibrated from his lips to my center before he tore himself away. His hand lashed out, grabbing the packet from my white-knuckle grip.

I watched the flex of the sinew on the back of his hands as he tore the package open, extracting the opaque rubber circle from its confines. He stared at it, almost as if he had forgotten how to put one on. Tossing aside the trash, he used two hands to ease the roll of the condom over his straining cock. Fuck, why was this hot? The slow stroke of the latex down his shaft, readying himself.

"I need you inside me." I rasped out, enticing him with an arch of my hips. A groan answered me back as he leaned back in close, stealing a kiss.

"What kind of man denies his lady?" He practically purred against my mouth

I cocked my brow at him, trying not to snicker. "I think you're going a little too…"

"Regency romance again?"

"…I created a monster."

That got an outright laugh out of Ender. "Historical smut not your kink huh?" He hovered above me, his knees nudging my thighs apart like it was an everyday occurrence.

"Only if it involves hot men in kilts."

"Kilts, hmm?" Ender glanced off in thought before his chocolate gaze moved back to mine with a new, wicked twinkle. "I could manage that."

My god he was so hot. Like a baseball god sent down from the heavens. The blonde highlights almost sparkled in the sunlight as he sat above me. All tall and rippled with lean muscles. I wondered if I could convince him to sit for an art class so I could get a painting of him, exactly like this. Well, sans hard on. That was all for me.

"At least claim me once before you go on planning other seduction techniques." I shot back at him, finally finding my voice. A gruff chuckle followed as he pressed his lips back to mine.

"Duly noted."

My breath caught as I felt the head of his manhood graze against my slit, sliding up the notch and bumping against my clit. I had to reach out and grab hold of him, one hand curling around the back of his neck while the other wrapped around his ribcage. I felt his smile against my lips as he pressed his forehead to mine.

"Are we really doing this? Again?" I whispered, my voice so close to giving out.

"I told you, Iffy. You're forever for me. Always have been, always will be."

I pulled him back down towards me, latching my mouth against his. Giving him full consent to take me. All of me.

Ender slanted his mouth against mine, drinking me in deep. I lost myself in the kiss. My body reacted to his as if it was second nature, my knees bending slightly to cradle his body. He responded with a subtle shift of his hips, pressing the head of his cock right where I needed him most.

My nails dug into his skin, and I held my breath in preparation. I'd had sex with other men, not recently, mind you, so I knew how this went. But I couldn't discredit the excited little flutter in my heart. Delicious anticipation pumped through my veins. Everything about this felt right. It gave me such comfort and peace.

I felt the subtle shift of Ender's body as he slipped inside, so achingly slow. Our sharp exhales intertwined in the sliver of space between our mouths. The stretch was delicious. The rounds of oral and his fingering me had made accommodating his girth so much easier. As much as I wanted to buck against him, the feel of him sliding deeper and deeper, inch by inch, had me in a chokehold.

Ender's lips recaptured mine, breathless and needy as he sunk straight to the hilt inside me. My hips shifted ever so slightly, adjusting the angle in which he penetrated me until it hit that sweet spot. A groan slid into my mouth and I swallowed it whole. My hands slid across his skin and through his hair, a desperate need to engage all of my senses at once.

"Still good?" He whispered. I quickly nodded.

"Yes, please move."

Slanting his mouth across my lips, he did as I asked. My back immediately arched as a jolt of pure pleasure shot up my spine. Somehow, Ender's hands made their way around my back, embracing me fully. Although he was sure not to squish me as he somehow braced himself on his elbows and knees.

The thrusts were slow and outright delicious. He made sure I could feel all of him before he slid back inside, making my breath catch. My hips answered in kind, rocking in the unhurried cadence as our bodies moved as one.

For some reason, I equated intensity with a good, hard fucking. But whatever was happening between Ender and me, in this steady dance, was the most intense thing I'd ever felt in my entire life. There was emotion here. Months, years of built-up longing and anticipation, now finally reaching a climax.

I felt his hand slip to my hip. The pads of his fingers dug into my skin, holding me down as he picked up the pace. My god this was incredible. The way he held me, kissed me, made me feel desired and present at this very moment. Most guys had a one-track mind when it came to the actual moment of copulation.

Not Ender. His hands and mouth were everywhere he could reach. Although he had to stop from time to time and slow it down. No need to rush.

"My god, you're amazing…" He mumbled against the curve of my neck. "Tell me what you need. Hard? Fast? Slow? New position?"

The checking in with me again. Fucking hell. My heart was ready to burst. "Tilt your hips a bit." I rasped out. "Grind into me." Adjusting the angle of his hips and his thrusts a bit, he tried a few times before the subtle change hit just the right spot, making my back arch clear off the bed. "Yep, that's the spot."

His soft chuckle didn't last long as he put all his effort into pressing his pelvic bone directly into my clit. I could see stars behind my eyelids as I whimpered. The noises only encouraged him further as he picked his speed back up. Fuck, maybe I shouldn't have given all my secrets away. But it's not like I could only have one good orgasm. I could have *lots*. Fuck, I loved being a woman.

"Fuck, Iffy. Fucking hell, I-I can *feel* you… So close…" He ground out between gritted teeth, pressing his temple to mine as he desperately tried to maintain. "Just let go," He begged. "Let go, *mi amor*."

The familiar and yet foreign sentiment hit my ears and sent me reeling straight over the edge into oblivion. I couldn't breathe for a moment as my pleasure had my body in a vice grip as the initial wave hit me. It was so intense and all-encompassing, so much more than any of my previous orgasms today. It took me by surprise as stars exploded in the corners of my vision.

I finally felt my body relax as the next pulsing wave hit me. Ender's rough groan hit my ears as I desperately held onto him. As if he were a life preserver on a stormy sea and my only chance at survival. My cries of his name exploded out of me as my back arched, my entire body writhing off the bed as my body couldn't contain the delicious chaos.

"Your turn." I gasped out, still choked up mid orgasm as I felt another wave hit. Ender's hips were the only thing that answered me as he chased me into the great beyond of bliss in just a few more thrusts.

Something darkened in his hazy gaze as he stole a quick kiss, a distraction for me even though I was still in the delicious middle of my climax. His hands grabbed a hold of my forearms, adjusting them so he could latch onto my wrists.

With the next thrust he threw my arms above my head, making me gasp in surprise. His large hand cuffed my wrists together as he pressed his nose against mine. The other hand dug into the mattress next to my head, gripping onto my floral comforter for dear life.

That's when all hell broke loose.

Ender grunted, a gruff tone that shook me right to my central nervous system. His hips quickened against mine, the pitcher's fit core fully coming into play. It took my breath away as he held me there, pinned beneath him like some female main character in one of my dark romances I loved so much.

It was sending me.

Sending me right back over the edge into oblivion. Only this time Ender was nipping at my heels, chasing me into the great beyond. His cock went rock hard inside me. With one final upward jerk, he moaned, collapsing atop me. Our foreheads pressed together as he kissed me, his thrusts easing off in intensity.

He slowed down with each thrust before coming to a stop. His hand loosened its grip on my wrists, and I immediately wrapped my arms around him in a tight embrace. There were so many emotions floating all around at once in my body. I wasn't sure how I was going to process them all.

Ender responded in kind, wrapping both of his arms around me, encompassing as much of my body as possible. He pulled me against him as he rolled us onto our sides. Another kiss graced my lips as I felt him slip out of me. I gave him a soft little whine in protest. Stupid condom.

"Wow." He breathed, a smile curling at his lips.

"That's putting it mildly." I huffed back at him. It got me a gruff chuckle.

"You're lucky you got that word out of me. Holy hell, Iffy." His smile had turned into a completely blitzed out grin. His frosted tips were all awry, thanks to them being an excellent handle when I was losing my mind during my orgasms.

In the afternoon glow, he almost looked like that boy I fell in love with in high school. The goofy little smile. The frosted tips on his dark hair.

I was falling in love all over again.

HAPPINESS

NEEDTOBREATHE

"Something is up with you."

I glanced over at Cadence, who was regarding me with a skeptical cocked brow and a hand on her hip. Besides being freshly and thoroughly fucked, nothing else had changed with me.

"I got a new book," I said as nonchalantly as possible.

"You get a new book every week. Hell, sometimes every day." Cadence rolled her eyes and shook her head as she leaned against the wall in my dressing room. "Even the newest special edition doesn't have you like this."

"Like what?"

"Smiling. Happy."

Shit.

"What, I'm not allowed to be happy?" I cast over my shoulder at her as I busied myself with getting the bell of Ding Dong onto a hanger.

"Girl, the last time you were happy resulted in someone getting accidentally maimed with a baseball bat."

I snickered, chancing a glance over at her. "That heckler deserved it. He should have been paying attention to the possibility of broken bats."

"So, who got maimed this time?" Cadence pursed her lips, crossing her arms in front of her. Ah shit. She meant business. I attempted to ignore it as I went to hang up the suit on the garment rack. "It wasn't Ender, was it?"

I missed the garment rack completely and almost lost my own footing. My misstep sent the suit into a metallic heap on the floor. If she didn't think I was guilty before, she sure as hell thought I was guilty about *something* now. Scrambling, I bent down, scooping up the suit and hanger. I attempted to cover my fluster by laughing at myself.

Cadence wasn't buying it.

"Ender makes you soft, Tiff."

"He does not."

"Oh yes he does." She pushed off the wall and stepped over to me. "Your hackles haven't been raised in weeks. No more of you sulking about with your nose buried in a book or your eReader. Lately, they've been *firmly* affixed to a certain set of tall pitcher buns." She pantomimed an ass tweak for good measure.

"Just because you're banging the former catcher does not mean that I'm sleeping with a player, too."

She cocked a brow. "Who said anything about sleeping with one of the guys?"

Shit.

My guilt was literally seeping from my pores. That was the only explanation for the slip of my tongue. I really needed to shut up as soon as possible.

"Uh…huh…" The skepticism in her voice wasn't promising. "So…are you ever going to tell me what's going on with Ender and why you hate him so much?"

"It's…not that interesting."

Cadence opened her mouth just as Cooper walked into my dressing room. Great. I swear the karma gods were against me today. Just when Ender and I get to figuring ourselves out again, the world had to come sniffing around for some fresh tea.

Except Cooper knew about Ender and my past. He was sworn to secrecy. He just didn't know about the fact that we kind of started dating again. And sleeping together. Not exactly something I wanted to talk about with my big brother.

"Hey, buttface, need a ride home today?"

Cadence sniggered. I rolled my eyes.

"What are you, twelve?"

"At heart!"

I love my brother, but I really wanted to punch him in the face on a daily basis. If only he weren't renting his basement to me for a whole lot less than he should. I had to keep my insults to a minimum.

"Yes, I would love a ride home. Especially since you were the one who fucking brought me to work today." I crossed my arms, shooting him a look. Of which he feigned complete innocence.

"Hey, I don't know what kind of plans you have with your nerd friends."

"Hey!" Cadence and I shot him a look simultaneously. At least she was back on my team. For now. Cooper was walking a thin fucking line. I was getting really close to asking for a ride from Cadence and just hoofing it home.

"You don't have to advertise the fact that you're a dick, you know."

"But then how will people know my charming qualities?" Cooper batted his eyelashes at me, with some sort of mock innocence. Cadence was really trying to hold it together in her little corner. I was ready to throw hands at my asshole brother. With love, of course.

"Oh, they figure that out as soon as you open your fucking mouth."

"Damn," Cooper pushed a drawn-out whistle between his lips. "What crawled up your ass and died?"

"Your sad attempt at being a decent human."

"And a 'fuck you' to you too. I even made Ender do an extra fifty crunches after practice today just for you." I had a sudden flash of a vision of said glistening, flexing biceps. Because I had a filthy front row seat to that body, just the other day. My hormones had some really awful timing.

I was distracted by the questioning look Cadence shot in my direction. Cooper needed to fucking shut up or I was in for another lengthy interrogation from my best friend. And I still needed a ride home.

Now I was stuck debating between getting a barrage of questions on the way home from Cadence or my brother picking on me. It was a lose-lose situation. But Cooper was still the safer choice.

"Well, my loveable asswipe, I'm leaving in like fifteen minutes. So be there or be square." Cooper shot finger guns in my direction before offering a polite tip of his head to Cadence.

"So, is there a reason your brother is still picking on Ender for you?"

"It's just, Ender–"

My mouth gaped open like a fish as my brain desperately tried to think of something. Only for karma to show up next in line, literally knocking at my door, ready to smack me around a bit.

"You rang?" Ender's head popped through my open door with a big ass dopey grin. Like Cooper, he was completely unaware of the fact that Cadence was there at first.

I couldn't help the immediate way my face lit up seeing my goofy, handsome giant of a baseball player. Cadence inhaled sharply, giving herself away as she pointed accusingly at me and mouthed *"soft"* in my direction.

"Oh hi, Ender." Cadence cooed, putting extra-long emphasis on the I in "hi". "Are you going to ask Tiffiny if she needs a ride too?"

Ender's handsome face softened with concern as he turned back to look at me. "You need a ride home?"

"I–"

Cadence was making faces at me from out of Ender's line of sight. The woman was like a cartoon character, trying to get her "I was right about something" point across in pantomime.

"Nope! I'm all good. Cooper is taking me home."

"Oh…good." Ender's face must have noticed my twisted expression as his voice reflected his confusion. He shrugged. "Oh well… See you tomorrow then, Iffy." He said casually, as if it was still second nature and the ballpark was just the halls of Garden Valley High School.

He suddenly realized his grave mistake. He had unassumingly used my very private nickname. In public. A nickname that was only between the two of us and one that no one else was akin to. Well, except his mom.

Until now.

Fucking dammit.

I had just gotten Cadence somewhat under control, and Ender just had to drop that fucking bomb. Thank fuck my brother had left already, or else I would have felt completely outnumbered in the barrage of questions that I knew would immediately follow.

Cadence's mouth was hanging open as she moved her stare back and forth between Ender and me. I had to sever this conversation while I still had a chance. Because I needed to make it out of this ballpark alive. Without dying from embarrassment or HR catching wind of Ender and me kind of sort of dating.

"Bye, Cadence, bye Ender!" I exclaimed as delightfully unperturbed as possible. I grabbed my purse and made a beeline for the door. "Gotta go catch up to my brother, he's my ride."

And I left it at that.

PINE

UNUSUAL DEMONT

"We have to be more careful at work."

Iffy's voice pulled me out of my daydream. I didn't realize that I'd been staring at her, perusing the bookshelves of The Broken Spine, a new to us romance bookstore in the Brewerytown area of Philadelphia. It was tucked inside an adorable artisan shop down a side street off Girard Avenue, just north of the Art Museum.

"Oh…yeah."

Fuck, I kind of sort of forgot about the whole forbidden romance trope aspect of our relationship. Coworkers dating wasn't exactly kosher. Cadence and Jamie were borderline. Because by the time everyone found out about it, officially anyway, Jamie was called back up to the majors.

"I don't want either of us to lose our jobs." She sighed, plucking a book off the shelf, admiring the cover. Our favorite dates of late have been picking a new local indie bookstore once a week to shop at. "But I'm…not ready to tell anyone. Not yet. I'm still getting used to the thought of *us* again, myself."

I knew I hurt Tiffiny when I broke up with her. I was doing everything in my power to make it up to her. To show her that I was hopelessly devoted to her. To us.

For many reasons, I didn't want to overwhelm her, so it was baby steps. More than anything, I wanted for her to break down her walls and let me in all the way. But this wasn't something we could rush.

"So, no more flirting at work. Got it."

"I mean," There was something in her tone that led me to believe that she wasn't overly fond of that idea. It made me smile. "Subtle flirting is okay. It just needs to be, you know… Discrete."

"Mmm, so you like my flirts, huh?"

She pursed her lips, trying to hide her smile as she playfully shoved my bicep. "Don't let it all go to your head."

"I mean, too late. Remember, I have a praise kink that needs to be fed, you know."

Tiffiny shot me a dark look as she moved on to the next shelf. We had already amassed a small pile that I was currently holding onto. Nothing like our first bookstore trip, but she was more than welcome to splurge if she wanted to. The Broken Spine was incredibly well curated. Even I was finding it difficult to narrow down my choices. They focused a lot on the harder-to-find indie authors. Plus, having them signed was too enticing to say no to.

"Speaking of kinks…" That got my attention immediately. "Has anything sounded fun to you in the books I recommended?"

"I think the shorter list is what *didn't* sound fun enough to try."

Iffy's gaze locked with mine. Something got deliciously dark in the depths, and I felt my cock stirring in my jeans.

I learned my lesson by now to not wear any loose-fitting clothing around Tiffiny. I couldn't trust how my body reacted to hers in public. This instance was the reason as to why I chose to wear jeans on a day when it was 90 degrees outside.

"Oh yeah? Interested in trying some *new* flavors other than vanilla?"

"I think so. Just none of that cuckholding stuff." Tiffiny blinked. "There's no fucking way I'm sharing you with anyone, let alone *watch* it happen." My voice had turned a bit growly and possessive. She quickly turned away, but I caught the rosy bloom on her cheeks. It only egged me on. "Although… Watching you, fucking yourself, now that's something else altogether."

Tiffiny whipped a book off the shelf and, without sparing it a glance, began to fan herself with it. She stayed quiet for a long moment, staring at the bookshelves in front of her. Her eyes were darting around too much to actually be reading the spines. She only managed a few more steps before she briskly turned towards me.

"Do you want to get out of here?"

She didn't have to ask me twice.

We checked out with our books. The shop owner was very sweet. She was sure to point out the shop's upcoming events and hoped we would come to some of them. Tiffiny opted for a printed copy of their events calendar, as I wasn't entirely sure the woman could think straight after our conversation. I couldn't either, but book events, and the possibility of future dates with Iffy sounded good to me. Depending on the team schedule.

I drove back to her place. We grabbed fast food on the way home, eating in the car, mostly in silence. I had a feeling we were going to need our strength for whatever Tiffiny was thinking about in that dirty brain of hers. The kink conversation still sat with me, along with my half-hard cock.

I found a spot down the block from her apartment. After parallel parking, I went to turn my car off, but her hand stopped me. Her head cocked thoughtfully for a moment, apparently listening to something. It was then that I realized what she figured out.

"Is this…" She glanced over at me, her gaze a bit glassy. "The song mix you made me back in high school?"

"One of them, yeah," I admitted, sheepishly.

"Wait, you kept them all?"

"Well…yeah. Why wouldn't I?"

Tiffiny melted into the passenger seat a little. I was serious every damn time I told her that she was my forever. I was going to have a playlist of all the songs I gave her throughout our relationship. Despite the hurt I felt listening to them, they were part of my regular rotation and made me feel something.

"I uh, added some new songs to the list since then. You know… Anything that reminded me of you."

Her hand flew to my chest, her hand grabbing a fist of my shirt before she pulled me to her for a kiss. Grinning against her eager mouth, I kissed her back. It suddenly got a lot more heated in my AC-cooled car.

"Can you like…stop being cute for a solid minute?" She murmured against my mouth as she took a moment to catch her breath.

"Nope. It's impossible."

Tiffiny let out a heated huff as she reluctantly let me go. Taking a moment to catch her breath, she grabbed her bag of books and purse and got out of the car. I scrambled after her, quickly turning off the ignition to my car before taking wide strides down the street to catch up with her.

Before I could open my mouth to say anything, she shot me a hard look. I swallowed, unsure of what she was thinking.

"You're making it hard to stay mad at you."

"Iffy, I'm more than willing to do anything to prove to you that I'm in this, head over heels."

She was quiet again as we stepped up to her front door. The silence continued as she unlocked the door and gestured me inside before closing it behind us. Did she not understand that I was absolutely one hundred percent serious about her? The dates, the text messages, me nabbing every single second of a chance to talk to her? To show her how much I cared for her with my words, my mouth, *my body*?

"Can you be quiet?"

The question hit me in the middle of my tailspin of thoughts about the only woman I ever truly wanted in my entire life.

"I...uh, yeah. Why?"

"Good, because my brother is probably upstairs and you have some begging to do."

Grabbing me by the hand, she dragged me down the familiar path to her bedroom. She dropped my hand as soon as we were through the doorway. Closing the door behind me, she marched over to some sort of white noise machine on her bedside table and turned it on. A soothing constant hush noise sounded. Something in her shoulders deflated a little.

"I want you to understand that what you did back in high school hurt me. A lot." I opened my mouth to speak, but she held a hand up, cutting me off. "These last few weeks have been blissful. Honestly, the happiest I've been in a while. Even Cadence noticed." I couldn't help but smile at that.

"But I just can't shake this feeling that history is going to repeat itself. That you're just going to find some hot girl in the stands, a wannabe WAG, a cleat-chaser that will fawn all over you, and you'll forget all about me all over again–"

"Tiffiny you have to understand–" I took a step forward, desperate to envelop this woman in my arms and give her all the comfort and reassurance that was humanly possible so she would never doubt me, even for a moment, ever again.

"More than anything, I want to be yours. Officially. Again. No more pretenses or hiding or any more of this bullshit." Tears were starting to pool in the corner of her eyes. I fisted my hands at my sides because her body language was screaming at me to keep my distance. "You keep doing all of this cute shit and going out of your way for me, and yet I still can't get the thought of you leaving out of my head."

"I said it once, and I'll say it again. I'm here for the long haul." I took one timid step towards her, and she didn't move. In fact, she looked defeated. Raw and open. I couldn't stand it any longer.

In two long strides, I scooped her into my arms, embracing her so hard that both of us had trouble breathing. I held on for dear life, not wanting to let go until she sucked every living breath out of me. Just so she could stop hurting for even a moment. My heart hurt. It hurt for her. For all the years of pain I'd given her because of one fleeting moment in my life.

I wasn't worthy of her. That was why I couldn't bring myself to go and ring her doorbell that night when I ran away from Regina. She was the most brilliantly beautiful woman to have ever walked the planet, and I messed that up.

Every part of her was amazing, inside and out. I loved her snarkiness, her knowledge, and her love of books. The fact that she could thrust random impressive vocab words into casual conversation without batting an eye always took my breath away. Even when the world thought she was dark and snarky, she had love and light on the inside for those she cared about.

"I love you, Tiffiny Campanaro." I breathed the words into her hair as I felt her body shake with the tears that I had no doubt were falling. "I've never stopped loving you. I knew it that day when I stood on your front sidewalk. I knew it to the very depths of my soul. So much so that it scared me."

We stood holding onto each other for a long moment. The wash of emotions surging between us was like waves against the shore. It was intense, but something in the air between us had changed. Something for the better. At least I hoped so.

Tiffiny slowly lifted her head. Her tear-stained cheeks and bloodshot eyes tugged at my heartstrings. Her lower lip trembled a bit. The ache in my heart from seeing her like this was almost too painful to bear.

Ever so gently, I cupped her face. I used the pad of my thumb to brush away a runaway tear rounding the convex peak of her cheek. It was warm.

"I love you," I whispered to her again as I pulled her face to mine. The kiss was deep, full-bodied. I put every ounce of my love and devotion to her in it. "I love you."

I only managed one more sentiment of love before the kissing became much more heated. Desperate. She was sending me such intense emotions each time our lips met that it left me breathless.

Suddenly, we were a blur of touches, kisses, and grabbing at clothing. Iffy grabbed a hold of my shirt, ripping it up and over me before tossing it away. Since her hands were busy, mine moved in the opposite direction of hers, reaching for the waistband of her leggings and shoving them down her thighs. I felt her body shift as she used her feet to kick the garment off the rest of the way.

Our bodies slotted back against one another as our kisses moved into fevered. The raw emotion passing between us had my heart almost beating out of my chest. I could only hope she felt some semblance of the same thing.

"I fucked up so badly back then. And I'm going to spend the rest of my life asking for your forgiveness and begging for you to love me back."

Because I was sorry.

So, fucking sorry.

Utterly beyond sorry.

With every kiss, it only cemented the fact that this woman was my everything. She always had been. That she always will be.

"We really are two idiots in love, aren't we?"

I couldn't help but laugh. "Yeah, I guess we are." My brow cocked as my brain finally caught up with her supposed connotation in her words. "Wait… Does that mean you love me back?"

Iffy stilled and avoided my questioning gaze. "Maybe?" She went quiet again. "You just have to do something first."

I blinked in surprise, thrilled that I had a moment to prove myself. "Anything."

She disengaged herself from my arms, shoving me back a bit as she turned and plopped down on her bed. I felt her gaze on me, caressing my bare torso with a heated gaze from ten feet or so away. My dick was going to go to full mast any second if she stared at me for any longer.

"I want you to get down on your knees…" I was a bit taken aback by the assertive demand with a sultry undertone. I honestly didn't know if I should be scared or turned on.

Or both.

"On your knees, Ender." She said, much more firmly that time as I'd been standing there, staring at her with my mouth agape. My spine went ramrod straight. Before she could say anything else, I lowered myself to my knees.

I watched as her eyes narrowed, drinking in the movement. Leaning back, she propped herself on her hands, stretched out behind her. She looked like some sort of delicious dark queen. The tear tracks were still evident on her face, but no more tears in sight.

"Crawl to me."

Okay.

I finally understood.

I finally understood why Tiffiny liked those dark romances. This shit? This shit was fucking hot.

"Crawl to me and apologize. Apologize and swear you'll never do that kind of shit to me again."

Swallowing my pride, I did as she asked. I lowered my fists to the floor, settling onto all fours for a moment before I made the slow but steady way over to her. I would do anything to prove to her that I was absolutely serious about her. About us.

Cocking her head to the side, her eyes were glued to my crawling form as I dug my knuckles and knees into the plush carpet of her bedroom. Her thighs parted ever so slightly, and from this angle I could see straight to heaven. Fuck, this was getting hotter by the second.

I arrived at her feet, locking eyes with her as I bent down, lower and lower as I watched her eyes grow wider and wider. I paused for only a moment before brushing a kiss against the top of her foot. Iffy seemed to stop breathing.

So, I did it again.

And again.

Slowly working up her shin, I paused at her knee.

"I will spend every," A kiss on the side of her knee. "Single." Another kiss. "Day." Yet another. "Making up for my past transgressions to you." One last kiss, right on the crown of her knee.

I felt her skin prickle more and more with each new kiss. She was so warm under my lips. Becoming more pliable by the second as I poured my heart out to her. She had to know.

"I'm sorry, Tiffiny. I'm sorry for being a self-centered asshole. I'm sorry for being scared. I'm sorry that I just didn't talk to you about my feelings. I'm sorry that I felt that I had to figure it out elsewhere."

Her eyes sparkled again as tears welled along her bottom lashes. Leaning forward, her hand reached out. It cupped my chin as she tilted my jaw up to catch her intense gaze. My god she was beautiful.

"I love you. I love you so fucking much. I've only been sure about two things in my life. Baseball, and you. But if I ever had to choose, it would always be you. I'd always choose you." I couldn't stop the words now. The dam had been broken. "I'll get a boring corporate job somewhere. Buy you a house in the suburbs and be home by six every night. Anything that would make you happy. I'm devoted to you, Tiffiny. Hopelessly and forever devoted to you."

A singular note of silence passed between us before she let out a breath she'd been holding. Tears began spilling down her face all over again. Her other hand joined the first on my face, cradling me right where she wanted.

I could taste the salt on her lips as she kissed me, soft and sweet. My hands curled around her wrists, holding her there as we got our fill of each other.

"Well, damn." She sniffled, pulling away from our kisses just a bit. "I wanted to be all hot and sexy and demanding. Instead, I'm a lovestruck, bumbling mess. So much for role play."

"Hell no, *mi amor*. You can boss me around any time." I turned my head, gracing her palm with a kiss. "Do you believe me now?"

A heavy sigh left her entire body before her lower lip started to tremble again. I stretched my thumb up to reach her cheek, brushing away the new tears. It broke my heart to see her cry like this, but at least they were happy tears.

"I do, Ender. I do. Honestly… I have since you told me. But there was just this doubt eating me away deep inside. I didn't want to give my heart away to you just for you to trample all over it again."

"Never." I kissed her forehead. "Never ever again."

"Promise?"

"I promise you forever and ever."

Her lips found mine again. This time, I felt her smile against my mouth, and my whole body relaxed. Slanting my mouth against hers, I deepened the kiss, feeling the warmth pass between us.

"I love you, Ender."

The moment she mumbled those words against my mouth I felt my heart stop. Never in a million years did I ever think I'd hear them again. That I had ruined the best thing I ever had, because it took me too long to realize that my love and devotion to Tiffiny was the real deal.

The forever kind of deal.

"I love you, Tiffiny." I murmured back through my grin. Standing quickly, my mouth stayed on hers as my hands scooped her up under her ass and tossed her further onto the middle of the bed. "And now that's out of the way," I crawled atop of her, caging her in, letting my voice get low and smoky. "Let's have some fun."

Her eyes went wide, tears all gone from her lashes as I dove in for a heated kiss. My hands moved to my jeans, making quick work of them and my boxer briefs so I could focus on her. I let out a sigh against her mouth as my cock sprang free, already hard. Just from the idea of physically showing this woman how much I loved her.

Tiffiny laughed into my kisses, a sound that set delicious fire to my body. "What kind of fun?"

With a grin in reply, I pressed my bare hips into the V of her thighs, slowly dragging the underside of my dick up and down right at her core.

"I have some ideas."

Another laugh filtered into my mouth as I pressed my body deeper into hers. This time, I got a heady groan out of her. What I wouldn't do to this woman. Curse the fact that men only got one good cumshot. Although perhaps that was the fail-safe. Because if I didn't have a conscious stopping point, I wouldn't stop making love to this woman. At least not until my heart gave out or my cock snapped off. Whichever came first.

The kisses grew to an obscene level, hot and heavy as I ground against her. The noises she was making were ones that I could get drunk on.

I went through the mental list of what she liked sexually. Using my pelvis to press my hard cock right up against her clothed clit. It sent a trail of fiery delight up my spine. Meanwhile, her kisses grew more desperate as she seemed bound and determined to suck my toenails from their roots through the connection of our mouths alone.

"I've been dying to fuck you again ever since you signed with the team." She groaned against my lips, the confessions falling with uninhibited ease from her mouth. "Those fucking frosted tips. Do you have any idea how hot you look? How sweet you are?"

Goddamn it if my cock wasn't harder than a piece of titanium outfitted for the space program, ready to withstand the dozen or so G-forces to shoot clear across space. Or withstand well, Tiffiny. What a way to boost a man's ego.

Did she mean that we could have been doing this all along? That I could have been drilling her clear through her mattress, into the concrete floor of her basement apartment, if only we had been upfront with each other sooner?

I needed to make up for lost time.

"On your back, Roche." Her voice was rough with want as she shoved her palms against my chest, nudging me back. The way she was assertive was doing nothing to help the *hard* situation in my crotch. Eager to see where this was going, I obliged her.

In two breaths she had her shirt up and over her head, her bra immediately following. Goddamn, she was incredible. Especially when she looked at me like she wanted to swallow me whole.

Licking her lips, she bent down, parting the side of her mouth as she encompassed my tip. I inhaled sharply, throwing my head back as I felt her tongue caress against the flushed head. She didn't allow me another breath as she swallowed me back, deeper and deeper until she bottomed out on me with a wet, choking sound.

Fuuuccckkkk.

GIVE YOU LOVE

FOREST BLAKK

"**S**o are we like boyfriend and girlfriend now?"

I asked Ender as I pulled off of his rigid dick with a brisk inhale, letting oxygen fill my lungs again. The man looked like he barely had two brain cells to rub together to form a coherent response. But there was a sparkle of surprise and delight in his eyes.

"I–If you'll have me…" Ender croaked out, haphazardly propping himself up on his elbows to look at me. "Again."

I brushed a kiss against the tip of his cock, watching it flex and bob with excitement. "I'd say that's a possibility."

"W–Will you be my girlfriend? Again?" I gave his erection a few slow pumps as I pondered the question. Ender made a noise as he gritted his teeth together. "And I'm not just asking because you have your hand on my dick."

I threw my head back with a laugh. "So romantic."

"Look, I will ask you again in the most romantic way possible, but right now I fucking need you, mi amor."

Damn, I loved a man who begged. I loved a begging Ender even more. Especially when he dropped sweet sentiments.

"It's so hot when you call me that."

"What? *Mi amor?*"

"Mmmhmm…" I nodded, my lips pursed as my eyes closed.

"But you are mi amor. Mi amor forever."

The words washed over me like a soothing balm. The sweet sincerity in his tone healing the wounds he had left in my heart. I knew at that moment I'd only be complete if I could hear that every day for the rest of our lives. But I wasn't going to tell him that. Not yet.

With my hand still on his dick, I crawled up his body. He welcomed me with open arms, tilting his chin up to give in to the kiss I sought out. Soft groans filtered past my lips as I pumped him, nice and slow, as my tongue slipped into his mouth.

I didn't give him a chance to return the favor as I backed away, settling back between his thighs. Flicking my tongue around in my mouth, I gathered all the saliva there. Tilting my head down, I pursed my lips and spat on his cock. It jerked as the hot liquid hit his tip. Using my fist, I worked the saliva up and down the shaft.

Ender was practically writhing on the bed at this point, watching me with fire in his eyes. I was going to get it for sure later. That much I was counting on.

Once his shaft was glistening, my hands moved to my breasts. My palms and fingertips caressed along the heaving masses, massaging and squeezing, getting a rise out of Ender with a few expletives.

Biting my lower lip, I cupped my breasts and leaned forward, slotting his dick between them.

I watched as he fell back to the bed, his back arching with the jolt of pleasure that for sure made its way up his spine. His head snapped back up, not wanting to miss a second of the show. Half a second later, his hips began to rock, following the slow bob of my torso. He was fucking my tits, looking positively wrecked as he did so.

The glistening, flushed tip sprang forth and disappeared into my cleavage for a few more strokes. I tipped my chin down, letting another gob of spit fly to lubricate the fun. Ender's groan almost shook the walls.

"Are you actively trying to kill me, Iffy?"

"No," I grinned. "Just egg you on so you'll punish me later when you show me what else you've studied in your reading material."

Ender had told me that after every book he read that I recommended, he looked up my reviews and annotations. They were public domain. But never in my entire life did I think I'd have a man reading through them and *taking notes* before implementing them on me.

So far, it's been rather fun. But with him so much bigger than me, I kind of had a feeling that he wasn't willing to push the limit. I wasn't going to break easily. Hell, I'd be happy if he did break me. So much so that I'd give him a hearty "thank you" from my puddle-like state.

He only lasted a few more thrusts before he moved so fast. I had barely registered his hands on my body, grabbing me and flipping me. I found myself face-first into the bedding. Unbelievably hot and bothered with how effortlessly he manhandled me.

I was still in awe at his strength and speed. His hips pressed me into the mattress, grinding his cock into the crevice of my ass. His hand reached over, haphazardly grabbing a few condoms from the box in my drawer, depositing them onto the bed like metallic confetti.

A sultry laugh escaped me as I felt my panties slide down over my ass, down my thighs, before disappearing completely. I felt a hazy sting against the plump skin of my ass as Ender's hand offered a glancing blow of a spank. Well, that was hot and came out of nowhere. Another soon followed, and I moaned, dropping my head back to the bedding as his thighs had mine pinned to the bed.

"Do you like that, mi amor?" Ender purred, and I vigorously nodded, not trusting the lust in my voice right now. Another slap against my ass, and I was almost a goner. "Good girl."

Oh my god, he did not just drop a loving "good girl" on me after spanking me.

I felt the third delicious sting of his palm against my ass as his hands gripped onto my hips, pulling me to my knees. He was being rougher, but the gentleness of Ender was prevalent. I moved to prop myself on my hands, but I felt Ender's hand against my shoulder blades, shoving me back now.

"Ah ah ah." He tutted as his hands went back to my ass. There was a bit of shyness to his words. But I knew the more I complied, the more he would get into this sexy new role he was trying out.

A gentle nudge of his knee left to right between my thighs, and I adjusted mine against the mattress, spreading myself wider for him. There was an approving noise that rumbled deep in his chest. I couldn't help but grin to myself.

"Do me a favor?" Ender's voice was gruff.

"Yeah?"

"Spread yourself open for me, Iffy. I want to admire you for a sec."

Jeezus fucking hell.

I took a slow inhale and shifted, reaching behind to grab my ass cheeks, doing as he asked. The stretch of my skin felt sinful. My cunt flexed with the feel of the cool air against my molten core.

"Mmm."

His guttural noise of approval was something I wish I had gotten a recording of, so I could listen to it on repeat. Because fuck all those dirty audiobooks. The noises my *boyfriend* made while looking at my bare center practically made me cum on the spot.

"Is that good?"

"Mmmhmm, just like that, mi amor." He praised. "I'm trying to memorize you exactly like this to keep me company for the road trip next week."

Fuck.

There was a hitch to his breath as I felt the subtle movement of the bed. Lifting my head to cast a glare behind me, I was blessed with an utter vision. Ender was on his knees, his core muscles engaged as he leaned back on one hand. All while the other slowly pumped his cock, licking his lips as he did so. Fucking hell. I sure hope he knew that what he was doing was doing the same thing my body was doing for him.

I felt the bed dip as he pressed his knee into the mattress right next to my leg. There was a subtle shift before I felt his thumb stroke up and down my slit. It was like throwing water on a live wire. The jolt was electric as it ran up my spine. Only for it to be joined by another one as he slowly rubbed the underside of his cock along my slit, coating his erection with my desire.

The man was going to be the death of me.

My ghost would have to come back from the great beyond to haunt him with my sincerest of thanks.

As quickly as he started, the sensation was gone, leaving me spread open, bare, and whimpering with the loss. The bed moved again, and suddenly I felt his ravenous mouth all over as he began to devour me. My legs shook from the immediate pleasure.

He spared no expense as his tongue and lips moved with such toe-curling purpose. My skin prickled as the tip of his tongue slipped out, flicking and wriggling against my clit. I saw ten million galaxies' worth of stars behind my eyes as he greedily sucked it into his mouth. The moment his thumb slipped under his lips and into me, I pressed my screams into the bedding. Hoping that between the fabric and white noise it would muffle it enough for my brother to never be the wiser to the fact that one of his pitchers was face-deep into my vagina.

I'd barely come off the high of my orgasm before Ender seamlessly slipped on a condom, grabbed my hips, and buried himself into the deepest recesses of me. That garnered a scream of pleasure, the comforter beneath my mouth moist from my hot breath and saliva.

He didn't stop there. His thrusts came sharp and quick. The uptick of his hips in this position sent him even deeper inside me.

"Yes, yes, yes…" I breathed out. The rhythm of the chant matched his thrusts. I tossed my head back so I could inhale a lungful of cold oxygen.

My scalp stung as he grabbed a fistful of my hair, holding my head in the arched back position so he could hear each ragged, whimpering breath. It took everything in my power not to scream like I wanted to. I couldn't help the yelp that fell from my parted lips as Ender spanked my ass again.

I felt myself tumbling into a much bigger oblivion in no time flat. My upper teeth clamped down for dear life on my bottom lip, using it as a filter to tamper the noise as I groaned out. Ender's approving noises only fueled the intimate fire that burned so deeply within me.

With only a moment to catch my breath, Ender disengaged himself as he spun me around, putting me on my back. I'd barely gotten my bearings before he pulled me with him as he fell backwards onto the bed. His hands with a firm touch on my hips, lining me up before dropping me right back down on his cock.

My hands shot out, propping myself up on his chest. The sensation of my entire body buzzing from the almost back-to-back orgasms was sending my body into an epic tailspin. Changing positions mid-orgasm had the room spinning. My pleasure receptors went straight into the stratosphere.

"Ride me, Iffy. Hard. Soft. I don't care. I just want to watch you come undone this time." The pads of his thumbs traced lazy circles at the jut of my hips, encouraging me to move. To chase my own pleasure at the expense of using his.

Leaning down, I kissed him. So rich and full of emotion as my hips slowly began to rock. I felt his fingertips dig into the heft of my ass as his pelvis rolled beneath mine.

"I love you," I whispered across his lips, using this softer interlude to my full advantage.

"I love you too." He grinned right back. His skin glowed from the perspiration of his previous efforts.

With one last kiss, I managed to prop myself up. My hands roamed his toned torso, tracing the lines of his muscles as my hips began their meticulously slow rock. Slow and thorough. I could see the strain on his features as he gritted his teeth, his hard gaze trained on my body.

How could one look at this man make me feel like an absolutely gorgeous and irresistible human? I'd never felt more beautiful and desired in my entire life. I was so hopelessly in love with this man. I had been ever since high school.

That was why the breakup hurt so much. I'd been so sure he was my forever. Sure, over the years, I touted it as a stupid high school love where you thought you were adult enough to have your whole life figured out. Anything to lessen the pain of him being out of my life.

Now that we were back together, officially, I felt the warmth of happiness flooding back through my veins. I felt put back together. I had found my missing half all over again. And it really was just as good as all those cheesy romance books touted it to be.

Our bodies moved as one, languid at first, but I quickened my pace, desperate for Ender and me to climax together. To truly engrain this reunion into one intimately physical moment. He followed my lead, pumping his hips up into me.

It seemed that our breaths and heartbeats were tuned in time as we both chased that sweet, sweet release in the pleasure we shared. My body jerked slightly as Ender's thumb found my clit between us, applying pressure and rubbing in gentle circles. My whimper sounded in the room as he worked me. Closer and closer to that oblivion.

"Cum with me, mi amor. I'm so close. Fuck… I want to feel you grip my cock inside you and don't let go until you are fucking satisfied." Ender panted out, desperate and begging all over again.

I did not have Ender talking dirty on my bingo card this year, but fucking hell, I was here for it. Leaning forward, I brace myself on my palms on either side of his head. It brought us almost nose to nose. He slipped his hand out from between us, giving me full leverage to chase our orgasms.

There was a hard set to his jaw. He must have been so close to his peak, holding out just for me. So I rode him. I rode him hard and fast, panting and moaning as I pulled him closer to oblivion. His moans mingled with mine.

He tipped me forward a bit, angling his hips in a way that gave him room to move. Once he was in position, he began to piston in and out of me. My jaw dropped open, unable to utter a sound as he sent me careening into the great beyond. The second he felt my walls clench around him, he let himself go, pumping hard and deep into me. All while his hips continued to move, but in shallower thrusts.

Thank fuck Ender took over because I was frozen on the spot. My body cumming and pulsing all around him as pleasure hit me in stormy waves. Little by little, I felt my body relax, all languid and pliable atop him as I slowly eased myself down to rest my body on his.

Ender stilled beneath me. A warm embrace settled around my body, holding me tight to him. Our breathing slowly evened out. I could feel myself already dozing, lulled by the steady beat of his heart beneath my ear.

"Everything feels right again," Ender whispered as his fingers stroked through my hair.

I couldn't agree more.

I MUST BE IN LOVE

AARON TAOS

All-Star break had been absolutely blissful.

Sexed up and blissful.

Cooper had gone on vacation with his wife's family to the Jersey shore. Which left Tiffiny and me with all the sexual freedoms we could want to have sex as often and as loudly as possible. It was hot. Freeing. Utterly euphoric.

Okay, so we hadn't exactly spent the *entire* time making love. We did binge a few television shows, watched a few movies, and took a few day trips to indie bookstores in Delaware and New Jersey. Just to pass the very short few days we had without a lick of baseball. Well, and of course, had dinner with Mamá.

She was all too thrilled that we were officially back together. The smile hadn't left her face the entire evening. Iffy and I couldn't get enough of each other. Always touching. Always smiling. Always happy.

I was happy.

Happy once *again*.

I felt whole for the first time in a long time. Complete. So utterly in love that the world seemed brighter.

The downside was the fact that the team seemed to catch on to something being different in my life. My pitches were sharper. My strike count had improved. Even with the distraction of a certain wandering mascot in the stands.

Tiffiny was proud of me. Proud of all I'd accomplished. She even got the crowd to cheer for me when I nabbed another strikeout. My favorite moments were when she waited by the dugout, just like old times, to give me a high five against the plush white Mickey Mouse-like glove of the Ding Dong costume.

It was a little weird to remind myself that, despite the giant hat and googly eyes that liked to rotate in their sockets, my girlfriend was the one who brought the character to life.

Heh.

My *girlfriend*.

Tiffiny was the only person that title was ever meant for. To think about her as my girlfriend again made me so insanely giddy on the inside. My skin prickled with delight and the implications.

I had formally asked her to be my girlfriend just a few days after the, well, rather *spicy*, vomit of words on my part when she had a hold of my dick. Surprised her with flowers and my dopey self on her doorstep with the question on my lips. While she probably thought it was silly, she didn't stop smiling for the rest of the night.

I had my girl. A career that I loved, and I was good at.

Life was perfect.

"Since Ender," I jerked from my daydream. *Oh fuck, right.* I was in the middle of a team meeting with the coach. "...missed our last big dance number, I think it's only fair that he gets to star in the next one." Hoots and hollers sounded across the locker room. I groaned.

"Look, that wasn't my fault I–" Not that I really wanted to explain the real reason why I got a concussion.

"You went and got a concussion just to get out of wearing a pink rhinestone jersey." Truitt's hand clapped onto my shoulder as he gave me a mock serious look. "We all know that's the reason." I swatted his hand away as he snickered, jumping back a few steps and back to his seat.

"So, anyway… I was thinking, and I came up with a great song selection for his big dance number." Cadence's gaze swept over to mine. Her lips pursed, trying to suppress a smile. Usually, her music selections were so on point that I wasn't exactly afraid of what she was going to suggest. *"Ring My Bell."*

Except that fucking one.

The absolute all-knowing look she shot me nailed me right onto the metal locker room bench seat. I felt color drain from my face. I mean, I had an inkling that Cadence was onto Tiffiny and me. I just didn't think she was going to make a mockery of it. I wonder who had put her up to this? Maybe Cooper. It sounded like a Cooper sort of thing to do.

"Hell yeah! Taking it old school!" Schmidt jumped out of his seat with his fists raised in the air. There were mutual cheers of excitement around the room.

"Two words: Bell bottoms," Camden added, and there was a mix of laughter and agreement. This was going downhill fast. Although at least no one made a snide comment about me making lovey dovey eyes on the daily at the mascot. Yet.

"Ender," My name on Cadence's lips pulled me back to face my coach. "You'll be having a little duet dance with Tiff in the Ding Dong costume. You know, to fit the theme and all."

Fuck me.

My choreography coach was a sadist. I was sure of it. Of course, she did hang out with Tiffany on the regular, so I shouldn't be surprised. Cadence just seemed like a more light-hearted person instead of a vindictive one.

"D–Does Tiffiny know about this?"

"Oh," a wicked little smile curled at her lips as she crossed her arms in front of her. "She will shortly."

Like clockwork, Iffy walked in, trying her best to ignore the locker room chaos as she tried to sneak off to her dressing room.

"Speak of the devil," Cadence murmured under her breath as she turned to address the beloved mascot. Tiffiny was just coming in from her after the game nonsense. Ding Dong's disembodied head was tucked under her arm. "Hey Tiffiny?"

I watched as she stopped, clearly annoyed to be distracted from her mission. She did look rather adorable in the shiny gold bell-shaped dress, looking cartoony from the neck down. Especially with the fact that each step sent her knees knocking into the very questionable ringer ball.

"What?"

Truitt and Camden sniggered in their corner at Tiffiny's attitude. Some of the other guys looked worried. I tried to remain neutral, considering that I'd been daydreaming about said mascot only a few minutes ago. Cadence looked absolutely smug.

"You have an assignment." Cadence grinned, her voice almost sing-song with her delight.

"For what?"

"A dance number."

"Oh no… I told you I didn't want–"

"Your theater talents going to waste? Don't worry, girl, I gotchu."

Tiffiny shot her a glare that was positively daggers. "Uh huh. And just what the hell do you have planned?"

"You're going to be the star of the next big dance number I'm working on!"

Iffy's brow dropped as her lips pressed into a thin line. She'd been an incredible dancer in all of the high school musicals. So I did not doubt her ability. But I assumed that the mascot costume wasn't the easiest thing to dance and move around in.

"Goody." She sighed, changing which arm had Ding Dong's head propped beneath it. "What will I be doing?"

"Dancing with Ender."

Tiffiny's face went white with surprise as her eyes shot to mine. I raised my hands and shook my head, silently promising that I had absolutely nothing to do with this. I directed all the blame to Cadence as I subtly pointed to her. Iffy's eyes narrowed as they moved back to Cadence.

"Extra fun."

Nothing in her tone showed that she thought any of this was fun. I tried to give her a small smile.

Hell, maybe our dance number would be romantic like Jamie and Cadence's had? Although how romantic could we get when there was a giant foam mascot head in the way?

"I think it sounds fun." I timidly offered. The guys were already talking about going full retro with outfits and everything. I even heard some chatter about going to the events team and putting on a full-blown Disco Theme Night. Okay, maybe they were onto something.

Tiffiny's brow furrowed as she moved her gaze to mine. The daggers in her eyes smoothed out to butter knives. We could have fun with this. Like old times.

"Uh huh. Well, alright, you crazies. I'm going to go get this obnoxious thing off of me and shower." Tiffiny grumbled as she turned, heading back down the path she had been set on.

Ah shit.

Suddenly, I was inundated with thoughts of Tiffiny in the shower. Naked.

My cock stirred to life, knocking on the sports cup in my crotch. The last thing I should be doing is chasing after my secret girlfriend at our place of employment, just because she was going to be naked in the next few minutes.

I glanced over at the guys, still chattering, now in various stages of undress. Cadence was talking with Schmidt about whatever crazy ideas I'm sure he had about the new dance number. She headed off to her office as the guys started to get undressed and head for the showers.

Might as well head there too.

RING MY BELL

ANITA WARD

My body was buzzing from all the eye-fucking Ender and I had done throughout the afternoon game. Thank fuck for the super obnoxious head with the camouflage mesh to see out of or else I was sure that I was going to get shit from Cadence. My bestie was starting to sniff me out. Which probably was fairly easy since I was a hormone-induced mess every time Ender walked by.

She really put the nails in the coffin with that dance number bullshit she pulled today. While she had been poking around the whole subject matter of Ender and me, she didn't press any further when I put my hackles up. My bark was worse than my bite.

I loved Ender, but why the hell did I give in to my damn body? Why couldn't we have waited until the off-season to figure this out? No, it had to have been a moment of weakness during ovulation when my innards barked at any half-decent man that walked by. The time of the month when women make some really stupid decisions just to scratch an ancient, biological need.

But now that I had a taste, and the fact that we were back together again, I couldn't stop. Ender was like a drug that I couldn't break the habit of. He was just so sweet, so…hot. Always hot. That's what kept getting me into trouble.

Pacing and deep in thought, perhaps even talking to myself, I didn't hear the soft squeak of my dressing room door. It wasn't until I heard that smooth, masculine voice that made my uterus turn into needy goo that I stopped in my tracks. Glancing over, I cursed my heart for joining in on the betrayal action as Ender grinned at me.

"Escaped the dance number planning chaos, hmm?" He surmised as he locked the door and stalked his way over to me.

"Tried to." I sighed, glancing over my shoulder at him as I put the Ding Dong head over on its stand to air out. "Looks like we're stuck being pawns in Cadence's nonsense."

"Oh, come on. It could be fun." He smiled as he walked over to me, awkwardly wrapping me up in his arms. The skirt of the bell flattened against my knees but tipped up in the back, smacking me across my shoulder blades. We both couldn't help but laugh. "This godforsaken costume, I swear–"

"I think it's pretty hot."

I laughed. Loudly. "Yeah okay. You're insane."

"What, you don't believe me? Again?" He shot back at her, smirking. It was a challenge.

"Who the hell would want this? I mean, it has *Mickey Mouse gloves*." I gestured down at my body before waving the rather large, cartoony, plush white gloves. "I'll tell you who. Nobody."

It was Ender's turn to laugh now. "Try me."

"What? No…" I blinked at him as he shot me a heated look. "You're–You're crazy."

"Maybe a bit." That grin of his turned a bit sensual. My heart started to flutter wildly in my chest as he leaned back in, kissing me. Those kisses quickly wandered. Across my jaw, down my throat, tonguing the high neckline of the black shapewear I wore under the suit. I probably smelled and was overly salty from sweating for the last hour.

"What? Ender, no. We can't do that here–" I protested, stumbling on my own words. He swallowed them down with a kiss that made my toes curl. It boggled my mind that kissing was anywhere on his to-do list because I was still in Ding Dong's costume from the neck down.

Shit.

Giving in to him had totally been a mistake. It was all going to his head. Er, *heads*.

"Why not? Your door is locked."

I snorted. "And that means nothing. Pretty sure rounding the bases *after* a game is called is typically frowned upon. Especially in the mascot's dressing room, where there are clearly zero bases."

My words didn't deter him as he looked me up and down. Something was different about him. He wasn't his timid, simpering self. He was confident. The scent of the ballfield clung to him, masculine and earthy. There was a flex of his forearms and biceps that tested the limits of his sleeves as his fisted hands rested casually on his hips. His tanned skin was still glossy with the remnants of sweat despite the overactive air conditioning in the room.

He was…

Hot.

Like, literally. Figuratively. Spiritually. *Hot.*

"It…it's still not a good idea, Ender." Thank fuck I wasn't ovulating or I would have let him spread me open on my desk by now. And I would have encouraged it wholeheartedly.

"I didn't say it was. I've…just been thinking about you." With every shuffle of his feet closer to me, he coerced me up against my desk, sending the skirt of Ding Dong's bell to flip up in the most inelegant way. Not that it looked like he cared. The way his voice dropped reverberated low in my belly. It made me forget about the stupid costume. "Missing you. *Wanting* you. Every damn day, Iffy."

It had been a few days since we'd managed any time together. The guys being on the road didn't help matters. I just didn't realize just how much until those words, Ender had been *craving* me.

"Ender… I—we shouldn't. What if we get caught? What if we—"

"Iffy, I don't fucking care. I let you go once," His hand shot up, fisting my humidity-riddled ponytail. I felt a sharp tug on my hair, just enough for my stalled half-assed protest to completely fade from my lips. "And now I'm going to go out of my way to remind you that I'm *never* going to do it again." A heated shiver ran down my spine as I felt his lips against the curve of my ear. "Even if it means I have to fuck you in this damn fuzzy suit every day for the rest of your life."

In my time with the Sillys, the stupid Ding Dong costume was nothing more than a deterrent when it came to dating. But it clearly wasn't a deterrent for the *right* kind of guy. Never in my life did I think this costume would be something I'd be fucked in. It was like some weird ass kink a character in a twisted, dark romcom would have. Or the author. But I suppose it could be worse.

He could have asked to fuck me in the Liberty Bell costume with the head *on*.

From there, I lost my train of thought as Ender's mouth found mine. The caress of his hand was insistent against my cheek before his fingers aggressively tangled deeper into my hair. He was doing his best to swallow me whole, kiss by kiss, breath by breath.

My brain could only focus on his mouth on mine as his hands wandered around, trying their best to feel me up through the layers of the Ding Dong costume. It wasn't an easy feat. But hell, I loved a determined man.

His frustration was apparent as he suddenly spun me in place, to face my metal desk. My eyeballs neglected to follow suit as they were still swimming in my skull from the sudden about-face. I didn't even have time to mentally right myself before Ender was already diving into the mascot suit to get to the creamy nougat inside: Me.

The lip of the bell's wired skirt dug into my shoulder blades as he upended the skirt to expose my ass to him. Basically that part of the costume was a pool noodle wrapped around a hoop skirt skeleton that gave the bottom of the bell its shape. I only knew because I had to dismantle the thing to get it dry-cleaned on a semi-regular basis. Which only made this more awkward. But weirdly, hot as fuck.

Ender's caressing lips danced their way down the side of my neck. My head tilted at his leisure, his fist curling tighter around the strands of my hair. I felt utterly cornered, but there was no fucking way I was moving even an inch. Especially as I felt his hard cock grinding into the curve of my ass.

With the costume, I was able to wear simple black shapewear leggings, but that was its only saving grace. My feet were still clad in the obscenely large, fuzzy yellow sneakers. And despite them, I was, hopefully, about to get railed into next week.

Keeping the cumbersome mascot costume at bay was almost a full-time job in and of itself. Ender seemed to have no issue dragging my leggings down over the curve of my ass, panties and all, while he unbuckled his uniform pants with the other. Nothing about this was kosher between two coworkers, but I at least had the smoke screen of my dressing room and bathroom. Both of which were behind a locked door.

I could feel Ender's trembling hands against my bare ass as he fumbled with the condom wrapper that he had someone magically pulled from thin air. Did he suddenly just start carrying them in his baseball pants since we started sleeping together again?

"Ender, please…"

I gasped out, begging for him just to do me already. Every hour that went by with us not joined together felt like a week. As desperate as I was to feel him inside me, Ender took his time to make sure that I was good and ready.

Shifting his hips, he grazed his hand along the inside of my thigh before his palm cupped my heat. The resulting groan had me assuming that he was rather content with what he found. I thought that was it. I thought he'd for sure bury that dick so hard the edge of my desk would leave bruises on my hips.

Despite the heated situation and our less-than-ideal surroundings, he still took his time. His fingers teasingly grazed along my slit as they made their way down towards my swollen clit. My knees nearly buckled as he teasingly swirled atop the bundle of nerves. I was so insanely wet from the very idea of this entire sudden situation that his fingertips glided with ease.

The slow twirl of his fingers had me hypnotized, guiding me closer and closer to a supernova kind of orgasm. But instead of letting me see stars behind my eyelids, he left me hanging on the precipice. My mouth dropped open, ready to plead with him again to stop teasing.

Instead, the normally docile Ender slipped inside of me in one smooth motion. Deep enough, and with enough force, that I felt his balls slap my clit. I let out an inhumane yelp of surprise and delight. Which only resulted in a hand being clamped over my mouth.

Holy shit.

Was I really living one of my darker romances right now?

Even if it was in some twisted, weird ass, romcom sort of way.

Ender let out a guttural groan, smothering the noise as he feasted on what skin he could around my black shapewear's neckline. I couldn't help it. With all the flusters, all at once, my orgasm suddenly gave way like the deprived bitch she was.

I was grateful for Ender's hand to hide my cries. His hand made a tight seal around my lips, and I just let loose. He then chose that moment to start thrusting into me. Giving me all he had.

My palm slammed against the desktop. The sound was muffled, thanks to the cartoony Mickey Mouse-like white gloves on my hands. The man moved fast. All I'd been able to remove was the mascot head. Which, thank fuck. Although it did remind me of that one episode of *Golden Girls* where Rose talked about dating the Goofy character actor. She only broke up with him because he took the Goofy head off.

I swallowed back a laugh as Ender rode out the rest of my orgasm that left me delightfully light-headed. My amusement only lasted half a second. The huffs of exertion behind me made my skin prickle in every delicious way. A delightful shiver shot up my spine as his thrusts got harder and more desperate.

"Oh fuck, Ender…" I whispered out against his slipping fingers. I felt myself spiraling towards a second orgasm that was utterly unexpected. Goddamn it.

A sharp thrust sent the edge of my desk digging into my hips. I gritted my teeth to distract from the pain before Ender's dick distracted me further. Until he laid a firm hand on the plump curve of my ass.

I jumped in surprise more than pain as he used the side of his hand to graze along the cheek for a slap of pleasure instead of punishment.

Holy shit.

Holy shit.

When he did it again, I was less surprised but more turned on than ever. The third time, I had to shove Ding Dong's plush white glove over my mouth and bite down on a digit to muffle my cries. This had actually gone down the road of my kinkier side of things, and I was fucking feral for it.

My body was too, as it felt the heated sting on my ass. His hand spanked me one more time, sending me careening over the edge into an orgasm that had my body blanking out. I stopped breathing, stopped moving. Hell, even my heart probably stopped beating. It was the orgasm to end all orgasms.

After giving me all that shit for being loud, Ender's moan filtered through his gritted teeth as he collapsed against my back. His hips were a bit sloppy as I was vaguely aware of his cock pulsing inside me, pouring every drop of cum into the tip of the condom. My eyes rolled back in my head as I felt ready to drown in a third orgasm just from the sensations of it all.

Minutes passed before arms embraced me, the barest hint of lazy kisses along the edge of my jaw. Ender was breathless as I felt his weight melt into the curve of my back. I would have relished in the comforting and satisfying feel of it all, but the metallic fabric of the Ding Dong costume was not doing us any favors. Nor was the fact that he was still dick-deep inside me. In my dressing room. At our place of *employment*.

I opened my mouth to say something to remind him, but an insistent knock at the door so rudely interrupted me. While at the same time gave me a fucking heart attack.

Shitfuckingdammit.

Ender jerked back, almost as if he had dozed off from the exertions of our sudden tryst that definitely shouldn't have happened. I felt his still half-hard cock slip out of me as he stumbled back, wrestling with his baseball pants around his knees. I swallowed back a whimper at the sudden feel of emptiness, and the lingering thoughts of how his delicious dick had just–

Another knock.

Fuck.

I moved to pull up my leggings only to find my hands still in the stupid, *confounded* plush mascot gloves. With a noise of frustration, I threw them off, hockey style, and somehow managed to wiggle my pants back up and over my ass. Pulling up his pants, Ender shot me a deer-in-the-headlights kind of look towards me as his fingers fumbled with his belt.

"Tiff?"

Both of us shared a look. Even though it was only Cadence at the door, it was going to open a whole can of worms, that I was currently ignoring at the moment if she saw what we'd just been doing.

I knew she'd have a thing or two to say. Ream me out. Do what girl besties do when the other makes bad decisions about good dick.

"Quick!" I hissed at Ender, shoving him into my tiny dressing room bathroom. Like a good boy, he hustled right into the stall shower, still shoving his uniform top into his pants. "Don't you make a fucking noise or else." I pantomimed a slash across my throat with my finger before pulling the shower curtain closed.

The knocking at the door was more insistent now. "Oh my god, don't get your panties all twisted in your camel toe," I called out, trying to smooth my loosened ponytail and not look so freshly fucked.

Cadence was still laughing when I whipped open the door. "What the hell took you so long?" Her amusement turned to questioning curiosity as her brow cocked in my direction. "You feeling okay?"

Shit. Think Tiff, think.

"I..uh… Life or death struggle with the hidden zipper."

"No wonder you're so sweaty." She made a motion for me to turn around. The zippers were undone with ease. If she suspected anything, she didn't say. I glanced to the bathroom, praying to goodness that Ender didn't make a peep. "I wanted to see if you wanted to go to the Phillies game tonight with me? Jamie gave me tickets."

"Oh…" Despite baseball being my least favorite thing in the world, I really needed to distance myself from Ender. Because if left to my own devices, I probably would do a stupid thing like invite him over for round two of sexy bang-bang times. "Yeah. I'm down. Drowning in beer and yelling at men playing with their balls is just what I need tonight."

Cadence let out an amused snort as she helped me out of the bell part of the Ding Dong costume. The air in the room instantly got at least ten degrees cooler. Someone really needed to figure out how to make mascot costumes breathable instead of being a personal sauna from the stuffy, manmade fabric.

"The first beer is on me. But after that it's all you." She teased as she headed towards the door. "See you in like 30?"

"Uh, yeah. Just let me take a shower and get out of my mascot Spanx." I waved her off with a forced smile. Closing the door behind her, I collapsed against it with a heavy sigh.

Ender peeked out from the door of the bathroom. "Is it clear?"

"Yes." I huffed at him. "I think you took about ten years off my life with your shenanigans."

"I'm pretty sure I heard no complaints from the bell." It wasn't fair that he already looked put together.

"Ha ha, very funny." I did my best to keep my face in its usual resting bitch configuration, but the adorably cheeky way he was staring at me had me unnecessarily unarmed. Why did he have to be so fucking cute?

"I know, I'm hilarious."

"Don't let it all go to your head, Screwball." Biting my lower lip, I did my best to suppress my smile. Although two Os after work was enough to make any girl smile.

"Screwball…?" Ender scoffed at me. I mean it just slipped out, but it suited him. He screwed me, had balls, and threw balls. I ignored his judgment of the nickname I had absentmindedly tested out.

"On the other hand… What you did back there? *Hot.*"

"Oh yeah?" Ender's cocky smirk almost did me in for another session. He stepped back into my space, aligning his body with mine. Then he had to go and to the sexy book boyfriend door lean, and I forgot to breathe all over again. "I don't know…seeing you in costume–"

"Don't you dare tell me you have a furry kink."

"A what?!"

"Those people that dress up in animal–" There was a sheer look of horror on his face. I couldn't help but laugh. "You know what, never mind. Technically, Ding Dong is more of a plush than a furry."

"I'm not even going to ask how or why you know that information."

"Oh, there's a whole community out there. If you feel bored one day, do an internet search. It should keep you busy for a few hours."

Ender gave me a slow, cautious look. "I'm slightly frightened by the fact that you know so much about such...*things*."

"You know what, don't judge my three am brain rot deep dives on the internet after reading some inanimate object smut. The furry thing is probably the more innocent of the shit I've seen online or read about." Ender looked more and more appalled each time I opened my mouth. I couldn't help but laugh. The man needed to get out more. Or maybe let me corrupt him. Just a little bit more. "You know what? Let me send you some books by Chuck Tingle."

30

WILDFIRE
CAUTIOUS CLAY

As hot as the sex we had in my dressing room was, that had to be the only time. Almost getting caught by Cadence was cutting it entirely too close. We couldn't get sloppy like that. Not now.

Thankfully, Cadence had been entirely too distracted by the exact shape and mass of Jamie's ass at the Phillies game that she hadn't done her normal interrogation of the interactions between Ender and me that she had witnessed. She also drank an extra beer than her usual two, so she was extra gone. Crooning to the masses about how hot her boyfriend was.

Well, my boyfriend was hotter.

I wish I could tell her about Ender and me. I wanted to go for tacos and frozen margaritas, and gush about how awesome our boyfriends were. Like best friends were supposed to do. I just needed to work up the courage first. And figure out how to broach the subject with the team. I couldn't do one without the other.

I knew I kept my mouth shut for Cadence and Jamie. And I would have until the end of time. But

Ender's and my situation was a little more delicate. He wasn't a moving part of the organization on loan. He was firmly a member of the current roster. If we fucked this up, he and I could lose our positions with the team.

Trying to distract myself from my tumultuous thoughts, I snuggled in closer to Ender. We were cuddled together on my couch, watching whatever *Schitt's Creek* episode I had left off on my continuous watch-throughs when nothing good was on television. Ender hadn't watched the series before, so it was amusing to feel him chuckle every so often.

His one arm was wrapped around my shoulder while the other traced nonsensical designs along the back of my hand that rested on his stomach. Aside from my whirlwind of thoughts, I was at peace just sitting here watching episodes of a show that I practically had memorized. It was safe here. Comfortable.

"You good, mi amor?" Ender's gentle voice pulled me from my never-ending anxiety-riddled worry list that seemed to almost constantly go through my mind.

"Oh, uh yeah." I sighed with a shrug, trying to shove aside everything I'd been thinking of. "I've…I've just got a lot of things on my mind."

"Anything you want to share?"

"No." I shook my head, trying to dismiss his questions with a haphazard smile.

"You sure?"

"Yep."

Ender cocked a questioning brow at me. He was quiet for a moment before a playful smirk rounded the one corner of his mouth. "Would you rather I distract you from said thoughts?"

I couldn't help the slow smile that played across my lips. "Maybe."

"Oh yeah?" Ender had shifted from his spot on the couch snuggled up next to me. He pressed his fisted hand into the cushion next to my thigh. His mouth was dangerously close to mine. Leaning in to nip at my bottom lip, he pulled away the second I tried to engage him.

Fuck, he was a good distraction.

With a smile, I grabbed the collar of his shirt, yanking him down towards me. Our mouths met and he took the diversion to grab ahold of me. He somehow twisted the both of us, landing on his back with me on top.

We broke out in a fit of giggles, caressing and kissing each other as the air grew more heated. It was a physical impossibility to keep my hands off of this man for longer than an hour. We'd probably forget to eat if we didn't have to stop.

"How are you so irresistible?" Ender groaned against my throat as his hands slipped under my shirt, gliding along my curves.

"I was literally just thinking the same thing about you." I chuckled, inhaling sharply as his hands found my breasts. "Your body is dangerous." His teeth nipped at the fleshy part of my neck to my shoulder.

"When we move in together, I'm suggesting we just don't wear clothes." Warmth flooded through my body so fast that it left me dizzy. Not only was the idea hot but the thought of us living together made me feel giddy for whatever reason.

I grabbed his face and kissed him hard. His mouth moved into a wide grin before he returned the favor. On his next breath he pulled away, tugging my shirt off and tossing it away somewhere.

Arching my back, I thrust my breasts towards him as he fumbled with the clasp of my bra. I let out a breath as they fell heavy and free. My bra followed my shirt somewhere into the expanse of my living room. Ender grabbed my breasts, massaging almost to a painful intensity.

It only spurred me on, rocking my hips against his, feeling his rigid cock like a monument in his shorts. With our positioning it hit me just right. Right in that sweet spot that sent jolts straight from my clit to the depths of my abdomen.

Somewhere in the tangle of limbs, I somehow ripped off his shirt and shimmied out of my leggings mere seconds before his hands gathered up heaping handfuls of my ass cheeks. He urged my hips to rock harder and harder against his cock.

I was left almost in a trance. So focused on the sensation of grinding against him. That familiar delicious haze started to warm my core, alerting my body that it was going the right way for an orgasm of epic proportions. And from the sounds that Ender was making, him too.

"Hey Tiff, you okay? You didn't answer your texts and Coop said you were–OH MY GOD."

I shot up like a Punxsutawney Phil on Groundhog Day, wide-eyed and in shock, only to see my best friend standing wide-eyed and open-mouthed in my kitchen. Of course Ender picked that moment to prop himself up off the couch to look over his bare shoulder. Which only morphed her surprised look into a scream.

Fuck.

As soon as we got into the apartment, we started sneaking kisses, which meant that neither of us remembered to lock the door. I did have a hidden key that Cadence knew where it was hidden, so it was a moot point. But that was besides the very large point that was happening right now.

I was currently topless, sitting atop of Ender, cowgirl style. My panties were hanging on for dear life as Ender's fingers were knotted with the straps that came across my hips. It's not like my best friend hadn't seen me topless before. Just not while making mutual deer-in-the-headlights eye contact with each other.

It was at that time that Ender decided to give me at least a shred of decency. His hands shot up to grab my breasts, hiding my pert nipples from view. I pursed my lips as I shot him a side eye.

"Not helping, Ender." I mumbled between clenched teeth.

He didn't have time to offer an alternative option. I heard the rumbling down the staircase that led to the main part of my brother's house, AKA the laundry stairs. I could only glance over my shoulder in horror to see my brother burst through the door. All as my heart came to a solid stop in the process.

Normally he would give me a heads up that he or his wife was on their way down. Normally I'd be wearing clothing while hanging out in my living room. Normally I wouldn't have an audience while trying to get freaky with my boyfriend.

Unfortunately, there was nothing normal about this situation.

"Tiff, what the hell is–OH DAMN MY EYES." Immediately, he slapped his palms to his face, placing an airtight seal around his vision that was certainly scarred for life.

Absolutely fuck my life into the end of times.

"OH MY GOD, COOPER GET OUT!" I screamed at the top of my lungs, chucking a throw pillow at his head.

"I didn't see anything I swear!" He yelled back, trying to inelegantly turn himself around enough to go back up the stairs. He ended up knocking over a small side table, sending a few of my stacked books tumbling to the floor. My head fell into my hands as I groaned, finally hearing the door close.

"I-I'm just gonna wait outside." Cadence stammered, feet quickly shuffling across the kitchen. I glanced over to her as she was slowly making her way over to the front door, but very clearly in no hurry. I didn't stop staring her down until she was true to her word, closing the outside door behind her.

Ugh, fuck. I suppose I had some explaining to do. To a lot of people.

Chewing on my lower lip, I looked down at Ender who looked adorably sheepish.

"I'm sorry…"

"For what?" A smile cracked around where my lower lip was stuck with my teeth. I was trying to bite back a laugh. Ender's chuckle joined me in the utter absurdity of it all. "Its not your fault we got found out."

"Yeah but–"

"Ender, really. It's not either of our faults. Its the faults of my nosy as fuck family and friends." I scowled at the front door. "I suppose…we'd better go and explain ourselves." My shoulders fell with a heavy sigh as I sat back.

Ender's hands were still on my breasts. Without the staring eyes of my brother and bestie, he took a hot second to massage the mounds in appreciation. I dismissed him with a noise of annoyance.

"Not the time or the place anymore, dude." I sighed, rolling off of him to go off in search of the bits and pieces of my clothing that had been scattered about. Like how the hell did my bra end up on my dining room hanging light? "If you hadn't noticed, the mood died in the most viciously violent of deaths."

"Hey," Ender sat up and I marveled at the flex of his muscles along his torso as he did so. Maybe a quickie wouldn't hurt. Afterall it was rather obvious as to what we were trying to do– "Raincheck?"

I couldn't help but laugh as I tried to un-lasso my bra from the light fixture. Ender was at my side in no time flat and used his height to his advantage to rescue my lingerie. He kissed my forehead as he handed me back the garment. I quickly scrambled back into it, much to his chagrin.

"Maybe you should go talk to Cooper. I'm sure the team isn't exactly going to be thrilled about this."

"Uh…"

Something in Ender's tone had me suspicious. "…What?"

"What if…Cooper already…kind of…*knows*…?"

"WHAT."

"Look, I was really distraught on the one road trip and he could tell so we talked about how I felt about us and—and he gave me some pointers about you—"

"Ender Gomez Roche!" Damn, I pulled his middle name out of the deepest recesses of my memories in the heat of the moment. "Don't you dare tell me—"

"Iffy," Ender took half a step closer, taking my hands into his. The rough pad of his thumb brushed slowly, reassuring circles on the back of my hand. "I'm not sure why any of this surprises you. I can't exactly help what my face does when I look at you." I smiled at that. "If your idiot older brother figured us out, I'm sure Cadence has a whole lot more to say."

Fuck. Right, Cadence.

I glanced at my front door and sure enough her silhouette was clear as day against the frosted glass of the sidelight. If my brother was observant enough to see how Ender felt about me, then Cadence must have a fucking treasure trove of annotations just ready to go. Might as well rip the bandage off.

"I guess we need to head to our corners."

"For now." Ender slowly grinned at me as he somehow found my t-shirt nearby and handed it to me. His shirt was still missing. Not that he really technically needed it. Besides, I was enjoying the eye candy. At least it was a good distraction from the fact that my best friend and brother saw me topless. "But when we're done, maybe they'll leave us alone for, oh I don't know, forever?"

I laughed. "Wishful thinking." My eyes drifted to his bare chest and my fingers soon followed, tracing along the top arch of definition of his abs. "Although maybe we scared them for a good decade or so." Ender's brows slowly rose on his forehead, but I didn't let him ask the question that I was so sure was on the tip of his tongue. "Hopefully Cooper has some insight on how to approach HR." That thought got him off the previous subject at least.

"Fuck, right. I didn't even think about that."

"Okay, rude. I am part of the team you know."

"Yes yes, that you are. Honestly, the heart of the team. I pursed my lips to contain my smile.

"Get a move on. Maybe we can put out this fire before it gets any worse." Taking one last long look at his handsome face, I turned him around and spanked his very fine ass, sending him on his way.

Which now left me to talk to Cadence.

I'd avoided this subject for so long that I knew it was going to rear its ugly head someday. I just had hoped that someday included me being fully clothed. Although Ender was right. I'm sure Cadence knew at least something.

I tried to psych myself up as I stepped up to the door. There was a sudden shuffle on the other side, and I assumed that Cadence had her ear pressed against the door, listening to nonsense. Oh, she was going to get such a razzing next time we hung out. I opened the door.

"Oh my god, Tiff! I'm so sorry! But girl, yes! Gettin' it."

The barrage of words hit me all at once. All I could do was stare at her in disbelief for a moment as I tried to pull myself back together. I half expected her to be pissed.

"So…uh, yeah. Ender and me…are together."

"Yeah, I gathered that." Cadence huffed as she crossed her arms in front of her. "I was able to put that together a while ago." She went quiet as she gave me a chastising look. "But…there's something you're not telling me about all of *this*. And I really wish I didn't need to catch you in a compromising position in order for you to tell me about it."

"Ugh. Right." I let out a long breath and shrugged. I should have known better than to be all cagey about this. Cadence was my best friend, I knew she wouldn't judge me. Maybe it was because I was in denial that this whole thing was happening. "So…uh… Ender and I used to date in high school…" I offered up with a wince, ready for whatever barrage she was going to bestow upon me. Whatever I said was the last thing she expected.

"Oh…" Surprise was etched on her face as she processed the information. "O-Oh shit."

"It was pretty serious, actually. I thought he was it for me. Which was stupid to think that way in fucking high school." I swallowed, realizing that I was going to trauma dump all over my friend if I didn't stop myself. "He ended up breaking up with me because he wanted to get with the popular girl in our school." I took a slow breath. "Turns out he never went through with it. He…loved me too much. Meanwhile I was holding a grudge, something just a hair short of cursing his family for five generations.

Anyway, after high school we both went to college. Ender got picked up in the MLB draft after he graduated, then got dropped by the team after Spring Training. Cooper called him up and offered him a spot with the Sillys. Ender started…*pursuing* me again. And when we finally ended up talking things out, well… All of this happened."

Cautiously I looked up at my friend, only to see her eyes had gone all glassy. Her hands were clasped tightly together against her chest. My brow cocked in silent question. But she hushed my curiosity that was bubbling up just below the surface.

"Oh my god, Tiff…" There was a warble in her voice. "That's like the most romantic thing ever."

I scoffed. "I think you and I have two very different definitions of romance."

"I mean, that's true. But I have seen you dabble in those cartoon cover romances a time or two."

I wanted to wipe the smug look right off her face. Because she was right. Ender and I were living our own special little romance. Not exactly the fairy tale sort of one that Cadence was living with her major league boyfriend. But it was a romance that suited Ender and me. A romance that was just…

Perfect.

Cadence took that moment to wrap her arms around me in a fierce hug that went straight to my bones. Oh I needed this. I returned the favor, hugging my best friend back. I could feel all the stress and the secrets melting away to nothing.

That's it. No more secrets between us. We could now share all the tawdry details of our relationships. As best friends. Like god intended.

"Hey, hands off. She's mine."

Ender's warm voice sounded behind us as he opened the front door to check on me. I couldn't help but chuckle. Cadence looked ready to cry again.

"Oh my god he really is a green flag." She whispered to me as she leaned in, glancing up at Ender.

"And a golden retriever too."

Cadence looked rather impressed as she looked at me. I couldn't help but smile. "He's been learning a lot at book club." That made her laugh outright.

"Holy shit, I thought the guys were kidding when I heard them talking about it."

"Nope. We will meet again next month. Schmidt is getting shirts made."

31

ONE LIFE

ED SHEERAN

"Its my understanding that you have something to tell us?" The woman from HR cocked her brow at me as we all sat crammed into her little office. All the admin offices were up on the club suite level of the ballpark. So if I had pushed aside the thought of potentially walking to our doom, it was pretty cool to be up in the fancy part of the ballpark on a game day. The only time I was up here was for the holiday party in December.

"Yes. We do."

The woman's eyes darted back to her computer screen, looking over the rim of her dark-rimmed glasses. Coach Bert Topper, Ender's boss, sat in the corner along with the entertainment manager, who was Cadence's and my boss.

I squirmed a bit in my seat. It was rather unnerving to admit to a group of people that Ender and I were in a serious relationship. Especially after hiding it for so long. What would they think? What would they say? Would we have to break up?

Cadence and I had pored over the employee handbook, looking for anything that might help us.

305

The legal jargon wasn't completely clear. But it didn't exactly sound all that good.

I glanced over at Ender, seated in the chair next to me. They were uncomfortable armchairs, meant for waiting only, instead of a long-term conversation. It only added to my anxiety.

"Well?" The HR lady looked at Ender and me.

In the email I'd sent her, I gave her a pretty vague explanation of the need for the meeting. Although it was fairly self-explanatory. At least now, since Ender couldn't keep his hand off my thigh. It was a subconscious move to reassure me, but it did nothing to help our case.

"Miss Campanaro and I are in a relationship."

"Is that so?" Her tone didn't reveal anything telling, but she didn't exactly sound thrilled either. "And how long have you and Miss Campanaro been seeing each other?"

"Since July." I added quietly.

"Actually," Ender butted in, casting me a look. "We've been in a relationship before. It was the team that brought us back together."

He was really laying it on thick, and I couldn't help but melt a little. I glanced at the HR lady. It seemed that his sweet sentiment had touched her in some way. Come to think of it, it was a little romantic. Well, if you take out the whole mutant Liberty Bell mascot part of it.

"So, you two did not meet because of the team?"

"No ma'am." I finally found my voice to contribute to the conversation. "We were in a relationship in high school. We…" My eyes flicked to Ender, wondering how best to explain the blip without opening more personal details.

"Lost touch after we graduated. We went to separate colleges. Tiffiny moved. I got drafted."

HR lady nodded, typing away at her computer. Her face was impassive as she typed, almost as if she had forgotten we were in the room. Topper and my manager were still quiet in the corner. They just needed to witness this private conversation. They didn't have to say anything. It was still unnerving to have them there.

"I made a note in both of your files of the relationship." She said suddenly, clicking around with her mouse. Her printer whirred to life, shuffling paper as it sat on the desktop next to her. "Since you two were previously involved before your employment here. I changed the language a bit in these disclosures you have to sign. That sort of thing isn't as common. But it makes my job a lot easier." It was then that we got the first semblance of a smile.

Ender and I exchanged looks as I let out an exhale.

"So, that's it? We just have to sign something?"

"Basically. The disclosure states that you both are in a consensual relationship that you have disclosed to HR. And that if anything goes wrong, we are not liable in any capacity. Just something to cover our asses."

I let out a snort, not expecting the prim woman to swear. But now that everything was all out in the open, she seemed more relaxed too.

"If you'll just both sign these disclosure agreements, I can put a copy in your file, and you can be on your way."

"That's it...?" Ender cautiously asked.

"That's it."

Phew.

Leaving the HR lady in her office, we all left. Coach Topper and my manager offered their congratulations with handshakes and smiles. It was rather odd to congratulate someone on just being together. It wasn't like we were getting married.

Married.

The word struck some chord deep inside me. I watched Ender as he spoke to his coach about something. His smile was brilliant, and his kindness was evident throughout all aspects of his life. My heart swelled, and I could have sworn that I sprouted wings and was floating in that moment.

Once upon a time, I'd dreamed of white dresses and picket fences and living in a cozy cottage with Ender by my side. But the years apart had turned them into bitter memories that never came to pass. Here I was, staring at the guy I fell in love with all those years ago. We were firmly in a second chance that had been greenlit by the universe. Not many people were as lucky as we were.

He turned, waving off his coach before heading in my direction. It was as if the whole world went into slow motion at that moment, letting me drink in his tall, lean form. The way the fluorescent lighting made his fading frosted tips sparkle like a golden halo on his head. With every step, his clothing ebbed and flowed over his muscles, giving me little peeks of their definition.

So yes, he was gorgeous. But not just on the outside, but on the inside too. The way he helped out his team. How he worked to better himself with every practice, every game. The fact that he did everything in his power to make me happy. To remind me that he was hopelessly devoted to me and that his love was never going to stop.

Was he really *the one*?

The universe had thrown us together again. Once it did, everything that had hardened my heart began to melt, leaving the warm, fleshy, beating muscle running at full capacity once again. All because of him.

It's not like I hadn't thought about the notion here and there since we started dating again. While yes it was so old-fashioned, deep down, way past my smut-loving heart, was a simple girl with dreams of being forever loved by someone who was endlessly infatuated with her. The antiquated romance of engagement and marriage. I was a sucker for it.

"So," Ender interrupted my runaway thoughts as he leaned towards me with a grin. "How should we celebrate?"

I laughed. "Celebrate? A meeting with HR is something to celebrate?"

"No, us being *official* official is something to celebrate. My family knows, your brother knows, Coach knows, your boss knows, and HR knows. Well," He lifted my hand to his mouth, caressing my knuckles with a kiss. "And you know."

That sent me into a fit of giggles. "Well, I would hope I'd know. Or else that HR meeting would have been real fucking weird." Letting out a relieved sigh, I squeezed his fingers. "We just have to let the rest of the team know."

"Something tells me that your big-mouthed brother probably said something while we were with HR."

I rolled my eyes. "Because of course. I swear those reality TV shows he watches with my sister-in-law have turned him into a dramatic gossip."

Ender threw his head back with a laugh. "Does that mean we can have fun at your place?" He emphasized that with a suggestive wiggle of his eyebrows.

"I'd say that's a possibility."

We escaped the ballpark thankfully unscathed. I got out of his car, grinning at him, as he followed me up to my front door. I hurried up the walk as he chased after me. We were free. No more hiding. No more secrets.

"Maybe order dinner in? Eat it in bed? Naked?"

This sexy banter made me feel rather giddy. It must have had the same effect on Ender as he pressed me against the brick wall outside of my front door, kissing me hard. It got a bit sloppy, something like our hurried kisses after our high school dates on my front stoop.

I managed to unlock the front door, dragging him inside. We were lost in a fit of giggles, kicking off our shoes. We pulled at each other's clothing, making our very familiar way to my bedroom. Each time we repeated this process, we ended up with fewer bruises from blindly running into things.

Perhaps it was better that we got a round or two out of our system. Maybe it would be different if we moved in together and had round-the-clock access. Or maybe this would never end. Well, until one of us breaks a hip.

My god. Was I already seeing myself growing old with this man? The vision of running home and falling back into his arms was something that I could so easily see every day for the future.

Did Ender have dreams like this? Did he sit and think of our future together? So many times he's told me that I was his forever. But did those words come with dreams of us sitting together on the couch, on some random Tuesday night, watching our same old comfort show, and it being just utterly perfect?

We'd spent our high school years together, and now we were here, diving headfirst back into the thick of it. So many years had been wasted all because of a stupid decision on Ender's part. Of which he had spent the better part of this baseball season making up for.

Why waste any more time? I'd already lost the love of my life once. I didn't want us to ever end up where we were again.

Without a second thought, I tackled Ender back onto the bed. We bounced as we both hit the mattress. My brain was screaming, my heart was racing, and my body wanted to consume every inch of the man all at once. Throwing my leg over his waist, I settled in to ride that pony.

My lips were on his before the second rebound. Tilting my head, I drank him in deeply before he finally came to terms with the fact that I was leading this nonsense. Within seconds, he was kissing me back twice as hard as we both consumed each other's atmosphere.

I'd never felt a feeling like this before. If I had fewer distractions from my deep thoughts, it was a feeling similar to the moment I first laid my eyes on Ender, way back when. For some reason, I knew then what I suddenly realized now.

Ender was my endgame. My forever. The happily ever after book boyfriend, but in real life. He was mine. He loved me. Adored me. If given the chance, he would transcend the depths of the galaxy or even jump through time to find me again. To find me again because it was our destiny.

No thoughts, only a sudden urge of incredible feelings of which I could only gasp out into the charged air between our kisses. Because at that moment, I could sum up my exact plans for Ender and myself into two words.

"Marry me."

Ender

"Marry me."

My entire body stalled as the words hit me like a warm sunbeam on the ballfield. In the breath immediately after, my body flooded with sparkling pinpricks as my heart began to race from excitement. The words reverberated in my head as my expression stalled in mid-kiss face. I thought my already-hard dick was going to explode from the sudden rush of blood throughout my body.

Throwing the M-word on top of my fluster as I stopped mid make-out session with the most beautiful woman on the planet had my organs fit to explode.

"W-What…?" I managed to finally croak out, my lashes blinking rapidly in my awe.

"You heard me." Iffy firmly replied, her lips pressed together in a vain effort to stop from smiling as her hand cupped my chin. Her lips found mine all over again, dreamy and passionate that it took almost a sheer force of will to pull away to readdress her question.

"Yeah but, uh… Iffy, are you serious?" I wasn't sure why I was even bothering to argue with her. Every ounce of my body wanted to scream YES at her.

"Why wouldn't I be?"

"Isn't it… You know, kind of sudden?"

"Ender, we dated for, like, what? Three years in high school?"

"I know. But we've only been together, this time, for sixty-eight days."

Tiffiny blinked at me before she narrowed her eyes. "That's… Oddly specific."

"What, a guy can't keep track of all the days he's felt whole? Happy?"

She sucked her bottom lip into her mouth, but I had noted the subtle tremor before she did so. Despite pressing her for her sincerity, I was only proving the point she was trying to make. That us dating was now just a formality.

"But like… I don't even have a ring or–"

Iffy hushed me with a quick kiss as she shook her head. "It's fine. It's not like we're a traditional couple anyway. At least, not really anymore." She made a huff of amusement.

I lay there, staring up at her in utter wonderment. The woman who had questioned my devotion to her was the one who sprung a random marriage proposal on me. Just two idiots in love.

Perfect for each other.

"Yes."

I answered simply. It took her aback so much that she suddenly pressed her hands into the bedding to either side of my head. Her gaze was intense as it darted around my face, looking for even a fraction of insincerity. To which there was one.

"Wait. Really?" Her lashes blinked rapidly as she started down at me, agape.

"Yes really." I laughed, wrapping my arms around the small of her back. The pressure of the hold pressed her face just a bit closer to mine. Grinning, I reached up and caressed her cheek. "Iffy, I've been in love with you from the start. As I said, I had to make the idiotic decision to break up with you to fully understand just how deeply my feelings went."

I gave her a gentle kiss. "I've never had this feeling with anyone else. It's like my body is full of electricity when I'm with you. That I feel alive. All while grinning like a dumb ass because everything about you makes me so insanely happy. You could fart, and I'll give you a standing ovation."

"Ender–"

"I'm not even kidding a little bit."

"I know you're not." She shook her head as she laughed. A sweet and hearty sound. I had the old Tiffiny back. The carefree woman. The deliriously happy one.

"So, what do you think? We get married in the off-season. Two months is enough time to get a wedding together, right?"

"I mean no." She scoffed, but her smile outshone her attitude. "Maybe it might be smarter if we pick a date right before the season begins?" I couldn't stop grinning at her. So much so it made her a bit unnerved. "What?"

"I just can't believe we're planning our wedding."

"Barely planning." Iffy rolled her eyes but there was a playful smirk there. "I don't want anything big. Something classy. Simple."

"Anything you want. Just as long as the team can be there."

She quirked a brow high on her head. "The whole team?"

"Well yeah. They are our family too, aren't they?"

"Okay fair." She rolled her eyes and despite the proposed attitude, she was smiling. "Shit, what are they all going to think about this?"

"I'm sure they'll get a kick out of it. I'll get to join the married men club with Schmidt and Martin."

"By getting a kick out of it, does that mean tease us mercilessly for as long as either of us are on the team?"

I thought for a moment. "Yeah probably. Or at least until the next guy gets married off. But the mascot banging the pitcher is a pretty saucy tale." A slow grin crept across my face. "Hey, it's like we have our very own romantic comedy or something."

"Yeah, a smutty one."

I laughed. "I love you, Tiffiny Campanaro."

She grinned. "I love you too."

Epilogue

FOREVER
MUMFORD & SONS

"Alright you two love birds," Cadence called from the top of the dugout stairs. "Are you ready for your big debut?"

"Yes!" Ender chimed in.

"No." I said in an annoyed huff.

"Hey Coach, can I get dibs as the headliner on the next new dance routine? I need me a woman." Truitt popped his head into the conversation as he stood with the other guys, waiting for their cue.

"Me next!" Added his partner in crime, Camden.

"Look, what? Guys just no–"

"Come on, you ended up with Jamie after your dance debut." Arlow chimed in.

"And, now, Ender and Tiffiny are dating!" Chirped Tomas.

"Guys, that happened *before* we started rehearsing the dance number." Ender corrected the chatter.

"Close enough!" Shrugged Roman.

I had to laugh. Ender was right. Our dating all started *before* Cadence asked us to be part of the dance routine. And I was still sure she did it out of spite. But the guys were insanely superstitious. Most athletes were.

The guys all looked good in their rip-away bell-bottoms for the Philly Sillys first ever Disco Night. Cadence insisted we dress up Ding Dong as well. She mentioned platform shoes, which I immediately vetoed. The next idea was a new hat, but the one that was part of the costume was permanently affixed.

It's not like Ding Dong had a gender. Some things were implied, but I touted the mascot as non-binary. Ding Dong was all-encompassing. Loud and proud of their identity. Which was just an unhinged bronze bell that ran around the stadium, causing chaos. Ding Dong identified as chaos. Just chaos.

Cadence did get Ender back into the pink rhinestone jersey. The team got their money's worth out of that extra accessory. She had somehow managed to also get him matching sparkly bellbottoms. Between his freshly retouched frosted tips and his outfit, he was a damn sight to behold. A sexy sight.

I shifted from overstuffed sneaker foot to overstuffed sneaker foot. Why was I nervous? I'd performed in front of crowds like this at college. Even when I did community theater for a bit over the summers, I was home from school. Something like this shouldn't bother me. Especially not when I was dating the lead man.

Ender shot me a dopey grin, and suddenly I was transported back to hiding off stage with him. We would sneak in a few kisses during theater practice, in between the layers of off-stage curtains. Now we're here, together again. Standing in the wings of an Entertainment Baseball League stadium. What a weirdly full circle moment.

For the dance number, the main focus was going to be on Ender and me. Something kind of like Ender admiring me from the pitcher's mound as I wandered the infield all nonchalant. The guys were backup dancers. Providing dancing entertainment as Ender and I did our storyline. The whole thing would conclude with Ender pulling me over to the pitcher's mound, where we would have our hot disco dance number duet finale dance.

Even though I was grumbly about it, Cadence always did a phenomenal job curating the theme and then teaching us the coordinating choreography for these dance numbers. They did make these ELB games a bit more fun to watch. They brought a younger crowd to the stadium. People who never watched a baseball game in their lives were now in the seats. My favorite part was that the league gave those guys who were still insanely talented at baseball but just couldn't quite make the cut a second chance. Guys like Ender. There were even rumblings about adding women to rosters. Now that would be awesome.

"Have everything you need, Ender?"

Cadenced addressed my boyfriend with a weird smile that made me narrow my eyes. Ender blushed with a nod, but not before looking in my direction. Just what the hell were those two up to?

The boom of the announcer's voice over the loudspeaker jolted me back to the present. Oh boy. Here we go.

"Okay, guys, you know the drill… Showtime!" Cadence gave the guys one last encouraging cheer before stepping out of the way. The beginning chords of the song sounded, and the team made their way up and out to the field. I was almost blinded by their rhinestone bellbottoms. And if the immediate cheer gave me any indication, the crowd was going crazy over their costumes.

"So… Nervous?" Ender stepped in next to me as we found ourselves alone in the dugout for the moment.

"Maybe a little. Wearing the head helps stave off most of the future mortification."

Ender laughed. His grin sparkled in the fading summer sunlight. Something about him was extra fidgety tonight. Although I couldn't put my finger on it. Thank goodness he wasn't the starting pitcher or else I might have had a word with his coach.

"Come on, mi amor. Time to woo the crowd."

With a sigh, I put my game face on. Not that it mattered much. I brought Ding Dong's foam head up and positioned it over my head, letting it settle onto my shoulders. There was a part of the faux wood bell hanger that was camouflaged with the viewing port, so I could see out. I could only see in front of me, which required me to have a handler, so I wasn't knocking out random kids or concessions.

Ender gave me an air kiss as he stopped at the top of the stairs. I had to laugh because I was still in awe of the fact that he still loved me, despite dressing up as a cartoon Liberty Bell for a living. But that finally got me to relax as I watched him run out onto the field for his cue.

With him gone, I made my way up the stairs, holding onto the metal railing with my oversized gloves. My equally oversized plush yellow sneakers toed the warning track as I got my own set of cheers and applause from those who saw me. As much as I was a grump about my job and the fact that I wasn't gracing the stages of Broadway or a famous actress, I really did love it.

Ding Dong was an extension of myself. Kids and adults adored me equally. It was a fun character to play and breathe life into. And I now get to work alongside the man I love because of it.

I shuffled my way out onto the field as the first "Ring my bell" chorus chimed in, along with most of the crowd. Dance numbers were always more fun when the spectators sang along or cheered extra loudly because of the song choice.

Finding my mark, I showed the guys how it was done. The crowd went absolutely bonkers. I could only imagine Cadence's face now. She'd been trying to get me to participate in one of the Sillys dance numbers since I started last year. I stepped in here or there, but nothing to this magnitude. It sounded like it wasn't going to be the last time I did this.

I threw in a few extra moves from my theater days to really ham it up for the crowd. I was pretty sure I got actual screams as I made my way to the pitcher's mound to meet up with Ender, who was doing his own efforts to schmooze the crowd.

My god, he looked hot, working those hips in rather sinful ways. He'd always been a fantastic dancer. But something about this dance routine had him really going for gusto.

A brilliant smile warmed his face when he grabbed onto my gloved hand. It made me feel warm and gooey on the inside, and not just from the summer heat and the mascot costume. He leaned in close, doing his best to romance Ding Dong on the dance floor, but really he was just flirting with me behind the mask. The crowd was eating up the winks and blown kisses.

Now there was an idea. Maybe Cadence and I could run with the idea of the pitcher having a crush on the mascot. That would make for some top-notch social media fodder with all the skits and nonsense we could do. We could–

Suddenly, Ender deviated from the routine, and I stuttered a bit in my dance moves, trying to make up for it. I know he couldn't see me under Ding Dong's head, but I was giving him a death glare for ad-libbing when we were so close to finishing the dance number.

I just didn't expect the reason as to why he dropped to one knee during our duet.

As I spun around, trying to disguise the fact that we were now doing our own thing, I found him not only on one knee, but holding up a velvet ring box with a rather gorgeous ring inside. My heart stopped right along with my feet.

"Ender?" I hissed, not that anyone in the crowd could hear us on the pitcher's mound. "What the–"

"I wanted to make it official." He grinned sheepishly as the crowd suddenly caught on as to what was *really* going on. Over his shoulder, I could see that the camera crew had focused solely on us on the big electronic videoboard. Why was it so hot in the suit all of a sudden? And who the fuck was cutting onions at a time like this?

I glanced up, seeing that the guys had stopped dancing to watch the spectacle. Sniffling, I looked back at Ender. He was looking up to me with the same adorable, loving look he always did. My heart was fit to explode.

My hands moved to the mask, lifting it up and off my head. I knew it was a cardinal rule not to unmask a character in front of a crowd, but there was no way I was going to say yes to this man as an unhinged overstuffed baseball team mascot. Shoving the mascot head under my arm, I whipped off my left glove, leaving my hand bare.

Tears were running down my face. But I was grinning. Grinning so much it hurt. The man of my dreams was doing a stupidly big gesture. A stupidly big romantic gesture. Complete with a full theatrical dance number. With costumes.

"Yes. Absolutely yes!"

Ender's eyes welled up with tears as he grabbed my hand, kissing the back of it before sliding the ring on. I didn't even have a chance to take a moment to admire him on his knees. I was in his arms, locked in a wildly charged kiss that I felt straight down to my toes.

"Figured it was my turn to ask you." He murmured against my mouth as we exchanged a few more kisses. Much to the crowd's enjoyment.

"And just how long have you been planning this?"

"Since the day after you asked me. Needed to make this, us, *official*, official."

All I could do was laugh through my tears.

"I love you, Ender Roche."

"And I you, mi amor. Welcome to the *official* start of our *forever*."

Stay tuned for
Benson's
love story in

Book 3

ACKNOWLEDGEMENTS

My readers. My gosh, where would this series be without you? You are the ones who made this series a sensation! I am eternally grateful for all the love and excitement you guys have for my books about a silly little baseball team in Philadelphia.

To the Banana Ball organization and the players, thank you for your enthusiasm for my books. It's been so incredibly fun to watch your reactions and delight when you see that your sport has its very own romance book series!

To my readers who have been here since the beginning, as always, thank you for your unyielding support. This book was done during a difficult mental time in my life. But with your encouragement and excitement for the new book, it gave me the strength to continue on until I wrote "THE END".

My love to the NEW indie bookstores who have given little ol' indie author me, a chance on their shelf. I take pride in featuring you on my retail stock list. I'm going to try to visit each and every one of you!

To my beloved Phillies organization, for the love of god, please give me a season to root for so I can write book 3 and not be so angry at baseball games. Got it?

About the Author

When K. Iwancio isn't attending a Phillies game or screaming at the Eagles on television, she's busy dreaming up her next book or creating…something. Born and raised in Northeast Philadelphia, her main food groups are soft pretzels, Dunkin', and wooder ice. Some of the fondest memories of her beloved late father are in front of the television yelling "Come on!" (in true Philly accent) at the umpires and referees. You can coax her from her writing cave with promises to visit indie bookstores and grab lattes. But if you want to win her over, ask her the number of the trash compactor on the Death Star where Luke, Han, Leia, and Chewbacca are trapped.